The Palace of Shadows

SANDEE COHEN was born in London and left school at fifteen after a 'less than distinguished' academic career. She worked for a design group for three years as a receptionist, writing short stories for women's magazines in her spare time. *All We Know of Heaven* and *A Woman's Choice* were her previous novels. She lives in London.

Also available in Fontana Paperbacks

**ALL WE KNOW OF HEAVEN
A WOMAN'S CHOICE**

SANDEE COHEN

The Palace of Shadows

FONTANA PAPERBACKS

First published by Fontana Paperbacks 1984

Copyright © Sandee Cohen 1984

Made and printed in Great Britain by
William Collins Sons & Co. Ltd, Glasgow

ACKNOWLEDGEMENTS

Lines from 'Song of the Barren Orange Tree' by Federico Garcia Lorca, *Selected Poems of Federico Garcia Lorca*. Copyright 1955. Reprinted by permission of New Directions Publishing Corporation, New York.

Lines from 'What is to be given' by Delmore Schwartz, from *Summer Knowledge*, copyright 1938, New Directions Publishing. Reprinted by permission of New Directions Publishing Corporation.

Lines from 'Contusion' by Sylvia Plath from her collection *Ariel*, published by Faber and Faber Ltd, London. Copyright Ted Hughes, 1965. Reprinted by permission of Ted Hughes.

Lines from 'A Mania for Solitude' by Cesare Pavese, from *Selected Poems*, translated by Margaret Crosland, published by Peter Owen, London and Boston, and reprinted by permission of Peter Owen.

Lines from 'Canto Amor' by John Berryman, from *Homage to Mistress Bradstreet*, reprinted by permission of Faber and Faber Ltd, London.

Lines from 'Fern Hill' by Dylan Thomas, from *Collected Poems*, published by J.M. Dent and reprinted by permission of David Higham Associates Ltd, London.

Lines from 'Conversations with Kafka' by Gustav Janouch, published by The Village Press and reprinted by permission of Gustav Janouch.

Lines from 'An Unpublished Journal' by Malcolm Lowry, copyright Douglas Day, reprinted by permission of Oxford University Press.

Lines from 'You Can't Go Home Again' by Thomas Wolfe, reprinted by permission of Charles Scribner Co., New York.

Lines from 'Last Poem' by Robert Desnos, from *European Poetry*, reprinted by permission of Bantam Books Inc., New York.

Lines from 'Paris' by Gertrud Kolmar, reprinted by permission of G.K. Magpie Press, London.

Lines from 'Live or Die' by Anne Sexton, reprinted by permission of Sterling Lord Agency Inc., New York.

Lines from 'Poem 113' by Osip Mandelstam, from *Selected Poems of Osip Mandelstam*, translated by Clarence Brown and W.S. Merwin (1973) and reprinted by permission of Oxford University Press.

Lines from 'A Slow Poem' by Frank O'Hara in *Poems Retrieved* (San Francisco: Grey Fox Press, 1977), reprinted by permission of Grey Fox Press, San Francisco.

Lines from 'Small Prayer' by Weldon Kees, from *The Collected Poems of Weldon Kees*, reprinted by permission of University of Nebraska Press. Copyright 1975, University of Nebraska Press.

Lines from 'Legend' by Hart Crane, from *The Collected Poems and Prose and Letters of Hart Crane*, reprinted by permission of Liveright Publishing Corporation, New York.

Lines from 'An Unwritten Novel' by Virginia Woolf, from *A Haunted House and Other Stories*, reprinted by permission of The Author's Literary Estate and The Hogarth Press Ltd.

Lines from 'Sonnet XI' by James Agee, from *The Collected Poems of James Agee*, copyright 1962, 1968 by The James Agee Trust. Reprinted by permission of Houghton Mifflin, Publishers, New York.

Lines from 'The Face' by Randall Jarrell reprinted by permission of Faber and Faber Ltd, London.

You cannot trust the ones who are too
careful. As writers or drinkers. Old
Goethe cannot have been so good a man
as Keats or Chatterton. Or Rimbaud.
The ones that burn.

Malcolm Lowry.

This book is dedicated to
The beloved memory of my mother and
father. As always . . .
To Josephina and Michelle in gratitude.
And to 'The ones that burn'.

All the poetry quoted in this book
was written by men and women who
lived for their art. Some of them even
died for it.

What is written illuminates the world,
but the writer disappears into darkness.
Franz Kafka, 1883–1924.
Gustav Janovch. *Conversations with
Kafka*

CHAPTER ONE

I want to live without seeing myself.

Federico Garcia Lorca, 1898–1936.
Song of the Barren Orange Tree

'Looks like your poet friend isn't going to show up,' the broad-shouldered American says, his shrewd grey eyes travelling speculatively over his companion's beautiful, but at this moment, unsmiling face.

'He isn't my friend,' Rebecca Farrell corrects, in her husky, slightly mannish voice. 'He's my client.'

'Not much of a client if he hasn't written anything in three years,' comes back the cynical reply.

'In this case the last thing which concerns me is my ten per cent.'

'Before you open your own literary agency, Rebecca, you'd better get rid of that dangerous idealism, otherwise you'll go broke within a year.'

Rebecca fixes him steadily with her startlingly blue eyes and raises her unfashionably thick, arching eyebrows. 'Oh you think so?'

Eliot Vaughan's strong, handsome features break into a smile of ungrudging admiration.

'No, as it happens I don't think so. I've known you long enough to realize you could sell freezers to the Eskimos.' He leans forward and kisses her mouth before asking, 'Do you want another bitter lemon or shall we forget Roth and have dinner?'

'Give him ten more minutes.'

'Whatever you say. I've got to make a phone call to Russ

Allen before he leaves for Hollywood in the morning. Order me another bourbon will you?'

Left alone, Rebecca takes the book off the seat beside her and reads one of the haunting poems. Nathan Roth has been called a genius, a man whose work ranks alongside that of Keats, Rimbaud and Whitman, a man who has been labelled impossible to know even by his oldest friends. Rebecca had been given a taste of that impenetrable personality this afternoon when she had met Nathan Roth for the first time. She stares at the photograph of the poet on the dust jacket of the book. It shows a gaunt-faced man with thick, black hair, turning grey, sitting before a typewriter and glancing up, startled, as though caught off guard by the camera. Five years out of date it was taken when the New York born Roth was thirty-four, but even then his narrow, deep set brown eyes behind the metal framed spectacles were sorrowful, as though the visionary was anticipating his own tragic future. He has changed since that photo was taken; his hair is now completely grey, his shoulders stoop, and he walks with the aid of a stick.

When Rebecca had learned through Roth's U.S. agent, Irving Kauffman, that Roth was coming to London for the funeral of an old friend she had written directly to him asking that he call in and see her in her office in Berkeley Square, not merely as a client, but as a man whose poems she has loved since she was old enough to comprehend their meaning. The letter, as all others to him had done in the past, went unanswered. Then that afternoon he had shown up in the reception of A.S. Greaves. He had limped into her office minus his spectacles, looking much older than his thirty-nine years and yet, paradoxically, almost boyish.

Although a cold November day with icy rain in the air, he had been wearing nothing but a tired looking tweed jacket, with the collar turned up to his stubbled chin, a shapeless sweat shirt and blue jeans that hung from his narrow hips. On his feet were a pair of worn down sneakers, and, another odd detail, he wasn't wearing any socks. She had offered her hand in awed greeting, proud to be meeting him at last, he had grasped her hand for only a second, admitting in his gentle Jewish accent that he had forgotten her name. His hand had been chilled, that and the deep pain in his eyes had made a shiver rush up her backbone. His neutral gaze had rested momentarily on her stunning face as she had offered tea or coffee, any hot drink.

He had sat down, his left leg jutting stiffly before him, the curved handled walking stick resting against his thigh. His bony hands, so pale, like his face, and lined in heavy blue veins, had searched his pockets until he located a pack of crushed cigarettes. When he had dropped his box of matches Rebecca had quickly retrieved them, putting them into his trembling hands. He had sat there smoking in silence, his eyes under fine, crescent shaped brows totally remote. Did he have a warm coat, she had asked him, to which his reply had been confusing. Not once did his distracted gaze come to her broad, dark face.

After ten minutes of her trying to start up a conversation, he had stood and limped to the window. The bleak scene, the trees standing in lonely isolation dropping their dead brown leaves onto the wet grass, had appeared to please him and something akin to a sad smile had turned up the corners of his sensitive mouth. Rebecca had joined him and standing there, she had seemed to tower above his hollowed out frame, though in reality at five feet ten inches she could only have been an inch or so taller than him. She knows so little about him, only the scant biographical details off the covers of his books; a brilliant Harvard graduate student, awards, degrees. In the end she had talked to him about New York, and poetry in general, but her voice had faded out in the gradually dawning knowledge that her words were simply not penetrating his self-imposed trance.

To draw him back from across the distance of his thoughts she had placed her hand on his shoulder. He had turned his head slowly to look at her and his hurt eyes had stared for the only time into hers. This had been one of the few occasions in her thirty years that she could ever recall being tongue-tied. His gaze had moved from her face to her hand, large and dark and strong, with colourless nail varnish on short, square nails. Her hand had evidently fascinated him because even after it had dropped from his shoulder he had stared at it, slightly unnerving her.

When eventually she had found her voice again she had asked him outright if he would care to join her and Eliot at his hotel for a drink this evening. He had said no, explaining gently that he was unhappy in company, so she had not pressed the issue. Before seeing him down to the street she had taken her expensive, checkered scarf and with characteristic generosity, wound it around his exposed and wrinkled neck, smiling at him, touched by his shy, withdrawn manner.

Outside on the terraced entrance he had said he would be in the lounge bar of the hotel at 8 p.m. He had said it without a trace of a smile, though his voice had been soft, and afraid. She had stood there, transfixed, as he limped down the street in the rain. Since then she had been unable to get him out of her thoughts. And the book; well, she had brought that along this evening in the faint hope that he would write something in the fly leaf. But it is now after nine o'clock, and Eliot appears to be correct, he isn't going to show up.

'Okay,' Eliot says, sitting down and taking her hand. 'Sorry I took so long. It's getting late, Rebecca, what would you like to do?'

Before she can answer their joint attention is drawn to a commotion at the entrance to the lounge bar. A frizzy haired blonde is rubbing vigorously at her twisted ankle while the disgruntled waiter picks up two glasses from the carpet. Beside her, his face completely expressionless, is Nathan Roth.

'That's him,' Rebecca says, trying to control the sudden tremor of excitement in her chest. 'But he didn't say anything about the girl.'

'Those two?' Eliot's deep voice betrays incredulity. The woman's metal bracelets jangle noisily as she wiggles toward their table in a tight red velour dress and high heels, with the poet following, wearing the same clothes as this afternoon and still needing a shave. Eliot stands up.

'Good evening, Mr Roth,' Rebecca says, her tone friendly, yet guarded, 'I'm pleased you could make it.'

'I brought a friend,' he says in his quiet, remote voice. 'Alice Kowaski.'

'Hello, Alice,' Rebecca manages, her wide mouth pulling back in a hesitant smile of greeting. 'This is Eliot Vaughan. Eliot, Alice Kowaski and Nathan Roth.'

'Pleased to make your acquaintance, I'm sure,' Alice pronounces in a broad Brooklyn accent, her teeth and gums emerging in a big, amiable grin as she looks first at Rebecca and then at Eliot.

The two men nod curtly at each other. If there is one virtue Eliot admires it is punctuality, so Nathan Roth, who has never worn a wristwatch in his life, has already got off on the wrong foot. His eyes move over Eliot's athletic six foot frame inside a charcoal grey, double breasted suit and a nerve begins to twitch ominously in his left cheek. When everyone is seated Eliot snaps his fingers and the waiter appears.

'I'm gonna have a pink gin,' Alice says, working a piece of chewing gum around her teeth as she speaks, and making her enormous hoop ear-rings dance against her jaw.

She crosses her legs treating Eliot to an unobstructed view of her smooth thigh. He coughs to stifle the birth of laughter in his throat. Roth lights a cigarette, his hands still trembling. He offers one to Alice and lights it for her.

'Thank you, Nathan,' she says winking at him intimately. His bitter-sweet, long, thin lips give a joyless little closed-mouth smile. Rebecca's eyes move over Alice's face, her curiosity about this odd relationship greatly aroused.

Alice could be any age from thirty to forty-five. The colour range of her cosmetics would make a rainbow look anaemic. A pleasant face, with bright enthusiastic eyes that protrude slightly, a nose with a pointed tip and nostrils that flare when she speaks. Her other charms are indisputable. The kind of figure that stops traffic, a pair of Vegas show girl legs, and a sexuality that leaves very little to the imagination. She moves in a cloud of cheap perfume.

'How are you enjoying London?' Rebecca asks her to start the conversation rolling.

'It's okay, I guess. I been watching the T.V. since I got here.' She gives an unrelated, high pitched giggle.

The waiter distributes the drinks. Alice lifts her glass.

'Thanks, Eliot,' she murmurs flirtatiously, giving him the full force of her pink and white smile.

'You're welcome, Alice,' he answers politely, inclining his head, obviously much amused. He looks at Roth. 'What do you think of this British weather?'

Rebecca watches Roth drink his scotch, wince and then touch his chest before replying.

'It doesn't bother me.'

'Nathan likes the rain,' Alice supplies, 'he even goes for long walks in the rain. Me, I don't care if it never rains again.'

'Is your hotel room comfortable, Mr Roth?'

The poet turns his vague gaze onto Rebecca's face and says in an unemotional voice, 'Yes, thank you.'

'What business are you in, Eliot?' Alice asks chummily.

'I make movies.' He blots his firm lips on the small napkin. 'I'm an independent producer.'

'You're kidding!' Alice bursts out excitedly. 'Nathan, did you hear that? Wow, I ain't never met a real life movie producer before. You here making a picture, huh?'

'Keep your voice down,' Eliot suggests, merely because her voice is loud.

'Oh yer, sure, sorry.' She puckers her face knowingly and taps the side of her nose. 'We don't want no one bothering you for your autograph.'

Rebecca covers her laughing mouth with her glass and looks at Eliot out of the corner of her eye. That last remark would have made his evening for him.

'Gee, me in the same company as a movie producer.'

Rebecca gives a mental shake of her head. There sits Alice beside a man who could arguably be called the world's greatest living poet and she is inordinately impressed because Eliot makes pictures – not very good ones in her own opinion. She steals a glance at Roth. She can feel him analysing them, putting first her, then Eliot under his microscope of a poet's eye, eyes that tonight are ringed in darkness like fading bruises. As the conversation drags itself sentence to sentence he repeatedly touches his chest just below the rib cage. She would ask him if he is in pain but somehow she thinks that enquiry would embarrass him in front of Eliot who looks like he has never suffered a day's illness in his life. Roth pushes the tumble of grey hair from his tired eyes. He tries to light a cigarette but his hands shake. Eliot leans over and lights it for him, making him blink rapidly as the heavy gold lighter snaps shut in his face.

'Tell me the names of some of the movies you've made,' Alice urges, sitting forward, hungry for the vicarious sense of pride Eliot's celluloid triumphs will give her.

He reels off the names of his last three pictures, all of dubious artistic merit but all natural box office hits. Alice's eyes strain further and further from their sockets.

'Wow, Nathan, did you hear that?'

When Roth remains silent Eliot observes disdainfully, 'Mr Roth is unimpressed. Maybe he doesn't think there is as much creative integrity in a movie as there is in one of his poems?'

'Eliot, do you mind,' Rebecca says warningly, concerned that his tone is gradually creeping closer to outright rudeness.

'Nathan don't like the movies,' Alice explains. 'He says they scramble your brains. But I watch them all the time and my brains ain't scrambled.'

Eliot opens his mouth to speak but Rebecca cuts across before he can deliver what she suspects would have been an unnecessarily cutting reply.

'Mr Roth, are you all right?' she asks, suddenly upset by the expression in his eyes.

'I'm fine,' he says, slightly hoarse, looking at Eliot who is staring at him critically.

'You an actress, Rebecca?' Alice's thin, pencilled-in brows furrow with the momentousness of this enquiry.

'No, I'm a literary agent.'

'A what?'

Rebecca glances impatiently at her. It was Nathan Roth's company she sought tonight, not this shop-soiled vamp from a bygone era. She catches herself resenting Alice's presence and then feels guilty because Roth's kind eyes are condemning her, her shortness.

'I negotiate contracts for authors,' she says, putting it as plainly as she can for Alice's benefit.

'That's nice, but I bet you'd rather be an actress, huh?'

'As a matter of fact, I wouldn't. I enjoy my work. Besides which I can't act,' she adds laughing toward Eliot.

'That never stopped anyone before,' he comments, joining in her laughter.

Nathan is trying to attract the waiter's attention. After three attempts he gives up. Eliot snaps his fingers and the waiter's response is instant. Roth touches his chest, his eyes beginning to blink with helpless embarrassment. He looks at Rebecca who smiles kindly, sensitive to his discomfort and wanting him to know it.

'I always wanted to be an actress,' Alice says, 'I guess

16

that's why I like my work. It's kinda like being in show business.'

'What line of work are you in?' Eliot asks.

'I'm a striptease artiste,' she announces not without a trace of genuine pride.

'I don't think I quite caught what you said,' Rebecca tells her, frowning.

'She said she's a stripper,' Eliot informs her with a smile that mocks her astonishment. 'She takes her clothes off to music.'

Alice draws heavily on her cigarette before saying, 'It's very artistic, none of that bump and grind stuff. I use real high-brow music, The Beatles, The Bee Gees, know what I mean?' Her gaze leaps eager and hopeful to Eliot's. 'I guess you're always on the look-out for new talent, huh? Why don't you take a look at my routine next time you get to New York? I work at the Blue Lagoon, come see me.'

'Oh I will,' Eliot assures her with comic enthusiasm. 'Do you ever watch Alice's performance?' he asks Roth, who is contributing nothing to the conversation.

'He don't need to,' Alice intervenes, 'he gets a private show every night.' She gives a burst of lascivious laughter but stops after one glance at Rebecca's stony face. 'Sorry. I got carried away. I guess I ain't used to being in polite company.'

Rebecca watches Roth over the top of her glass. He looks as though he hasn't slept properly for weeks and there is a history of suffering in those premature lines on his forehead that go back into some immutable, private hell. Surely Alice can offer no comfort to a man like him?

Puzzled, she stares from one to the other and when her gaze collides with his he looks away, blinking.

'I got this terrific stage name off the race card at Belmont,' Alice says. 'I call myself Fifi Laverne. Ain't that great? Hey, you two, wanna see what Nathan bought me?' From her large imitation leather bag she produces a fluffy blue rabbit. She touches a switch concealed in the animal's back and sets it on the table where it bangs a drum and blows a whistle making her giggle uncontrollably.

'Jesus Christ,' Eliot mutters under his breath.

'I'm gonna treasure it always,' Alice says, squeezing Nathan's pale hand. Their hands remain locked together in her lap. Rebecca finds her gaze compelled to the knot of fingers, unable to define the twist of emotion that makes her want to push the mechanical toy off the table and tell Alice Kowaski to grow up. After a moment she raises her gaze to Roth's face. Their eyes meet and this time it is she who has to look away. When the rabbit stops its repetitive noise Alice puts it away with a satisfied smile.

'I'm aching to go to the john,' she confesses. 'Do you think they got one down here?'

'I'll join you,' Rebecca volunteers, wanting to escape for a moment. 'Will you take care of Mr Roth?'

'Go ahead,' Eliot says, lighting a cigarette.

In the cubicle Alice sings an old Beatles favourite. The door is unbolted and she emerges. She removes the half dozen dress rings from her bitten down fingers and washes her hands. From her bag she takes a large holdall from whose murky and faintly aromatic depths she brings a selection of small pots, cartons and tubes. She applies the contents to her face, layer upon layer, talking all the time, changing direction in mid sentence but remaining loyal to the same subject, herself.

'Do you think I could ever be an actress, Rebecca?'

'Why not?' she answers evasively. 'How did you meet Nathan?'

Alice removes one piece of gum from her mouth and replaces it with a fresh strip, offering one to Rebecca who shakes her head.

'In a bar.' She gives Rebecca the once-over. 'That's a nice dress you're wearing.' It is black with long, tight sleeves, a

18

neat silver motif design and a wide white collar beneath which Rebecca has put a single, short row of delicate pearls. 'Of course it wouldn't look good on me. I gotta wear something with more dazzle, know what I mean?' She tugs her own dress down from the waist then peers closely at herself in the mirror. 'Do you think I oughta get a nose job?'

'A nose job?' Rebecca repeats blankly.

'Yer, you know, plastic surgery. Marilyn Monroe had a nose job and look where it got her.'

'Your nose is fine. So you met Nathan in a bar?'

'Yer, I had nowhere to live so he let me move in with him.' She halts the paintwork a moment to clarify her words. 'It ain't like it sounds. He always treats me real decent and respectful. He ain't always trying to paw me. Take most guys, they find out I take my clothes off for a living and they think that gives them the right to treat me like dirt. But not Nathan.' She goes back to studying her handiwork in the mirror. 'You sure I don't need a nose job?'

'I'm sure,' Rebecca confirms impatiently. 'Have you known him very long?'

'Four, no, five months now. He gets these moods, real queer, know what I mean? Take me, I'm one a those people who can see the good side of everything. But Nathan, he gets depressed and sick. Know something?'

'What?' Rebecca says anxiously.

'I ain't so sure about not needing a nose job.'

When they get back to the table Eliot is sitting alone.

'Mr Roth had to leave,' he says indifferently.

'Oh gee, I was just beginning to enjoy myself.' Alice looks at Rebecca. 'See, like I said, he gets these moods. I'd better go. See you around.' With manifest regret she walks away from the table, her hips swinging seductively. Rebecca sits down.

'What did you say to him?'

'What makes you think I said anything to him?'

'I know you. Diplomacy isn't one of your strong points.'

'He's oversensitive.'

'What did you say?' she persists.

'All I did was ask him about his wife.'

'Eliot . . . ' She breaks off with an angry sigh.

He turns to look at her, a puzzled expression on his face.

'There was an odd smell about him, did you notice that?'

'No,' she says almost inaudibly.

'You must have noticed it. My brother always smelled that way. It's the smell of death.'

CHAPTER TWO

What do you fear?
Being found out.
Then why do you always give yourself away?

Malcolm Lowry, 1909–1957.
Lines From An Unpublished Journal

Later that evening across the table in the restaurant Rebecca
touches Eliot's hand consolingly. A few months ago he had
told her about his brother Scott who had died at fifteen after
a long history of illness. An illness that had eaten away at
his parents' energy and savings, an illness that made the
neglected older son grow up with more hostility than sympathy toward the sick.

'I was sorry when Scott died, but I hated what he did to
my parents, I hated how they got old before their time,'
Eliot reflects bitterly. 'In the bar, with Roth, I could see
Scott sitting there, that same smell, that same colourless
skin, that same look in his eyes.' He swallows hard and then
smiles apologetically. 'Crazy.'

'No,' Rebecca demurs, 'we all have our little obsessions.'
She draws in a deep breath and releases it slowly. She tastes
her coffee. 'I suppose it was thoughtless of me to invite
Roth to meet you. It must have brought back all his bad
memories of Hollywood.'

'Hollywood didn't kill his wife, it could have happened
anywhere.' He pauses to light one of his thin, brown cigarettes, exhaling the slightly aromatic smoke with satisfaction. 'Did you know Roth was driving that night?'

'No,' Rebecca says quietly. 'I didn't. I read a brief report

21

in the newspaper. French movie actress killed and her husband, poet Nathan Roth, seriously injured when their car went off the road during a storm.'

'You memorized it,' Eliot observes with something of the contempt that is present in his tone when he discusses Nathan Roth now.

'I seem to have done, don't I? I'd only just gone to work for Greaves.' She shakes her head. 'He must have been inconsolable. That was three years ago, just about the time he stopped writing.'

'You think Madeline was his inspiration?' Eliot asks sceptically in a manner that makes Rebecca suspect he knows more than he is saying.

'Virginia Woolf said, "Women have burnt like beacons in all the works of all the poets from the beginning of time." '

'I don't know anything about that. I only know there was a lot of bad talk after her death.'

She looks at him sharply. 'You've never mentioned that before.'

'I never mentioned it because you've always admired Roth's poems and who am I, a humble mass culture man, to poison your mind against a genius?'

'By bad talk you mean Hollywood gossip,' Rebecca states in contempt. 'I thought you were above that sort of thing.'

'I'm only human.' Eliot's expression is full of mock humility.

'I sometimes have my doubts,' she says smiling, and then turning serious again before asking, 'What was she like, Madeline Boucher, did you ever meet her?'

'Once or twice. She was much in demand as an actress but she hadn't made any films outside France. She didn't impress me, on or off the screen, not my type. She had that popular waif look of the time, white skin, straight blonde hair, big empty eyes, thin as one of these.' He holds up one of his cigarettes. 'About as opposite from you as it is possible to get,' he adds, looking at her long black hair falling

22

in loose curls over her broad shoulders, and thinking about her strong, dark, shapely body and large breasts.

Rebecca Farrell has the kind of face men dream about and women can but envy. Even Eliot, who had met some of the world's most beautiful women, had been forced to stare the first time he had seen those deep blue eyes fringed with dark lashes and that rather large, straight nose. There is so much more to her face than bland beauty. There is that striking cleft in her chin, the soft, full lower lip that could have the most unimaginative men engaging in sexual fantasies. But for Eliot she had a quality in her face that most of those other beauties lacked, strength of character; in fact Rebecca Farrell is a woman strong in mind and body.

'What do you think Roth sees in Alice?' Rebecca enquires, keeping her voice casual.

'Some men feel inadequate with women of beauty and brains. Since Miss Laverne has neither, Roth probably feels very relaxed in her company.'

'That's unfair to Roth. You might not appreciate his work but I do, and I'm in very good company. Do you know he has three Pulitzer Prizes, three.' She holds up the equivalent fingers.

'I can count,' Eliot says, grabbing her hand and kissing it.

'You're just jealous because you don't even have an Oscar.'

'Oscars don't necessarily equal good box office. I'm not in this business to win prizes.' He calls the waiter for the check. 'If Roth is so successful why doesn't he buy himself some decent clothes? He wasn't wearing any socks, did you notice that?'

'You show me a rich poet and I'll show you a philanthropic publisher. In fact the real visionary, the true genius doesn't give a damn about money.'

'There it is again, that dangerous idealism. What do geniuses live on, welfare? Right, so let them get a job. Roth

23

could park cars, anything.' He helps her on with her coat. 'He doesn't write anymore. How does he live?'

'With great difficulty I expect, and men like Nathan Roth do not park cars. Though I am surprised he doesn't have a teaching post in a university.'

'Maybe no university would have him.'

'You must be joking. Mr Roth could be on the faculty of any university he chose.'

'Okay, don't get upset.' He puts his hands on her shoulders and sways her back and forth, kissing her haughty left eyebrow that had risen in prompt and earnest defence of the poet.

She wakes with a start and listens. It can't be morning already? She props herself on one elbow and reads the time on the illuminated face of her travelling clock: 2.45 a.m. She could have sworn the alarm bell woke her. Then she hears it again, not the alarm bell but the one on her front door.

'Eliot.' She shakes him by the shoulder. 'Eliot, wake up,' she whispers insistently, 'there's someone at the door.'

He lies there, a stone in slumber, breathing noisily. She gets out of bed and into her kimono. She puts on the light in the hall and squints through the spy-hole in the front door. On the other side, the distorted image of Nathan Roth looms up in front of her. Quickly she opens the door.

'What's happened? What are you doing here?'

'Can I come in?' His voice is hoarse as though he has a sore throat.

'Of course.' She reaches out for his arm and draws him inside, closing the door. 'How did you find me?'

'Irving gave me your home address before I left the States. He said I should have it in case I got in trouble.'

'And are you?'

Before he can answer Eliot's irritable voice booms out from the bedroom. 'Rebecca?'

'I'm sorry,' Roth says, speaking with evident discomfort

24

as he touches his chest. 'I didn't realise ...' He turns to leave. Rebecca grabs his arm.

'Wait a minute, he doesn't live here. You'd better sit down.'

'Rebecca, what the hell is going on?' Eliot halts abruptly halfway into the room, his face hardening. 'Roth,' he spits out angrily.

'Don't shout,' Rebecca tells him, 'you'll wake the neighbours.' She looks at Roth who is standing there with a vague expression on his drained face. 'I'll get you a hot drink.'

'Thank you,' he says before slumping to the carpet at her feet.

'My God, he's fainted. Help me get him onto the couch.' Rebecca grips his legs and waits for Eliot to take his shoulders but he remains stubbornly motionless, his hands in his bathrobe pockets. 'Eliot? All right, damn you, I'll lift him myself.'

Eliot comes forward with an undisguised look of repugnance on his face. He grips the poet's jacket and together they lift him onto the couch. Rebecca touches his hair.

'He's soaked. He must have been walking around in the rain. Please take off his shoes.'

'Some chance,' Eliot says with a chilly laugh.

'Then get a blanket from the cupboard in the bedroom.' He hesitates. 'Well go on!' she urges, losing her temper.

When he returns she is sitting on the edge of the couch with the upper part of Roth's body leaning against her as she removes his jacket. He waits there with the blanket, his eyes hostile, yet curious, he has never seen Rebecca in this role before and his irritation is aggravated by jealousy. She snatches the blanket from his hand and uses it to cover the poet. She rubs his chilled hands between both of hers, first one, then the other, briskly, to aid his circulation. Calm, efficient and, above all, gentle.

'The first aid books tell you to put the victim's head between his legs but I'm not going to risk that.'

She rests her palm against his forehead. She goes to the bathroom and returns with a damp flannel which she places over his brow. He moans softly and she goes back to rubbing his hands.

'I wish I had some of those old fashioned smelling salts.' She glances up at Eliot's arrogant face. 'You're a lot of help.'

Roth's eyelids flutter rapidly and then open, his confused eyes focusing on Rebecca's anxious face.

'Would you like me to call a doctor?' she asks softly.

'He doesn't need a doctor, he's not sick, he's plastered.'

'No . . . I'm fine . . . ' Roth croaks.

'Ask him what he's doing here. Did you give him your address? Did Alice throw him out or something?' His lips twist into a cruel knot of interrogation.

'Instead of asking stupid questions why don't you make us all some tea?'

'The Goddamn English and their tea. I don't want tea, I want sleep.'

'Then go to bed, I'm not stopping you.'

'No, he is.' He points an accusing finger at Roth who tries to lever himself off the couch with a weak, 'I'd better . . . be going.'

'You stay where you are.' She covers him with the blanket. 'This is my flat and I'll decide who stays and who leaves.'

'I'm going to bed,' Eliot says in disgust.

'Good. I'll try not to wake you when I come in.'

Roth's eyes slant to look at Eliot's sturdy, well exercised legs and at his broad back as he strides to the door and slams it behind him.

'Take no notice,' Rebecca advises. 'He hates anyone to disturb his beauty sleep. I'll get you that tea.'

When she comes back into the room he is leaning against the wall clutching at his stomach.

'Nathan,' she says in alarm, putting down the tea. 'What is it?'

'Where ... where is the bathroom?' He heaves himself off the wall, stumbles against a chair and drops his stick. Rebecca supports him across the hall and into the bathroom. 'Get ... out ...' he says, the colour draining from his face. He retches into the sink, his entire frail body racked with the effort. He grips the bowl while Rebecca holds him around the waist. When the first spasm has passed he looks sideways at her, expecting to see revulsion in her eyes and finding only anxiety. He vomits again, feeling it come up through his chest, burning like fire, thick in his throat. When he vomits a third time there is nothing more to bring up except saliva and he begins to cough as though he is choking.

'Swallow some of this water,' Rebecca instructs, remaining totally calm.

She puts her hand on the back of his neck as he bends over the sink, spent, bent almost double with pain and gasping as he tries to breathe. She holds the glass to his lips as he drinks. She uses a paper tissue to wipe some vomit from his chin and another to wipe the tears from his eyes. She holds him, his head on her shoulder, rubbing her hands over his back until he is breathing more easily, speaking comfortingly to him, supporting the meagre weight of his body. When he can walk she takes him back to the couch and covers him with the blanket. The veins in his neck and forehead are standing out, throbbing with their tiny, independent pulse. She combs the hair off his face with her fingers.

'Lie quietly, you'll be fine now.'

'Where is ... my scarf?'

'It was damp. I ...'

'I want my scarf.' His face muscles twitch.

27

She puts it on the blanket and he clutches it with his skeletal fingers, trembling violently. She sits down on the couch and embraces him, trying to warm him with her own body heat. She makes him fresh tea which he sips slowly from the cup which she holds. In time he stops shaking. Rebecca watches him with deep concern. His face looks like a skull. She blinks. Not it doesn't, that is simply her imagination and a trick of the shaded light behind his head. It looks like a face, the face of a very sick man.

'How do you feel now, Nathan?'

'The pain goes . . . ' he says, drawing his arm across his deeply furrowed brow, ' . . . it always goes finally.'

'You ought to see a doctor.'

He nods without looking at her, as though acknowledging the wisdom of her suggestion but reserving the right not to adopt it.

'Do you know what causes it?'

'Indigestion.'

She stares at him wondering if this is a serious answer or a joke. He doesn't smile. He never smiles. She hates the way he never smiles. He smiled once this evening at Alice, but that wasn't a smile of pleasure, it was a shape made by his sculptured lips, the smile of an ascetic. She makes her voice light and conversational.

'Perhaps if we talk it will take your mind off the pain. What was so urgent that you had to see me tonight?'

For a moment he is lost in thought, then he says, 'I don't know.' His lidless eyes show weariness.

'Perhaps you'll remember by the morning.'

He gives a jerky motion of his head and touches his stomach inside the blanket.

'You ought to get some sleep. I'd better . . . '

'No, wait, please.'

She looks at his hand on her arm, one white and thin, the other strong and brown.

'It's always difficult to get to sleep . . . I don't sleep. I just want some company.'

She holds his hand and looks into his eyes under which the spidering of fine blue veins is covered by a layer of translucent skin. He has the saddest eyes she has ever seen, sad and compassionate as though all mankind's pain were his own.

'I'll sit here with you until you sleep,' she says in a comfortable, unhurried way.

He doesn't close his eyes, he stares into the distance as she strokes the hair off his forehead. His inward gaze is constantly focused upon something or someone no one else can see. A mysterious, dark, unfathomable place that his poems evoke in the most lyrical language. Even now Rebecca can sense a ceaseless, alert tension in his mind, the mind of a man who has no peace. The poet eternally engaged in a lonely struggle to find a personal vision that can be transformed, miraculously, into a universal message.

Rebecca speaks suddenly, words she has been longing to say since he walked into her office.

'Nathan, I love your poetry. I have every poem you've ever written. I read them all the time. They share my every emotion.'

He turns his head to look at her, his fine brows peaking to a frown. There is an odd pressure in Rebecca's chest, just below her left breast and her throat feels very tight when she swallows.

'I know how you feel,' Rebecca says, offering him a painful smile, some kind of tangible condolence. 'I lost my mother when I was fourteen. It takes a long, long time to recover.'

A strange brooding hurt comes into his eyes as they move over her uncombed, raven black hair tumbling around her broad shoulders. She smells of sex, sex with another man, a man strong in body and mind. He has never seen eyes this colour before, not that kingfisher colour. The cleft in her square chin deepens when she speaks, and she has a habit of trapping her lower lip between her teeth while she thinks and releasing it when the thought is complete.

'Do you have a cigarette?'

'No, I don't smoke, and neither should you, at least not anymore tonight. You should be trying to sleep,' she says solicitously.

'I'm sorry about your mother,' he says with the simplicity of genuine association with another's pain.

'Would you like me to call your hotel and tell Alice where you are?'

'No,' he says softly with a melancholy smile. 'Alice is used to me being out all night. She won't worry.' He blinks rapidly. 'I don't want anyone to worry over me.'

There is no posturing in this statement, none of the suffering martyr that such a declaration would seem to require. His delicate, bluish eyelids droop closed. Rebecca tucks the blanket in around his neck and shoulders. He does have a certain smell about him, the aroma of frail humanity, of a man whose bones show through his flesh, whose eyes blaze one moment with the intensity of his thoughts and grow unbearably sad the next with some secret pain. She presses a kiss to his forehead, her lips soft and warm on his pale skin. His eyes open.

'I'm pleased you came to see me tonight, for whatever reason,' she says in a respectful voice. 'I'm pleased I had this opportunity to tell you that I believe your loss as a poet and a man to our world is a tragedy. I hope that one day soon you will find it in your heart to come back to us.'

Eliot groans and turns over restlessly as Rebecca climbs into bed. She rubs her eyes and moisture comes away on her hands. Tears? How rarely she cries these days. How rarely she has cried even as a child. Lying there in the darkness she finds her mind suddenly filled with thoughts of her parents. Why now, after all these years, should she suddenly be analysing her feelings toward her mother and father and their strange love for one another?

Her mother, Lillian Bickel, had come from a respectable and wealthy Jewish home. Her father, Sean, had been brought up in a very poor district of Dublin. They had met, of all places, on a London bus. Young Lillian, frightened and excited at being spoken to by a handsome, silver tongued stranger with dark blue twinkling eyes, had allowed him to walk her home. After two meetings she had fallen hopelessly in love with him, this charmer with a grin to melt any girl's heart. Who could blame her, her weakness, when she had been accustomed to keeping company with sombre minded solicitors and antiquated accountants? Who could fault her for being entranced by an impractical dreamer whose sole concept of supporting a family was closing the door behind him on his way out?

When Lillian had told her mother that she wanted to marry Sean the woman was understandably scandalized. Her father, a diamond merchant, had died in his mid forties. Lillian had been a delicate child, she was a sensitive young woman, Mrs Bickel feared that withholding permission would only make matters worse and alienate her only child altogether. But Sean was a wanderer and, as he was so fond of telling his long-suffering wife, you cannot teach an old dog new tricks. He loved Lillian with all the confused idealism only an Irish romantic can feel while never losing his desire for taking off on some wild adventure, temporarily leaving his wife, and then their two children, in the care of his intensely disapproving mother-in-law.

A mad Irishman, Grandmother Bickel called him as often as possible, deserting his family to run around the world searching for Inca gold or the treasures of the Pharaohs. It would be a blessing from God, she would declare, if the itinerant Farrell was eaten by savages or tumbled into an unexcavated tomb. But whatever anyone said about her beloved Sean, Lillian, the devoted wife, continued to pray for

31

his safe return. Which she did for twelve years. Despite her cursing, Grandmother Bickel was a realist, a practical woman. She loved her daughter and was concerned for her grandchildren.

When Sean departed at a moment's notice Grandmother shepherded in her sad flock. The memory of being uprooted from their own home would remain with both children for life. It left Rebecca and her brother Patrick with a deep sense of rootlessness, a constant searching for somewhere to belong and a paradoxical urge not to remain in one place for more than the briefest time. The both wanted a real home and yet they had both inherited their father's wanderlust. Night after night in their grandmother's house Rebecca and Patrick would discuss their own futures.

'I'm never going to feel that way about any man,' Rebecca would declare, remembering her mother's sad face every time her father left. Her dark blue eyes would flash in her already beautiful face. 'Look what love is doing to Mummy. I'm never going to allow a mere man to rule my life. I'm never going to depend on anyone or let anyone depend on me. It makes people unhappy.'

'I'm going to be a famous pilot and own my very own airline,' Patrick would say, his handsome open features taking on his father's dreamy look. 'I'm never going to get married. I'm going to fly around the world and see all those places Daddy talks about.'

'Before or after you become a famous airline pilot?' Rebecca would enquire, ruffling his thatch of black hair and his pride. She was older than he by three years and despite her vow never to become involved, she was Patrick's natural protector. She had to be, their poor mother was unable to protect herself, let alone her confused children.

One day after sixteen years of what, to most women, would have been an intolerable situation, Sean Farrell packed a suitcase and left for the last time. He was caught up in one of those African coups, a not particularly bright, apolitical Irishman, who loved everyone, and he was never heard from again. Of course Grandmother Bickel set the wheels of diplomacy in motion. Her motives were somewhat mixed. She could not let Sean rot in a foreign jail, and if he were dead she wanted to know, how else could she marry her distraught Lillian off to a very nice middle-aged widower who was excitedly awaiting the prospect of becoming Grandmother Bickel's second son-in-law.

The parliamentary probings into Sean's fate were unsatisfactory. No trace could be found of him. Lillian, wasting away with grief, began to crumble before her children's helpless gaze. She could not live without him, she said, taking to her bed. Before her thirty-seventh birthday she died of a broken heart.

When Rebecca was eighteen and Patrick fifteen they found themselves having to make their own decisions and rely on their own judgements. Grandmother Bickel had passed away leaving the two children a great deal of money. For a time Rebecca and Patrick lived with their father's sister, but their characters were too formed, too strengthened by adversity to be bent into obedience by a well meaning but old fashioned Catholic lady. As soon as Rebecca had found a flat she had moved out taking Patrick with her. Rebecca had gone from being a child to being a woman. She had never been allowed the privilege of that irresponsible time when life is light hearted and the most momentous choice a teenager can make is deciding between two party frocks.

Patrick, too, was a man at sixteen. In time he formed a friendship with a Canadian boy and they went back to Montreal together, taking his half of the inheritance and opening a small aviation business. Rebecca and her brother kept up a somewhat sporadic correspondence, why should it be otherwise, after all, they didn't need anyone, even each other. They were free, independent spirits. Then one day out of the blue a letter arrived from Patrick. He was getting married. He was head over heels in love with a Canadian girl called Sally, who was sweet and childlike and Patrick 'just wanted to protect her for the rest of life'. There had been a more sombre postscript. Patrick had, in halting words, tried to tell Rebecca that he had 'succumbed to the same weakness as our mother. If anything happened to Sally I doubt if I could go on living. Is there such shame in caring?' he had asked. 'Everyone pays a price for love, me, I'll have to forget flying around the world, our poor mother paid a high price. She could have married a more suitable man and pleased everyone, but would she have known the joy as well as the heartache, or true love? I'm responsible for the happiness of another human being and I couldn't be more pleased. Try it sometime, Rebecca, do yourself a favour, fall in love.'

Rebecca had not been able to ignore the glimmer of truth in his words. She enjoyed relationships with men, but that was such a strangely cold and distant word. Besides the men she always found attractive were mentally and physically strong, independent types who knew where they were going and wasted no time getting there. Rather like Eliot. She was pleased for Patrick but she had doubts as to whether or not that would be her fate. She simply could not see herself living for another, however much she loved him. Why now, after all these years, should she be suddenly analysing her feelings toward her mother and father and their strange love for each other? Any why does she feel so very cold, cold and indescribably sad? She turns onto her side and goes to sleep.

CHAPTER THREE

There is no word
which can possess or stop you. You gather
wounds as the earth does,
give them life, caressing
breath, silence.

Cesare Pavese, 1908–1950. *A Mania for Solitude*

Rebecca sits in the bed and watches Eliot getting dressed. He is in a predictably surly temper this morning, they still have an unexpected guest on the couch. He takes his jacket out of the wardrobe and the hanger clatters to the floor.

'Shsh . . . you'll wake Nathan.'

He brushes his thick brown hair vigorously and throws the brush on the dressing table.

Rebecca gets out of the bed. She puts one arm around his waist and slips the other hand into his pocket lifting a packet of cigarettes. She kisses his mouth.

'Go edit your movie or whatever it is you do in that little dark room.'

As he opens the bedroom door she calls softly, 'Don't make a noise on your way out.'

He bangs the front door thunderously. 'And the same to you!'

After a shower she dresses, pours two cups of coffee from the percolator and takes them into the living room. Nathan is still sleeping, the blanket wrapped around his thin body, his right arm dangling on the carpet and his head tipped sideways at a severe, unnatural angle. She studies his face, the skin is stretched taut over his prominent cheek bones and those premature age lines on his forehead never relax, even in slumber. Evidently he had a fitful night. She lifts his head carefully to the centre of the armrest and inserts a cushion. He moans, then he coughs, then his eyes open. He rubs them with the backs of his hands, negligently, like a child. He stares at the beautiful woman standing over him in tight brown jeans and a beige tailored shirt.

'Good morning.' She holds out the coffee. He struggles to sit up and gazes around the room.

'Your apartment?' he asks in bewilderment, unable to reconcile this discovery to anything in his immediate memory.

'How is your stomach?'

He puts his hand over his mouth, down over his prickly chin and onto his throat. His hollow face becomes strained as he tries to remember what happened the night before. He takes the coffee and drinks it thirstily, not stopping until the cup is drained. Rebecca refills it for him. She puts her hand on his forehead and he ducks out of her reach. She stares at him in surprise.

'I just wanted to see if you have a temperature.'

'Do you . . . ' he has to clear his throat and even then it sounds hoarse. 'Do you have a cigarette?'

She lights it for him because his hands shake.

He murmurs a shy, diffident thank you, his eyelids flickering rapidly. He looks at the unusual cigarette which makes him cough.

'They're Eliot's, specially blended for people with cast iron lungs. But there is a tobacconist's shop not far from here if you want to buy some of your own brand after breakfast.'

'Where is Eliot?' he asks nervously.

'Gone to the studio. Don't worry about him. His bark is worse than his bite. In his business you have to cultivate an aggressive personality or they eat you alive.' She laughs her husky laughter. Roth's whole face is suffused by a deep, stony calm. Rebecca sighs. 'Mr Roth, I'm not trying to hurt you. What I am trying to do is put you at your ease. It's an unfortunate coincidence that Eliot is in movies and so was Mrs Roth . . . '

'Don't call her that.'

Rebecca makes a pained face. 'I'm sorry, all I did was call her . . . '

'I know,' he interrupts again, never raising his voice or allowing his expression to display anger. 'I just don't want you . . . ' he appears to struggle for a moment with a thought that will not become words. He touches his forehead. ' . . . I just don't want to talk about her.' His bony fingers tremble against his temples. 'It's difficult . . . for me.'

'Yes, of course. I'm truly sorry.' She takes a step closer to comfort him but he waves her off with an awkward, meaningless gesture.

'I'll get out of your way,' he says in a subdued voice. 'You'll be late for work.'

'I don't go into the office on Friday.' She indicates a dog-eared manuscript, a pen and a notebook on the coffee table. 'I read submissions.'

The phone rings. 'Excuse me.' It is her secretary. He listens as she discusses a letter that was in the morning post. She is polite and confident, and when she bestows a concerned smile in his direction he turns away. He pushes his fingers through his untidy hair. Where did he put his shoes? Was he wearing any damn shoes? These days it is increasingly difficult for him to remember. He can smell her, even from across the room, an earthy perfume smell and the woman herself. He can't find his shoes. His search becomes ever more frantic as though time is running out and he must make his escape.

'Mr Roth?'

He leans against the back of the couch because his stick is on the carpet and he doesn't want her to watch him limp awkwardly the way he does without its support.

'Have you lost something?'

He stares at her as she walks across the room toward him, her body moulded by the tight fitting clothes, her breasts straining against the shirt fabric and the shape of her nipples outlined plainly beneath. She tosses the thick hair casually off her face and stands before him with her hands on her hips, saying cheerfully, 'Well now?'

Roth's expression is a curious blend of melancholy and scorn. His mouth hardens and his eyes turn cold.

'I'd better go.'

'Oh no you don't,' she says, narrowing her dark blue eyes to look directly at him as if issuing a challenge. 'Not before a shower and some breakfast.' She picks up his stick and offers it to him. He grasps the curved handle, his suspicious eyes on her face.

'I'm doing all this because I'm after your money,' she says in answer to his mute enquiry.

In due course he emerges from the bathroom fully dressed except for his jacket and shoes. Rebecca is lying across the arms of the chair reading the manuscript and making copious notes as she progresses. She cranes her long neck to look at his naked white feet.

'You could do for the sock industry what Clark Gable did for vests.'

'I beg your pardon?'

'It doesn't matter. Feel more refreshed?'

'As I squeezed the toothpaste it came out too fast. So I tried to get it back in the tube and it went all over your sink.'

Rebecca puts the top of the pen to her lips. His seriousness in making this confession can be in no doubt, but not unnaturally it confuses her.

'I'm not certain I heard you correctly. Did you say you tried to get the toothpaste back into the tube?'

'Do you remember where I put those cigarettes?' He looks around remotely.

'On the couch.' When his back is turned she shakes her head and shrugs her shoulders. 'Back in the tube?' she mutters under her breath.

'I'm holding you up. Please go on.'

'That's all right, I'm used to interruptions,' she smiles at him, her wide mouth parting to reveal her strong, white teeth. 'Besides, do you really expect me to concentrate on work I can do any day when I have Nathan Roth in my home?' She says this so seriously, so sincerely that Nathan looks away from her and limps to the mantelshelf where he lifts a photo frame and squints at the picture of a beautiful dark haired woman with a baby in her arms and a small girl at her feet.

'That's my mother holding Patrick. I'm the one with the ringlets.'

Nathan puts the photo back without comment and rubs his eyes.

'Nathan,' Rebecca says with concern, 'why don't you wear your spectacles?'

'They're broken.' He takes them from his pocket and shows her, like a child showing a broken toy to its mother. One arm is missing.

'I can fix that for you temporarily. But you must get yourself a new pair of frames.'

Nathan sits on the couch and watches her perform a minor operation on his spectacles. She makes an arm from a length of stiff wire, attaches it to the frame and winds cotton wool around the curved end so that it doesn't cut the skin behind his ear. She fits them on him, pushing them gently up over the bump on the bridge of his nose. His eyes blink rapidly behind the lenses.

'How does that feel?'

She is sitting so close that her knees touch his thigh and her fragrant breath fans his gaunt cheek. He nods.

39

The phone rings. This time it is Eliot demanding to know if Roth has left yet.

'As it happens we are just about to have breakfast together. What a pity you can't join us.' She glances over at Nathan who is engrossed in her collection of books.

'Rebecca, get rid of him, and I'm not playing games with you. I don't trust him. You never know what a guy like him could do next. Please, for me.'

'Bye, Eliot.' She drops the receiver in the cradle.

'You have a good collection of biographies,' Nathan says admiringly. 'All literary men?'

'Mostly. Some day I'd like to write a biography but it would have to be of someone I greatly admired, and whose permission I could ask first. I would hate to think the subject was unhappy about what I'd written. I would try to celebrate the person and the creative spirit that makes them what they are. I would be a worshipper, not a detractor.'

'Do you have anyone in mind?'

'No,' she says, joining him in front of the bookshelf. 'It's just an ambition for the future.' Her smile turns ambiguous. 'No one has ever done a biography of you.'

'They wait until you die.'

'Is that what you want?'

'I don't care.' He runs his delicate fingers over the names on the spines. Scott Fitzgerald, Malcolm Lowry, Byron, Joyce, Keats, Dickinson and many more. 'I worked in a book shop on Fifth Avenue once.' He speaks slowly as though his thoughts are straining up to the surface of his memory trying to clarify themselves. 'They wanted Philip Marlowe and I tried to sell them Kafka.'

Rebecca laughs. Nathan looks down at his toes. After a second the corners of his mouth twitch.

'I got fired.'

'There is no justice in this world,' Rebecca says, touching his arm affectionately. 'How about some breakfast?'

'You're busy. I'll get myself another cup of coffee then I'll go.'

She watches him limp into the kitchen. She glances regretfully at the manuscript lying open on the table. She really ought to be getting on with her work but his voice had lacked any conviction. Then suddenly the decision is made for her. She hears something clatter to the kitchen floor. 'Nathan?' she calls in alarm, crossing the hall. She pauses at the kitchen door in amazement. The large bread knife is on the floor and a loaf of bread is on the laminated work top. Standing in the centre of the room is Roth staring at the blood which is oozing up out of a deep cut in the palm of his hand.

'My God, what have you done?' Rebecca rushes him toward the sink and moves his hand under the stream of cold water.

'Stay there. Nathan, do you hear me?' She grips his chin and turns his face around. His eyes stare but see nothing. 'Nathan!' He blinks rapidly, his eyes coming into focus. 'Stay here with your hand under the water,' she commands. She comes back with a small first aid box and has him sit down on a chair with a towel on his lap and his hand on the towel.

'It will stop bleeding in a moment,' she tells him soothingly because his eyes are fixed on the wound as though hypnotized by it.

'It doesn't matter,' he says in an oddly detached voice.

'This is going to sting,' she warns him, dabbing his hand with a mild disinfectant. 'You're lucky, just a little higher and you would have cut the vein.'

'It *was* an accident. I wanted some toast.'

She looks up into his face. His eyes are overbright, restless, far too alert, like someone gripped by a fever.

'I know you didn't do it deliberately.' Even while Rebecca is saying this she is aware of a strange coldness creeping through her limbs. You never know what a guy like him

41

could do next, Eliot had said. She shakes the thought off. What does Eliot know about a man like Nathan Roth? They are as different as Marlowe and Kafka.

'How do you know that?'

'What?'

'How do you know I didn't do it deliberately?'

'Be quiet,' she says, becoming annoyed, but genuine anxiety invades her dispassionate tone. She lays a strip of lint over the wound and winds a bandage around his hand leaving the thumb and fingers free. He really is a most unnerving individual and it takes a lot to shake Rebecca Farrell.

'Have you noticed that they never actually get the blood the right colour in the movies? Have you noticed that?' He passes his other hand wearily across his face, as he says in a tired voice, 'Maybe I should have saved my blood and given it to Eliot.'

'Your interest in blood leads me to suspect that you are descended from vampires.'

His lips give a pitiful twitch of a smile that fades far too soon. They stare into each other's eyes intensely before Roth has to avert his gaze.

'God knows why you even needed a knife – it's a sliced loaf.'

They sit together at the small kitchen table.

'Don't you like bacon?' Rebecca asks, biting into a slice of toast.

Nathan turns his diffused gaze onto her face, wrinkling his narrow forehead like someone gradually awakening from a trance.

'I beg your pardon?'

'Bacon,' she says, indicating same, and smiling.

'I don't eat meat.'

'Oh, you're a vegetarian. Why on earth didn't you say so?'

'Vegetarian?' he repeats, frowning. 'I don't put any name to it. I just don't eat another animal's flesh.'

Rebecca looks down at the solitary slice of bacon left on her plate and receives the mental image of a cheerfully grunting pig oblivious of what fate and the farmer has in store for him. She pushes the plate away, asking hoarsely, 'More coffee?'

Nathan is gazing around the kitchen. Somehow he had expected her to inhabit a more affluent apartment than this one which is perfectly clean and tidy but full of rather shabby, old fashioned furniture like a third rate hotel.

'Nasty, isn't it?' Rebecca comments, reading his thoughts. 'I took it furnished so I accept no blame for the contents. I've been here just over a month and I'm moving out as soon as possible.' She butters him another slice of toast, the first, like the bacon, lies untouched on his plate and is now cold and soggy. She lifts his hand and puts the toast into his fingers and urges the hand toward his lips. 'Not flesh, nor fish, nor fowl. Please?'

Nathan chews mechanically, food has no taste for him. He eats what he must when forced but he might just as well be chewing cardboard.

'Will you take just a little of the egg?' Rebecca suggests, resting her head in her hand on the table. 'Do you like cereal?' she asks hopefully. 'Cornflakes? Porridge with hot milk?'

'When you move out of here where will you go?'

'I don't know yet. Anywhere as long as it's better than this place. I took it as a stop gap. The truth is I'm a nomad. I never stay in any place for very long. I've had a lot of different jobs in many different countries. I even went to stay with Patrick in Montreal for a time but I got so restless. God knows what I'm looking for in life because I certainly don't.' She checks his face for attentiveness. 'Are you really interested in the Life and Times of Rebecca Farrell?' He nods gravely. 'Well, I travelled around Europe.

43

Decided I was getting nowhere fast and came back to London to work for Greaves. I'd worked there before as a secretary to one of the authors' agents so I knew the ropes and, even if I say so myself, I'm damn good at what I do. My problem is too much energy. I have to be constantly stimulated by life. When I learn to do something well it ceases to hold any challenge for me. Though I must admit being a literary agent is the closest I've ever got to having a vocation, albeit frustrating at times.'

Nathan makes a move toward the cigarettes on the table. Rebecca draws them out of his reach.

'Toast first, then cigarettes.'

'Have you found what you're looking for?' Nathan asks in his gentle persuasive voice.

'No,' Rebecca admits with difficulty, made uncomfortable by the poet's perceptive gaze. She shrugs and bites her lower lip. 'I want my life to have meaning. Perhaps I'm destined to wander the world for eternity like my father.'

'Life has meaning only when you look inside yourself,' Nathan states rubbing his finger along the curve of his semitic nose. 'You have to make up your mind if you're looking for a material or a spiritual home.'

'Both,' Rebecca replies without hesitation. 'I've never had a real home since I was a child, nor any real spiritual guidance.'

'Why don't you live with Eliot?'

'Because I'm not ready to live with any man. Old Buddhist principle say: Never search for salvation in anybody else. Old Rebecca principle say: Never become addicted to anyone so that if you lose them . . . ' Her voice fades out lamely. She drinks some coffee to allow the moment to pass before saying softly, 'I'm sorry, that was insensitive of me. But you see my mother never got over the death of my father. She died because he gave her her reason to live That's never going to happen to me.'

Nathan stares at her abstractedly before asking, 'How did you and Eliot meet?'

'At a press showing of his latest picture. I thought it was bad and I told him so. You could say that formed the basis for a beautiful friendship.'

'Are you in love with him?'

'You are nosy,' she says, laughing at his frank question.

Nathan gets up from his chair and limps out of the kitchen.

'Hey, come on back here,' she calls, 'I'm only teasing you.' She follows him into the living room. 'Nathan, I am teasing you. Don't be hurt or angry. Hasn't anyone ever told you teasing is a sign of affection?'

He sits down on the couch and with awkward movements pulls on his moccasins. Rebecca stares at them from three different angles before coming to the unavoidable conclusion that her eyes are not deceiving her. He has put them on the wrong feet. She gets the cigarettes.

'Please don't be hurt.'

'I'm not.' He looks into her eyes over the match flame. She blows it out before it can burn his fingers. He starts to cough. She sits close to him and rubs his back, her warm breath touching his face. He pushes her away, gently but firmly, and reaches for his jacket.

'You're not going yet, are you?' she asks, not bothering to disguise her disappointment. 'I was hoping to discuss your work with you.'

Nathan's eye alights on the manuscript.

'When they come into your office do you read them all?'

'No. There are several of us who read submissions.'

'So you and your colleagues effectively pass judgement on the writer's talent?' he asks in a measured voice.

'If you're implying that the system is wrong I totally agree. But until someone comes up with another idea it's the only way of handling the submissions. I see my work in a positive sense. I'm there to discover talent, not to disillusion those who have none. If I believe a writer has that certain spark I encourage it. Perhaps the book needs more work before I show it to an editor. If I don't want to represent the book I return it with a polite letter suggesting they try another agent.'

'Wouldn't it be kinder to tell the truth?'

'What is the truth? I've given that a lot of thought. Suppose my opinion is unconsciously prejudicial? I can only be subjective. They ought to seek a second, or even a third, opinion. I've turned away books that have subsequently been published. I've also taken on books after my colleagues at other agencies had turned them down. As I said before, it's frustrating, not only for the writer, but for me. It have a great deal of trouble persuading a paperback editor to buy anything of literary merit unless it also has commercial potential. I'm not saying I don't enjoy making a profit for all concerned, but it's profoundly satisfying to sell something of lasting value, such as your poems. I'm very proud to be your U.K. agent and I wish there was more I could do for you.'

The phone rings. Rebecca swears softly under her breath. It had to ring now, just when she had managed to steer the conversation around to his poems. On the other end of the line is a friend of Eliot's inviting them for drinks on Sunday after their regular squash game. She makes a note and terminates the conversation as quickly as she can. When she returns to Nathan his eyes are turned inward upon himself in a kind of introspective stare.

'You play squash?'

'Not very well,' she lies, unable to prevent herself from glancing at his stiff leg. 'I play for Eliot's sake.' Another lie, she played long before he ever came onto the scene.

He stands up.

'Where are you going?'

'To get some cigarettes,' he says, avoiding contact with her stunning blue eyes.

'Would you like me to come with you?' She helps him into his jacket and winds the scarf around his neck. The familiar, not unpleasant odour of his frail body fills her nostrils.

'Nathan, are you hurt by what I said before?'

'No. Nothing hurts me, and everything hurts me. It no longer matters.'

She tries to take his hand but he pushes it into his pocket. He has a pinched look around his nose and mouth.

'You turn left outside the entrance. Be careful of the road. Keep your mind on what you're doing,' she advises.

He leaves the flat and he doesn't return. Rebecca, acting on a hunch calls the hotel. A lazy voice answers with a yawn.

'Yer . . . hello . . . who is it?'

'Alice, this is Rebecca Farrell. Has Nathan contacted you?'

'Sure. He just walked in. Wanna speak with him?'

'No,' she says hastily, relieved and then angry. 'I just wanted to know he was safe.' She hangs up.

She has dreams about him, dreams during which he calls to her across a great and lonely landscape, a distance which grows wider with every dream. Sometimes she awakens in the night because she thinks he is standing in the room, asking her for something, his lips moving without sound. She goes for weeks without thinking about him, at least consciously, but the dreams persist and in moments of solitude or sadness she recalls his gaunt face, his tragic eyes, and his quiet, gentle voice.

CHAPTER FOUR

I saw a man pursuing the horizon;
Round and round they sped.
I was disturbed at this;
I accosted the man.
'It is futile,' I said,
'You can never—'
'You lie,' he cried,
And ran on.

Stephen Crane, 1871–1900. *The Collected Poems*

Three months later Rebecca Farrell is walking across the lobby of the San Francisco Hilton when a shrill, female voice arrests her progress.

'Hey, Rebecca, Rebecca, wait a second!' A young woman with long, dark hair comes hurtling toward her, grabs her hand and shakes it vigorously. 'Hey, Rebecca, don't you remember me?'

The shock of recognition hits Rebecca squarely in her chest. 'Alice?' she says in astonishment.

Alice's gums and teeth emerge in a gleaming pink and white parade of gratification.

'I thought for a second there I had you fooled with this wig. How do yer like it, huh? It's the latest gypsy style.' She does a 360 degree turn in the manner of the great Mae West, showing off her flowing hair and saucer-sized earrings.

'It's very . . . very . . .' Rebecca, still reeling under the shock of finding herself in the same hotel as Alice, hesitates.

searching for precisely the right word. ' . . . startling,' she says uncertainly.

'Startling, huh?' Alice is evidently happy with this description. 'Startling? Yer, I guess it is.' She gives a contented giggle. 'Hey, how about some coffee?'

Without waiting for an answer she takes Rebecca's arm in a quick, proprietary gesture and leads her away to the coffee shop on the other side of the lobby.

As soon as they are seated at their table a waiter appears and fills their cups.

'I'm gonna have a Danish,' Alice says, scanning the menu with her slightly protruding eyes. 'You wanna Danish, Rebecca?'

'No thank you, just coffee,' she tells the waiter.

'Okay, then I won't have no Danish.' She transfers her earnest gaze to Rebecca's face. 'What you doin' in Frisco?'

'I'm here with Eliot. He's on a business trip and I'm having a brief holiday. What brings you to California?'

'I'm here with Nathan and his friend Professor Adler.'

At these words the blood drains from Rebecca's face and a tiny jolt of shock shoots through her heart. She uses both hands to steady her cup on its saucer.

'Nathan is here in San Francisco?' She tries to keep her voice objective but Alice is too self-absorbed to notice any change in Rebecca's tone.

'Alice?' Rebecca calls insistently, and repeats her question.

'Oh yer, he's gonna get some kinda award or sumpin'. I don't know nuthin' about it. They brought me along for the ride. I don't get to travel much. But gee, ain't it some coincidence me and you being here at the same time?'

Alice rambles on and on about the uncertain nature of fate but Rebecca has ceased to listen. Her thoughts are on Nathan Roth. In the departure lounge at Heathrow on the day she and Eliot had flown out her attention had been captured by a frail, gently attractive man in a wheelchair

49

parked close to the boarding gate by a steward of the airline in readiness to board the aircraft. At first when she had looked at him she had seen Nathan's pale, narrow face and her heart had contracted, but on more rational examination the only thing the two men had had in common was that vulnerable look around the eyes. She had spoken of him to Eliot, unable to understand why a man like that should be travelling alone, sitting there, trapped helplessly in the wheelchair, obviously ill at ease, stared at by the other passengers, nervously smoking a cigarette and at the mercy of a uniformed stranger's charity – not even charity, the steward had been paid to do a job. Eliot had looked away and changed the subject. Rebecca had seen nothing more of him, he had been seated in another part of the aircraft.

'. . . so I said, Nathan, this ain't no good, you really gotta take more care of yourself . . . '

'What? What did you say?' Rebecca's thoughts return with a jolt to the present.

'You sure you don't wanna Danish?'

Rebecca waits with admirable patience as Alice unwraps a strip of banana-flavoured chewing gum and pushes it into her mouth.

'Alice, please, you were telling me about Nathan.'

'Oh yer, sure, right. See, he gets sick a lot, I mean real sick and I told him he oughta see a doctor. Mrs Adler told him too but he don't take no notice.'

'Mrs Adler?'

'The professor's wife. They're like parents to Nathan. He's a nice old guy, you'd like him. Hey, I got a great idea, why don't you, me and the boys get together tonight for a drink right here in the hotel?'

'No, it's out of the question. Eliot wouldn't . . . '

'Oh come on, Rebecca, please. I get so lonely, that's the truth. I got no one to talk to see, the professor and Nathan they ain't good fun. I never get a chance to talk with no other female, not like you. The girls at the Club they ain't like you. Oh please, Rebecca.'

Alice's enthusiastic smile and eager gaze conspire to melt what is quite truthfully only a token resistance. Can she possibly resist the urge to see Nathan Roth again, now, after fate has so graciously, or capriciously brought them together again?

'All right.'

'Wow, that's great! Wait until I tell Nathan.'

'Wow . . .' Rebecca echoes softly, '. . . wait until I tell Eliot.'

Surprisingly Eliot does not go through the roof of their room when she tells him, mainly because his eyes tell her he thinks she is teasing him.

'Of all the hotels in all the world they had to be staying in this one,' he drawls, Bogart style.

'I knew you wouldn't mind,' Rebecca says confidently.

'You had me going there for a second, Rebecca.' He kisses her cheek and smiles before going on with adjusting his neck tie.

'Eliot, I wasn't joking. We're meeting them at nine p.m.'

From then on the conversation has only one direction in which to go, down hill all the way.

'Jesus, you could have gotten out of it.'

'I tried.'

'Well maybe you didn't try hard enough.'

'Well maybe I didn't want to.'

Eliot lights one of his cigarettes and sits down heavily on the bed. Rebecca sits beside him.

'Is it because he reminds you of Scott?' she asks reasonably.

'No, it isn't that he reminds me of Scott, damn it, I just can't figure out what you find so attractive about that guy's company. When we were with him in London he hardly said one damn word.'

'He did to me. He's shy. I can't explain it, but I would just like to see him again. One drink, that's all, please.'

Eliot looks at her long black hair, at the indent in her square chin, at the way her left eyebrow curves higher than her right giving her an unintentionally haughty expression.

'If it means that much to you . . .'

'Thank you,' she says, guilt making her avoid his direct gaze.

In the semi-darkness of the Cable Car Bar at nine p.m. Eliot orders a tomato juice for Rebecca and a bourbon for himself. His eyes move over Rebecca's flushed face. If it were possible she looks even more beautiful tonight in a cherry red dress cut deep into her broad shoulders and flaring out from her small waist. She appears unusually nervous, or is it his imagination? Has she ever been nervous?

'Miss Farrell?'

Rebecca turns her head to look at a heavy set man of just over middle height, sporting a short, trimmed beard.

'Yes.'

'I'm Bernard Adler. Nathan's friend,' he adds as if to complete the introduction. He has the lined face of a man who would have been handsome in his youth, bright twinkling eyes, full of gentle and wise humour behind metal rimmed bifocals, and although he is going bald on the crown he has thick, white wings of hair brushed back over his ears. He extends a generously freckled hand which Rebecca grasps, trusting him immediately.

'I'm Rebecca,' she smiles deeply, 'and this is Eliot Vaughan. Eliot, Professor Adler.'

The two men shake hands briefly.

'I'm afraid I'm here as Nathan's emissary. He wonders if you would mind cancelling this evening's plans, only he doesn't feel well.' He gives an embarrassed smile, obviously unhappy with being the bearer of this message. 'He does have a very bad chill, and an early night would benefit him.'

Rebecca's smile is automatic. Damn him, she thinks, damn his cowardice, he's hiding from me. He probably even considered moving hotels. Well let him, let him move planets for all I care. Weak and cowardly, two characteristics she has always despised in a man.

'Won't you join us for a drink, professor?' she hears herself saying.

'Thank you, I'd like that very much, but just one.'

Rebecca looks at Eliot's face resentfully, he need not be so relieved, damned if she is going to leave San Francisco without just once telling Nathan Roth what she thinks of him. Adler is peering at her over the half lenses of his glasses in deep contemplation.

'You said Nathan is unwell, professor, is it anything serious?'

'No, no, really, only a chill.'

'Well I don't think it was too polite of him,' Eliot comments, slipping his arm behind Rebecca's back on her chair and relaxing. 'Though pretty much in character from what I've seen of him.'

'He isn't the most reliable of men,' Adler agrees amiably, 'but then who would deny the prerogative of a genius to be unreliable at times?'

The lines of Eliot's mouth become contemptuous as he says, 'Are you another of Roth's nursemaids?'

'Eliot,' Rebecca rebukes him warningly.

'It's perfectly all right, my dear, as a matter of fact my wife and I do consider ourselves responsible for Nathan's welfare, as far as that is possible under the circumstances.'

'And what circumstances are those?' Eliot enquires with disdain.

'You can lead a horse to water but you can't make him drink,' Rebecca says with a knowledgeable smile.

'Precisely,' Adler says with a nod and an appreciative smile.

'But you can make the "water" so inviting that the "horse" is unable to resist.'

Eliot looks at Rebecca. 'And what does that mean exactly?'

'The professor knows.'

'Indeed I do.'

Eliot offers him a cigarette, but he has his pipe.

'Do you mind, my dear?'

'Please, go ahead. I was wondering, if Nathan is unwell should he be alone?'

'Alice is with him.'

'The blind leading the blind,' Eliot says with a rueful smile.

Rebecca stares at the flame in the rose bowl on the table. When she raises her eyes Adler is watching her. She colours slightly.

'How long have you known Nathan?' she asks.

'Since he was sixteen. We met at New York University, at Washington Square College. I was teaching a course on philosophy and Nathan was one of my students. You might say Joan and I adopted him. He was very thin and intense, very shy and very brilliant. Much as he is now.'

'Does he have a family?'

'His parents were not, let us say, impressed by their son's talent. They would have preferred him to show more tangible gifts, those which matter in a world where men are judged by their wealth.'

'It's the American way,' Eliot interposes, raising his glass in a solitary toast.

Adler ignores him.

'He has a brother living in Philadelphia and a sister in New Jersey, both very much older than himself. His parents were quite elderly when Nathan came along so there was always a wide gap between himself and the other two children. When his father died his mother went to live with her eldest son.'

'This is all very interesting,' Eliot says, pretending to stifle a yawn.

By unspoken and mutual agreement Rebecca and Adler both ignore him.

'After he obtained his PhD and went to Harvard as a graduate student he wrote regularly to Joan and I and came to stay with us at vacation time. I remember so clearly, after his first collection of poems was published he gave a reading at Harvard. There was standing room only. It brought tears to my eyes to see that frail boy transport and thrill that audience with the beauty of his words.'

'You make him sound like Billy Graham,' Eliot says, finishing his drink. 'It must be quite a burden, being a genius.'

There is a strained silence before Adler says kindly, 'I can understand your confusion and scepticism, Mr Vaughan, it requires a truly developed spirit to appreciate the Nathan Roths of this world.'

'Are you trying to put me in my place, professor?'

'Trying?' Adler sips his sherry. 'I thought I had succeeded.'

Rebecca laughs. She takes Eliot's hand and holds it to her lips, kissing it affectionately.

'You are both very clever men in your own special ways,' she says to placate him. 'It would be a very boring world if all the inhabitants were alike. Isn't that so, professor?'

'Oh yes.' He looks at Eliot. 'A man with your physical attributes and obvious ability should not resent my pride in Nathan's talent, even if I do make him sound like Billy Graham,' he raises his eyes to heaven, 'though God forbid it were true.'

Rebecca gazes off past Eliot's strong profile to the lobby beyond, and blinks in disbelief. Nathan Roth is standing there watching her. Before she can utter a sound he has limped away in the direction of the Taylor Street exit with the speed of a man who knows where he is going. For a second she thinks her eyes were deceiving her, but one look at Adler's face dispels any suspicion on that score.

'Will you excuse me a moment? I have to get something from my room.' She stands up.

'Rebecca?' Eliot says.

'I won't be a moment.' A confusion of conflicting emotions is concealed behind her calm voice.

She follows Nathan out of the hotel and into a crowded, smoke filled bar only a block away. She stands behind him as he orders a straight scotch and then, as he lifts it to his lips, he sees her through the mirror. He pauses only a second before drinking the contents of the glass. He looks terrible, thinner, drained of colour, hollowed out. The grey smudges of shadow under his eyes have darkened to black circles. He is wearing jeans, the same jacket, her scarf and as usual he needs a shave. His hands shake as he places the empty glass on the bar top and tries to attract the bartender's attention.

'Don't you have anything to say?' Rebecca asks, contracting her heavy brows.

He lights a cigarette. 'What do you want me to say?'

'You could begin with an apology or an explanation.'

She makes her voice rise on an edge of contempt but she has too much respect and affection for him to make it sound convincing. The bartender looks at her questioningly.

'I don't want anything,' she says dismissively.

The man looks at Nathan who pushes the empty glass toward him and nods.

'Since you're here, have a drink.'

'I don't drink alcohol.'

'And you don't smoke. Is that the pious Jew or the devout Catholic in you? I thought the Irish liked a drop of the hard stuff?' He empties his glass and makes a gesture toward the bartender.

'You make me sick, Nathan, do you know that? You

make me want to slap you all around this floor until you realize what you are doing to your God given talent.'

Noisy laughter rises at the other end of the long room.

'Come back to the hotel,' Rebecca says, raising her voice to be heard above the din. 'We can't talk here.'

'I don't want to talk. Go away.' His quiet voice sounds thick and nasal. He takes a handkerchief from his pocket and wipes his nose, looking at her self-consciously.

'Why didn't you come down and see me this evening?'

He lifts the glass to his lips, his Adam's apple rising and falling in his throat as the liquid passes through his gullet.

'Nathan, did you hear me?'

'I needed a drink.'

'You could have got one of those in the hotel.'

'I wasn't in the mood for company.'

'Damn you, talk to me!' she shouts, grabbing his shoulder and pulling him around on the stool. He breaks into a dry, compulsive cough, wincing as a stab of pain shoots through the area of his stomach. 'Nathan,' she says with sudden exasperation, her voice betraying her alarm, 'what are you trying to do to yourself?'

She lifts her hand to his silver grey hair and he stops it in mid air, with a shake of his head, telling her, 'Stay out of my life.' He blinks his perpetually hurt eyes. 'I never asked for your concern and I don't want it. Just stay out of my life.'

'Why, when I can help you?'

'I'm beyond help. I just want to be left alone.'

'My God, you are so full of self-pity.'

His frown deepens to a scowl, his eyes darkening until the darkness within is indistinguishable from the shadows encircling them. He shakes himself free of her hand and limps out of the bar. By the time Rebecca can push her way through the tightly packed groups of men unwilling to allow her to pass without some dubious comment he has vanished.

When she returns to the hotel Eliot and the professor are waiting for her in the lobby.

'Where have you been?' Eliot demands.

'I told you, I had to get something from my room.'

'You never said your room in London.'

Rebecca looks at Adler and it is very obvious from his expression that he knows she has been poet hunting without success.

'I'm sorry, professor, it was very rude of me to leave you. Are you going now?'

'Thank you, yes. I enjoyed my sherry.' He takes her hand. 'Be patient, my dear, I beg of you, and don't judge him too harshly. Kafka said, "A man's embittered features are often only the petrified bewilderment of a boy." '

CHAPTER FIVE

I wonder if you can die of
sadness – what a way to go.

Frank O'Hara, 1926–1966. *A Slow Poem*

The next morning after she and Eliot have eaten breakfast
and he has left for an appointment with a man called Harvey Klein, Rebecca takes the elevator back up to the fif-
teenth floor. She knocks quietly on Nathan Roth's door and
after a second it is opened by the professor, looking dishev-
elled and distracted.

'Rebecca, my dear,' he lifts a hand in an abortive, helpless
gesture and shakes his head, 'Nathan didn't return to the
hotel last night and I've just had a call from the hospital. He
was admitted at one a.m. this morning after falling down
some stairs outside a bar.'

'Oh no!'

'He's all right,' the professor assures her quickly, reaching
for the hand she has lifted to her open mouth and holding it
tightly. 'Just some bruising. They kept him in overnight for
observation. I was just about to go and collect him.'

'I'd like to come with you,' Rebecca says earnestly.

'You're very kind.' He takes her arm.

As the cab travels down Taylor Street and into Union
Square Rebecca looks at Adler's tense face. He seems very
nervous as he fidgets with his unlit pipe.

'Are you sure Nathan's injuries aren't more serious than
you've told me, professor?'

He gazes at her absently and frowns. She repeats her question.

'Yes, yes, I'm sure.'

'Then don't worry,' she tells him with a consoling smile.

'I'm not worried. These little dramas are no longer a shock to my nervous system. He has them with predictable regularity.' He punctuates his words with a resigned sigh. 'He has always been a prey to his psychological demons but since the accident he is like a man possessed.' He removes his spectacles and cleans them with his pocket handkerchief.

Rebecca can't help feeling that there is something Adler is not telling her, and his preoccupied air seems to bear out that theory.

'Where is Alice?' she asks.

'At the beauty parlour I believe.'

'Shouldn't she be going to collect Nathan?'

'Alice cannot take care of herself, so the guardianship of a highly emotional poet who walks the streets at night is out of the question.'

'Then why does he stay with her?'

'Companionship. Who knows? What can one say about Alice that doesn't speak for itself? Her last boyfriend treated her harshly. Nathan recognized a kindred spirit, another of what he calls "nature's rejects". She's cheerful, kind hearted, if somewhat vain, but I would choose her any day over the late Madeline Boucher.'

Rebecca stares at him unable to make sense of this last, unmistakably acrimonious remark. He takes his wallet from his jacket and shows her a photograph of his wife, a small, curly haired woman in trousers, perched jauntily on the lip of a fountain.

'That was taken in Rome last year. We went there on our honeymoon so we thought we'd like to go back again.'

A nostalgic smile flickers over his face. Adler turns the plastic cover over in her hands. Back to back with the photo of Joan is a snapshot of Nathan trying to conceal himself from the camera.

'That was taken in Central Park. He's shy, what can you do?' The question is purely rhetorical so Rebecca returns the wallet without comment. 'Joan and I were never blessed with children.'

'You have Nathan,' she says seriously.

'Thank you for that, my dear.'

'Professor, you made a remark before about Madeline . . .'

'Ah, it seems we are here.'

The cab pulls up outside the main entrance of the hospital. Adler pays the fare. Inside Rebecca makes enquiries at the reception desk and they are directed to the first floor. After yet more enquiries, during which Adler's highly coloured face drains of blood, making Rebecca certain that he hasn't told her everything, they are sent to the next floor. Rebecca waylays a nurse who conducts them to a room down the corridor. She knocks and enters. Nathan is sitting on the bed fully dressed and looking no more tired and sick than usual.

'The doctor would like to speak with you before you leave,' the nurse tells Adler and closes the door.

Nathan lifts his head and looks at Rebecca.

'What are you doing here?' His voice is gentle but strained.

'I asked her to accompany me,' Adler answers. 'I wanted her to see what you are doing to yourself.'

Nathan reaches out for his stick. Rebecca offers her hand. He ignores it.

'Nathan,' Adler murmurs, shaking his head.

Nathan limps to the door and opens it.

'You can't go yet, the doctor asked us to wait,' Rebecca reminds him.

'You wait. I already know what he's going to say.'

'He's right,' Adler states firmly, 'they are only going to

61

say he should take more care of himself. Something I've been telling him for years.'

Nathan looks at Adler and then limps out of the room. Rebecca and the professor follow him down the corridor then she allows them to go on ahead and she stops at the nurses' station.

'Excuse me, I'm with Mr Roth. I wondered what the doctor wanted to see us about?'

'Are you a relative?'

'Fiancée,' she says without hesitation and bringing forth an appropriately proud smile.

The nurse consults her records.

'I believe Dr Eastman wanted Mr Roth to remain here for a series of tests.'

Rebecca swallows. Her stomach gives a jerk of fear.

'What kind of tests? For what purpose?'

'I'm afraid you would have to speak to Dr Eastman personally. He shouldn't be very long.'

'Rebecca,' the professor comes hurrying along toward her, 'please, my dear, can we go?' His agitation has risen to the surface and he tugs on her arm.

'But the doctor?'

'Nothing, it's nothing. Come along before we lose him again.'

Rebecca obeys, but strictly against her better judgement.

Nathan doesn't say a word the entire way back to the hotel. He sits there and smokes in thoughtful silence while Adler points out places of interest through the window and Rebecca tries to concentrate on his words.

'You ought to go straight to bed,' Rebecca tells the poet as the cab pulls up and the doorman approaches.

'I'm not tired.'

'To rest, not sleep,' her voice becomes annoyed making the professor's beard twitch delightedly. 'Read a book.'

Nathan gets out of the cab and goes into the hotel.

'Follow him,' Adler begs, paying off the driver.

She runs down the escalator after him and halts him physically on his way to the bar.

'That's enough!' Her eyes blaze. 'Do you know what pain you are causing that man out there?'

'I don't want to hurt Bernard. I love Bernard.'

'Then stop trying to destroy yourself.'

The professor remains a little way to the side, listening but not joining in.

'Let me take you up to your room and see you comfortably in bed with a book.'

Nathan looks at the professor who nods imperceptibly, his eyes deeply sad behind his lenses. Rebecca slips her arm through the poet's.

'We'll all go up together. The professor wants to shower and change his clothes.'

Outside Nathan's room Rebecca and Adler arrange to meet in the restaurant downstairs so that he can have a late breakfast or an early lunch. Rebecca unlocks the door to Nathan's room. Alice is sitting at the dressing table preening herself.

'Oh hi, how do you like my new hairdo? I got my nails done too. I wanna look real pretty.'

'You rival Venus no less,' Nathan says, bowing to her.

'You're crazy, Nathan, ain't he crazy, Rebecca?'

'Certifiable,' she agrees without smiling. 'Alice, would you mind going out for a while? Nathan doesn't feel very well and he wants to rest.'

'Well, gee, I only just got in myself. I mean where could I go? I don't know this town.'

Rebecca gives her six ten dollar bills.

'Go and buy a new dress at Macy's.'

'Wow! Are you sure?'

'Positive.'

Alice looks at Nathan who is sitting on the bed laughing softly to himself.

'You okay, honey? You been sick again? Can I get you anything?'

'Alice, go,' Rebecca says, pointing to the door.

'Sure, right, terrific. See yer.' She grabs her bag and her orange coney coat and is gone.

Rebecca places herself in front of Nathan.

'Shoes off, and as usual you've got your left shoe on your right foot and vice versa. Didn't they teach you anything at Harvard?'

He kicks off his shoes lethargically. Her scarf is draped around his neck, considerably more grubby than when she gave it to him.

'Are you bashful?' she asks.

'Very.'

'Then I'll turn my back while you get undressed.'

He removes his clothes and gets under the covers. Rebecca puts them neatly on a chair.

'Do you have a book?'

'In the drawer.'

She brings out the hardback copy of *The Diaries of Franz Kafka*, very thumbed, very annotated, inscribed in the fly leaf 'To my "son", Nathan, from Bernard with everlasting pride', and his glasses. She puts them on the bed and sits down beside them. He makes a move toward them and she arrests his hand. He blinks rapidly as their hands make contact and then he puts both of his under the cover.

'First we talk. Did the doctor tell you he wanted to do some tests?'

'Why should you care about me?' he enquires without rancour.

'Now that, Mr Roth, is a good question.' She looks at his untidy hair, his thin face, and hurt eyes. Why should she care? Why should she feel right now like lifting his frail body from the bed and holding it against her breasts? Why should she want to protect him from a world too cruel and hostile for the sensitive breed known as poet? Why should she lose sleep and have odd dreams? One look into those strange, Jewish eyes and something stirs in her, wanting him, sensing his tentative hold on life, a hold which he himself seems dedicated to loosening. Is there such a narrow dividing line between moral obligation and physical attraction?

'Could I have my glasses please?'

She cleans the lenses for him.

'When do you intend to get these frames fixed?'

'I like them that way,' he says obstinately, like a child.

She puts them over the bridge of his nose, her eyes dropping to his exquisitely moulded, bitter-sweet lips. She rests her hands on the pillow and leans forward to kiss his mouth. He turns his head away, his eyes going dead. She kisses it anyway, stroking his hair and passing her fingers tenderly over the shadows in his gaunt cheeks.

'I told you last night, I'm going to help you. I don't need your permission, but it would be pleasant if you consented. But either way I'm in your life now so you might as well get used to that fact.'

She closes the door softly behind her. He presses his face into the pillow, his body racked by sobs.

Rebecca joins the professor just in time for coffee.

'How is he?'

'Fighting me all the way. But I'm not so easily discouraged.'

Adler laughs heartily. 'You do not know how wonderful it makes me feel to hear you say that, my dear.'

'Oh I think I can guess.'

'He told me what happened in London,' Adler says, studying her face for a reaction. 'He was very grateful.'

'He has a very funny way of showing it.'

'He has his reasons. You are very beautiful and he is no Adonis. You are strong and he is frail. He doesn't yet trust you, you might be laughing at him.'

Rebecca's chin juts out indignantly.

'I tease him, yes, but I would never laugh at him. Would you laugh at a man you admire and respect?'

'He is so different from your young man.'

'Eliot is primarily a business man with a business man's philosophies and ideals. He dropped out of college before graduating because of problems in his family. He has a tendency to mistrust, even despise those whom he considers put too much emphasis on education, the feeding of the soul, and too little on personal achievement. As Eliot is fond of saying, "I got my education at the university of life." '

'Do you feel the same?'

'No. I never went to college, but then it's much less of a stigma in Britain than it is in the U.S. I went to night school to learn shorthand and typing. But I don't resent those who went to a university. My talents are of the more practical variety.' She smiles suddenly. 'Why do I get the impression that you are testing me?'

'Perish the thought,' Adler exclaims, throwing his hands up with horror. He drinks his coffee, his eyes watching her over the rim of his lenses. 'Forgive me,' he begs, by way of admission.

'I don't think I will, not unless you explain something you said about Madeline in the cab going to the hospital.'

Adler brings out his pipe and turns it over and over on the tablecloth.

'You must miss her very much,' Rebecca says, misinterpreting the reason for his grieving expression.

The professor's grey, balding head rises abruptly and he stares at her as sudden insight floods his eyes.

'You think . . . of course, you only know the story from the newspapers. How foolish of me not to realize . . . I could kick myself.' His wise eyes travel over Rebecca's sombre but bewildered face. 'Would you like to know all about Madeline Boucher and Nathan Roth?'

'Please,' Rebecca says softly.

'I shall be brief, but you will forgive me if I become emotional.' He clears his throat. 'In 1976 the American Academy of Arts and Letters awarded Nathan a seven thousand dollar travelling scholarship to spend one year abroad. He chose Paris. The year went off smoothly, he made many new friends, and drew many admirers for his work. Then six weeks before he was due to come home he met Madeline Boucher. After what I believe they call a "whirlwind courtship", four weeks to be precise, they were married. Joan and I flew to Paris for the wedding. From the moment I was introduced to that woman I knew deep in my heart that he was making a terrible mistake.'

The professor removes his glasses and pinches the corners of his eyes. 'Subsequent meetings only confirmed my first impressions. She was a cruel and shallow woman,' he says in a voice full of hatred. 'Cruelty came as naturally to her as breathing. She had the face of an angel and a capacity for hurting her fellow human beings that I cannot begin to describe. Not physical cruelty, you understand, the mental kind, which destroys slowly, relentlessly, over a long period of time.' He looks into Rebecca's shocked eyes. 'She treated Nathan the way no human being should be allowed to treat another, and he loved her.'

Rebecca is so stunned by these words that she is unable to do more than shake her head and stare at the professor.

'Joan tells me I should not speak ill of the dead, but I remember what she did to Nathan, the most gentle of men, and I cannot forgive her, even in death.' At the end of a long pause he says in a more normal voice, 'It was evident that he worshipped her, as only a Brooklyn born, Jewish boy could worship a beautiful, gentile, Parisian movie star. I admit, I could not help but ask myself why she was marrying Nathan.' Rebecca lowers her gaze. 'My dear,' he puts his hand over hers on the table, 'you are different.' His expression becomes bitterly reflective. 'As I said, she was shallow, superficial. Anyway, I prayed it was love, but I knew her motives lay elsewhere. Joan and I gave our blessing, played our parts. It was what Nathan wanted, so be it. The most difficult thing for me to understand in relation to Nathan's love for her was her complete disregard for his work. She had never read a single line of his poetry, and never did. Not a single line. Can you believe that, Rebecca?' He finishes in a quiet, puzzled voice.

'No,' she answers soberly, 'I can't.'

'To me it seemed like a negation of all Nathan stood for. A dismissal of the man's very essence, his soul. How can you be emotionally involved with a visionary and not be involved with his visions? He is poetry. If you do not know his work you do not know the man. It is like marrying Michelangelo and not knowing what he does with himself all day in the Sistine Chapel.'

Rebecca doesn't laugh. Adler isn't trying to be funny.

'There was a man, a director of films, Jacques-Louis something or other . . . ' he concludes dismissively.

'Jacques-Louis Michelet.'

'You know him?'

'No, but I've heard of him.'

'He was this woman's Svengali. I was assured by everyone, including the man himself, that he was a great talent in the avant garde cinema. I thought him a very stupid, insensitive man, lacking any psychological insight, and infinitely more suited to Madeline than Nathan.' His features tighten. 'It was obvious to everyone except Nathan, that Madeline and Michelet were having an affair. It had begun long before Nathan arrived and was still going on long after preparations were made for the wedding. I learned much later that Madeline had tried to blackmail Michelet into marrying her. He never believed she would actually go through with the wedding. Love, marriage, all a game to these people.'

He stops fidgeting with his pipe and looks once more into Rebecca's intensely compassionate eyes.

'After a honeymoon in Mexico City, paid for by Nathan, they came back to New York where she held court in a ludicrously large and expensive apartment, which she filled with equally shallow film people of Michelet's calibre. Nathan tried to write while she entertained. We, that is Joan and myself, began to see less and less of Nathan, but that was to be expected, he was married now and had a wife with whom to share his dreams. On the occasions when I did see Nathan he never complained although I knew his work was suffering because that woman had turned their home into a zoo.

'Then one day Michelet turned up. He had followed her all the way from Paris hoping that she would leave Nathan and go back to him. She did better than that, she moved her lover into the apartment. Of course I was not aware of all this happening until afterwards, after the accident. I knew that Nathan was unhappy but I did not know the extent to which she made him suffer. He began to behave strangely, he stayed out all night, started to drink heavily, something he had never done before. Can you imagine how easily a man of his sensibilities has the balance of his mind and nerves impaired? I was afraid for his sanity. I begged him to move in with us, this frail man, this poet whose psychic powers have to be nourished and nurtured. He would not listen. He said he loved her. There was nothing wrong with the relationship. He was the selfish one. He was the bad husband.

'After a year of this torture Madeline announced that she intended to go to Hollywood and make movies. She went with Michelet and I rejoiced. Two weeks later Nathan followed. I pleaded with him not to go. I believed I would never see him again. He wrote us letters, everything was wonderful between him and this woman laughingly called his wife. He talked of having children, there was nothing he more fervently desired. Then one day I pick up a newspaper and there staring me in the face is a picture of a wrecked car. Joan and I were on the next plane to Los Angeles. I could not recognize him, this shell of a man. A man who lives to write and who had not written anything in sixteen months.' Rebecca's hand trembles as she lifts her cup. She sips slowly, tasting nothing, merely wanting to moisten her dry lips. Adler touches his temple in an uncertain gesture. 'Should I go on?'

Rebecca nods.

'Madeline had been killed instantly. Nathan had received head injuries and multiple fractures to his leg. He was never a vain man, the walking stick made no difference to him, at least at that time. In the hospital we talked. He said he was finished with living, he wanted only to write, to exist as a poet, nothing more.'

'Then why did he stop? What happened?' Rebecca asks knitting her brows.

'He never stopped writing, my dear, he stopped caring about reality, about publishers, agents, royalties. There is over two years' intensely crafted work in his apartment, work I am permitted to read but not to present to the world.'

'My God . . . ' A hot wetness wells up into Rebecca's eyes, ' . . . you'll have to give me a moment to realize what you're saying to me.' She stares into the bottom of her empty cup, making a concerted effort to assimilate the professor's words. Nathan Roth is still writing. He has always written. 'Professor, he has to be made to publish his work.'

'I've tried. Joan has tried. His friends have tried, pleaded, argued, shouted, to no avail. He simply does not care. The poem is a source of joy and redemption in itself. Publication would require the kind of energy and concern for the exterior world he no longer possesses. Madeline Boucher robbed him of his desire to live in the world as we know it. I cannot put it more simply, he no longer cares.'

'Professor, do you know what causes those stomach pains?'

'No,' he says flatly.

'Have you ever tried to find out?'

'There is nothing wrong with Nathan that rest, good food and a lot of love will not put right.' He is so blatantly avoiding contact with Rebecca's eyes that even though his statement has the ring of truth it makes a hollow sound in her ears. 'As I said last night, he needs the kind of devotion Joan and I cannot give him, the devotion of a strong, intelligent woman. No man should have to live without once experiencing the joy I have known with Joan as comfort and companion.'

'I'm coming to New York in May,' Rebecca announces.

'For a visit?' the elderly man says excitedly.

'To work, to live. Irving Kauffman offered me a job in his agency and I accepted.'

'This is too wonderful,' he cries, looking around the almost deserted restaurant for someone with whom he can share this unexpectedly good news, 'does Nathan know?'

She shakes her head, smiling at his delight.

'Please, let me be the one to tell him. I cannot wait to see his face.'

'Tell him I intend to raid his apartment looking for those unpublished poems.'

'You are not leaving San Francisco until Saturday, that gives us two more days in your company.'

'I think you're forgetting Eliot.'

'No, I was hoping you would forget Eliot.'

'Professor, that isn't very nice.' She looks at him reproachfully. 'He may not be the kind of man you would normally have as a friend, but he is my ... my ... ' she searches for a delicate word and Adler rescues her chivalrously.

'Point taken, my dear. I apologize.'

'And talking of Eliot I really ought to go up to the room and change. We're going over to Sausalito this afternoon.'

She stands up.

'You really are coming to live in New York?' Adler asks, unable to restrain his pleasure.

'Really.'

'I think I will celebrate. Waiter!'

She leaves him ordering more coffee and the stickiest Danish pastry on the tray.

She sits down on the bed in the room, her heart beating ludicrously fast. Nathan Roth still writes. She wants to laugh out loud with the sheer ecstasy of it. Then she remembers Madeline Boucher. Boucher. She will never again think of that woman as Mrs Roth. Now it all begins to make sense. His attitude to her, the fear in his eyes when she goes close to, or touches him, and Alice, a woman without ambivalence, whose every feminine emotion lies on the surface. A woman so open and honest in her manner that no man could fail to trust her, or be certain of her motives, however simple or mercenary they might be. Suddenly, coming to a decision, she lifts the receiver and dials. After a few moments a quiet voice says, 'Hello?'

'Nathan, it's me, Rebecca.' She tries to conceal the tremor in her tone. 'How do you feel?'

'Better, thank you.'

'Eliot has appointments tomorrow morning and I plan to go to Fisherman's Wharf. I was thinking, if you feel up to it, would you like to go with me?'

An indefinable silence makes the instrument heavy in her hand. The wicked, irrepressible weapon of sarcasm jumps into her throat.

'I would appreciate an answer before I reach pensionable age.'

'No,' he says suddenly, hoarsely, 'I have things to do in the morning.'

Shock robs her of a suitable departing comment, and before she can recover her composure he has put the phone down. Seconds later Eliot walks in.

'Hi.' He kisses her upturned mouth. 'Good day?'

'Very nice, and you?'

'I think I'm getting there. I've got to see Klein again tomorrow. But it looks . . . '

The phone comes to life by Rebecca's elbow. She lifts the receiver.

'It's probably Klein for me,' Eliot says confidently as he loosens his tie.

'Hello?' Rebecca says.

'I've changed my mind. Please, I'd like to go with you.' Eliot reaches out for the receiver.

'No,' Rebecca tells him quickly, 'it's for me.'

He gives her a surprised who-would-call-you-here kind of look and sits down on the edge of the bed to remove his shoes.

'Rebecca?' Is this the first time she has heard her name on his lips? She can't remember, so much is crowding into her head at once. 'Are you there?' He speaks so irresolutely, as though experience has taught him to expect disappointment.

'I'm here.' She cannot even say his name because Eliot is beside her, smoking, his eyes telling her that her conversation is being listened to with fascination. 'Meet me downstairs in the lobby at ten a.m.'

'Is Eliot there?' He guessed.

'Yes.'

'Okay.' Click.

Rebecca holds the receiver in her hand as Eliot stares at her troubled face through the dressing table mirror.

'Who was that?'

'What?' she says vaguely.

'On the phone. Who are you meeting tomorrow at ten?'

'Oh, Alice.' She drops the receiver casually into the cradle. 'We're going down to Fisherman's Wharf together.' She turns to Eliot. 'What's the matter? Why are you staring at me like that?'

'No reason. Better get ready. We'll be late.'

CHAPTER SIX

It is to be learned—
This cleaving and this burning,
But only by one who
Spends out himself again.

Hart Crane, 1899–1932. *Legend*

She waits patiently in the lobby and he is late by twenty minutes but he looks as though he had a bad night so she says nothing, only gives him a sympathetic smile. As they make their way carefully over the uneven iron tracks on Powell Street toward the trolley stop they can hear the warning clang of the approaching cable car. The car trundles to a clumsy halt. Nathan and Rebecca await their turn and then mount the platform at the rear. Concerned for his safety in such a tightly wedged mass Rebecca tries to protect her frail companion from a bulky rucksack on one side mounted high on the back of a student, and a fat woman whose sharply tipped umbrella is dangerously close to Nathan's left ear. Rebecca pushes the 'weapon' unceremoniously aside with a most telling expression aimed at the owner's indignant face. Nathan is watching her, he knows what she is doing and he cannot help but be touched by her concern.

'Let me through! Move down inside!' shouts the conductor, elbowing his way into the packed centre aisle. 'Come on, make room, sit on someone's lap. Have your fare ready!'

The trolley gives a bone jarring jolt as the brakeman releases the hefty brake rod and with a piercing series of clangs on his most effective warning bell the trolley moves along the level stretch of ground on the east side of Union Square to begin the stiff haul up Stockton Street and the first of a series of steep hills.

'Are you all right there?' Rebecca asks.

'I'm fine, thank you.' He takes his hand off the rail to briefly touch her arm. Rebecca stares at him in surprise. He blinks and swallows, a nervous smile flickering over his drawn features. He is wearing one of those soft tweed caps with a button on the crown that were so popular in the depression era and which are popular again now. It suits him marvellously, his old fashioned Jewish face, his rather crumpled and battered aspect, and he knows how to wear it, perched there, over his forehead, cockily, on top of that thick silver grey hair, his strange, sad eyes watching her from beneath the broken peak. Just past the St Francis Hotel the trolley shudders to a halt. Nathan falls against her shoulder. She puts her arm around his waist to steady him and he murmurs a shy thank you. A light cool breeze is blowing as they ascend Telegraph Hill, but a wintry sun attempts to warm their faces.

'Next stop Nob Hill!' shouts the conductor. 'Here we go!'

Then at the stop closest to Chinatown elderly, wizened Chinese board the car, along with their tiny, beautiful children. When it seems that not another person can be squeezed inside someone will rush to hang on the steps, squat on the running boards or hook their arms through the safety rails along the side of the car.

'I'm sorry . . . ' Nathan says, unavoidably close.

'Don't worry, it takes a lot to crush me.'

Their eyes meet. She looks at the furrows in his forehead, the permanent indent on his large nose where the frames of his glasses rest, and the gauntness of his cheeks, and once more she is struck by the vulnerability of his existence. She raises her hand to his cheek and touches it lightly, her expression summed up in a quizzical frown.

'What do you see?' Nathan Roth asks in his quiet voice.

'Pain, a lot of pain, in the mind and the body, and I see beauty.'

He turns his face away and she turns it back again. She kisses him at the corner of his thin, chiselled lips.

'Nathan, quickly, look, over there!' She points. A glimpse of the Golden Gate Bridge gleaming red in the distance as the trolley breasts the crest of a hill. 'It's magnificent!' she cries excitedly.

When she looks at Nathan he is staring not at the bridge, which he has seen many times before, but at her. She is so beautiful, so gentle in her manner toward him that it is impossible for him to look anywhere else or admire any other sight. He blinks and looks away, an old, irrational fear rising to haunt him, a spectre of his past suffering on the horizon of his faint hope. There are experiences locked into his soul that he will never forget, pains buried deep in his flesh like splinters that fester and poison his existence.

'Nathan, please . . .' Her plaintive concerned words penetrate his consciousness, even though he doesn't want them to, even though he would wish to be struck deaf so that her husky voice could never again stir his blood and move him to believe in the tenderness of a woman's tone.

'We walk from here,' he says unemotionally, as the trolley rattles to a halt at Victorian Plaza.

They pause to examine the merchandise displayed on stalls along the pavements, to admire the ancient Chinese artisans applying delicate spots of colour on fans, pottery, and miniature paintings, undisturbed by the tourists' fascinated gaze. Rebecca looks at a selection of printed sweat shirts and listens as a Chinese woman attempts to persuade her to make a purchase. Rebecca holds up one for Nathan's attention bearing the inscription 'Property of Alcatraz'.

'For Eliot?' he suggests.

'Perfect,' she agrees, laughing.

The main thoroughfare of Jefferson Street along the wharf proper is packed with thronging tourists, splashes of colour beneath a blue sky broken intermittently by patches of white cloud hung over the Bay. Above them is the famous ship's wheel sign with the crab motif, bearing the words 'Fisherman's Wharf of San Francisco'. Up on the red and brown wooden ramp along Jefferson the atmosphere is more reminiscent of a fun fair than a wharf, with 'live' shows, waxwork effigies of the famous, and the infamous, and the spine-chilling 'Chamber of Horrors'. The 'barkers' are recorded voices, blaring out from the depths of the buildings, selling the virtues of their own unique brand of entertainment. 'The Guinness Book of Records' has a somewhat sad, but comical display featuring grotesque, shiny plastic replicas of the World's Fattest and the World's Tallest Man. Children run eagerly to measure themselves against these unfortunate freaks while their parents click away enthusiastically with their cameras.

At 'Ripley's Believe It or Not' Museum they cast a sceptical eye over the world's only living werewolf, dead over 200 hundred years. Rebecca laughs and Nathan gives a short, almost apologetic imitation of a man trying to laugh, of a man learning how to regain his capacity for laughter after years of redundancy. He shows her a wax effigy of the emaciated body of a Fakir on his bed of nails inside a glass case, with the self-contemptuous remark, 'Looks like me.'

'Don't be ridiculous.' Rebecca runs her hand intimately over his back. 'Hey, look, want your horoscope read?'

'No,' he limps quickly away, 'I already know my fate.'

Rebecca follows him to the first of the exits. The powerful, unpleasant smell of steaming crabmeat accosts her nostrils. She peers into the tank where live crabs give the occasional listless twitch of a pincer. She joins the queue for something less offensive to her palate and returns to Nathan with giant cardboard cups of hot chocolate and homemade cookies generously spotted with chocolate chips. They stand a little to one side, out of the way of the crowds and Nathan holds his cup of chocolate in his free hand. Rebecca lifts a cookie to his mouth. As his lips close over the soft biscuit their eyes meet, and unable to bear the sadness of his gaze she says flippantly, 'You've got nice teeth. Are they your own?'

'No, I borrowed them for the day.'

'A joke?' Her eyes open in mock astonishment. 'Now if I'm not mistaken that was the first joke I've ever heard you make.' He takes another bite of her cookie. 'They're good aren't they?'

His head jerks in affirmation.

'Finish the hot chocolate, please,' she instructs, urging it toward his lips. 'Come on.'

He obeys and she takes the empty cups to the waste bin.

At 'The Haunted Goldmine' they stand amidst a group of laughing children to watch an animated model of an old prospector in a wire lift cage whose shaky hillbilly voice is rendering 'Clementine' while the cage descends slowly to the 'goldmine' below. A timid smile plays around the corners of Nathan's lips. Rebecca puts her arm through his and gives a gentle tug. He looks at her.

'It's like riding a bicycle,' she tells him wisely, 'once you know how, you never forget the knack. Go on, laugh.'

A strange kind of creaking sound emerges from his throat.

'It's improving, but we have to work on it.'

As they walk slowly down the sloping ramp past the display of Old San Francisco he leans on her, as though literally testing her strength. Rebecca finds herself suppressing a smile of gratification.

They cross the wide road to the wharfside and stop at Pier 41 where the boat leaves periodically for sightseeing trips of the now disused and abandoned Alcatraz Island. The queue winds around the corner of the building and includes many impatient children, apparently eager to see the soulless place at first hand, or perhaps confront the ghost of Ma Barker or Al Capone.

'Would you think so many people wanted to visit Alcatraz, knowing its history?' Rebecca asks Nathan.

The poet's voice and expression make no judgements as he replies, 'It gives them a good feeling to know they can return immediately to the mainland. It gives them a renewed sense of the glory of their own freedom.'

He mounts the steps and goes out onto the pier, to the guard rail overlooking the water where the smell of salt and fish is very strong. A couple of seagulls swoop over the boarding ramp screeching dementedly as they fight for something bobbing about in the dark shadow of the rotting pier supports.

As Rebecca joins him a helicopter moves through the sky overhead, its propellers throbbing and pulsing. She tries to control her hair which blows around her face and Nathan makes a grab at his cap. He laughs and his laughter is followed by an ugly cough. He covers his mouth with his handkerchief until the coughing subsides and then he wipes his nose and pushes the handkerchief into his jeans pocket. Rebecca touches his shoulder.

'I'm fine,' he assures her, keeping his face down.

She looks out at the grey stone building of the prison set high on the secluded island. To the left is a lighthouse, its single light blinking every few seconds, the only sign of life in a bleak and chill landscape. She shivers.

'Most of us live in a prison of one sort or another,' Nathan says, with a hard look into the distance. 'We forge the bars and throw away the key.' His face becomes distorted as though he is staring into bright sunlight or hears distant voices he cannot identify.

'You're a poet, Nathan, surely your mind is always free?'

'Poets know less about freedom than most men alive.'

He searches the pockets of his jacket and comes up empty handed. 'Do you have any cigarettes?'

'I don't smoke,' she reminds him with a patient smile.

Nathan coughs and the utter frailty of him, the profound

mystery of his existence touches her deep in her soul. She lifts one end of the scarf and winds it around his exposed neck. His eyes hold hers.

'Nathan, why do you look at me that way? Is it so strange that I care about you?'

'Yes,' he answers honestly, 'but that doesn't mean I appreciate it any less.'

'Well,' she says with a wry little smile, 'thank you for that, at least.'

The air from the Bay is chill and she stops to button Nathan's jacket, to turn up the collar under the scarf – her scarf that he wears all the time. He moves in closer to her, as though wanting something he cannot yet articulate, or even understand, in relation to his own painful emotions. She traces the lines on his furrowed forehead, touches the darkness beneath his eyes. His tightly pressed lips are framed by two deeply cut lines at the corners of his mouth.

'How can you say you have no feelings? You are feeling, pure feeling. Look at you. I've never known a more emotional man.'

He puts his fingers against her arm, letting his hand slide down slowly to her hand, winding his fingers around hers. She lifts the tangle of fingers to her soft lips and kisses his knuckles reverently, a thrill of tenderness melting her heart.

They wander in and out of the myriad of fascinating but predictable souvenir shops to be found along Jefferson where Rebecca searches for gifts of a less common variety. By now she is accustomed to the irregular rhythm of Nathan's walk, the slight dragging motion of his once shattered left leg. She walks slowly, or waits for him, showing him something, asking his opinion, his advice, trying to involve him, to bring back his waning interest in life.

On the pavement a young man wearing the costume of a musketeer is performing tricks on a card table surrounded by wide eyed children. Nathan limps away from her side and edges his way to the front of the audience. She watches from a slight distance but even so the boy's sleight of hand seems clumsy and amateurishly executed. But Nathan's expression is one of ardent curiosity and unlimited admiration. With all the ingenuousness of a child at a party he begs of the magician, 'Do the trick with the ball and the cups again.'

'Now watch very closely. Three small cups, one pea sized ball, cover, uncover, first you see it, then you don't.' Elementary, basic, and simple, the first trick any prospective member of the Magic Circle could do standing on his head. Nathan hooks his walking stick over his arm and applauds loudly, louder than anyone else.

'Marvellous!' he exclaims, his mouth stretching back in a youthful boyish grin. He puts a five dollar bill on the table.

'Thank you, sir.'

'I wish I could perform magic tricks,' he confesses to Rebecca as they continue their investigations of the sights.

'Nathan, does it ever occur to you that when people speak your name they call you a genius?'

'To be able to perform tricks like that boy just did,' he says, having not even heard her question, 'that would really be something.'

Rebecca pauses on the sidewalk, staring at his back as he limps away. Didn't she read somewhere that one of Albert Einstein's favourite ways to relax was to watch a Laurel and Hardy movie? But did that particular genius ever express a desire to be in one?

The Anchorage is a complex of shops on various levels overlooking a kind of amphitheatre where at this moment two waif-like girls of about sixteen in white jeans and sweaters are coaxing music from their violins with all the sweet-tempered concentration of those who know they will never grow up to be a virtuoso. Rebecca and Nathan sit on the steps among the small crowd to listen. Nathan closes his eyes as the girls play a poignant passage from Mozart. On his thin lips is a delicate smile which is more the reflection of some distant, alien joy, than an expression of his own happiness.

'There was a time when I would go to a concert every week,' he says in a resigned voice, 'but that was another life.'

'It doesn't have to be, Nathan. Why don't you and I go to a concert together? I would be honoured.'

'Here . . . in San Francisco?' he asks falteringly, as though fearing a trick.

'Well, no, I can hardly desert Eliot for the evening. I was thinking about New York. It's not so long to wait until May.'

'It doesn't matter.'

'Nathan, be reasonable, how can I tell Eliot I'm going to spend an —'

'I said it doesn't matter.'

It is not so much the words which anger and upset her as his tone, his flat, unemotional tone. A tone that seems to say it really doesn't matter.

'Look, the first week I'm in New York we'll go to a concert together. You can even book the seats if you wish. My treat.'

He says nothing. He is listening to the music. She lifts her hand and runs her fingers over his thick silver hair.

'Is it a date?'

'Yes,' he says softly, not looking at her.

He negotiates the steep steps and drops a five dollar bill into one of the open violin cases then he rejoins her on the pavement.

Ghiradelli Square is a series of stately red brick buildings where it is possible to buy anything from Persian rugs to Chinese kites, with outdoor cafés and art galleries. Dominant among the unusual attractions is a restaurant called Maxwell's Plum. Stained glass, ornate crystal chandeliers, red carpets, embossed wallpaper of maroon and grey chevrons, Art Nouveau fixtures and fittings and a fountain set into the wall. Rebecca studies the menu in the glass and gilt frame on the entrance. Nathan limps up beside her.

'Are you hungry? What do you think?' she asks him.

'They won't let me in without a tie.'

'They let him in.' She indicates a fat man in short sleeves and open collar shovelling food into his mouth. A head waiter meets them with a mechanical smile. There are no tables immediately but if they would like to wait in the bar they will be called.

'We must have a drink while we're waiting,' Rebecca says. She turns around. 'Nathan?' Her bewildered gaze searches the immediate area. Then she grabs her bag and rushes out into the bright sunlight of the Square. Nathan is sitting at an empty table outside one of the cafés.

'I've heard of men who leave after the meal and before they pick up the tab but not before they've eaten.'

'All those people . . .' he says inconclusively, his hands shaking, ' . . . I hate crowds.'

Rebecca runs her hand over his shoulder.

'It was my fault, I should have realized that wasn't your kind of place.'

'Madeline always liked to go to that sort of restaurant. I was never comfortable, but she still made me go.' He raises his eyes to her face. 'You see I wanted to please her, so I went but I can't do it anymore, not anymore.'

Rebecca draws a chair up close to his and sits down with her arm around his shoulders. She presses her face against his cold cheek and rocks him slowly to and fro until his body stops shaking.

At Pier 39 they discover a pleasant, quiet restaurant serving freshly caught sea foods and delicious desserts, with a superb view of the Bay, so that from their table in the intimate interior it seems they are suspended over the water. Rebecca studies the menu.

'What are we going to eat?'

Nathan glances at his menu card, pretending an interest he doesn't enjoy. 'Lobster?' he says because it is top of the list.

'We could have char broiled lobster and chocolate cake to follow. This sea air makes me hungry, how about you?'

He smiles closed mouthed because she looks at him from under lowered brows. When she looks away he presses his chest and winces. He gazes out at the small fishing boats moored at the wooden marina.

'I always thought I'd like to go fishing sometime.'

'Then why don't you? You could hire a rod and anything else you needed.'

He turns his face to her, his own face sad and withdrawn.

'I never got around to it. It's just something I thought I'd like to do.'

The waitress comes to their table. 'What can I get you?'

'Is it possible to order dessert only?' Rebecca asks her. 'We'd love some of that chocolate cake with fruit and fresh cream.'

'Sure.' The waitress notes the order. 'You want anything to drink?'

'Two large glasses of milk.'

When the waitress has gone Nathan says, 'What happened to the lobster?'

'He got away.'

'Good for the lobster.' He takes out his new pack of cigarettes, his trembling fingers working at the cellophane.

'Don't smoke now, Nathan,' Rebecca says in a voice of genial authority. 'Not before you eat.'

He looks at her and she holds his gaze unflinchingly. He puts the cigarettes on the table, unopened. He pushes the hair nervously off his face and it falls forward again. He looks at Rebecca and smiles but the smile doesn't quite make contact with the corners of his sensitive mouth.

The waitress serves them. Nathan drinks his milk and

wipes his mouth with the back of his hand like a small boy who has forgotten his table manners.

'When I was in Hollywood with Madeline it was full of men like Eliot. Confident, ambitious, assertive.'

'You missed out ruthless,' Rebecca says, meaning to be ironic. 'Surely no caricature of a Hollywood movie producer is complete without that streak of ruthlessness?'

'Eliot can't be all bad, otherwise you wouldn't like him.'

Rebecca laughs. Sometimes this man, this genius, this prophet and visionary can sound as naive and inexperienced as a schoolboy the first time he is allowed to enter the closed and confusing world of the adults. Not just his statements, but the tone of his voice.

'Eliot can be very kind, but he does tend to present one face to the business world and another to his friends and family. He was married when he was twenty and divorced at twenty-six. By then he had two sons. His wife married again and now the boys call someone else Daddy. That hurts him more than he cares to admit, because he believes it was his fault his marriage failed and his sons hardly know him. He was too busy proving to himself and the world that he had what it takes to be somebody in Hollywood. Well he proved it, up to a point. Now this next one is the biggest and the most ambitious as far as he is concerned. This next picture will make him if it's a success. That's why he came to San Francisco, there is a man here called Harvey Klein who has a great deal of money to invest and he wants to invest it in Eliot's picture, if Eliot can persuade him he wouldn't be better off putting his money in a building society. If Klein agrees, then the other half of the money has to come from Gerry Shapiro who is Head of Production at Pantheon Pictures in Hollywood. Eliot has to do a kind of diplomatic balancing act, he gets backers interested in each other so that if one agrees to give his money the others will follow. If one pulls out they all pull out.'

He looks at her vaguely, saying, 'Forgive me, I'm not that interested in Eliot's career.'

'Okay,' she takes his hand, 'let's talk about us and what we're going to do together in New York.'

They stand alone together in the warm silence of the hotel corridor outside his room. Rebecca leans forward and puts a kiss to his pale lips. He goes slowly and wordlessly into her embrace and she holds him tight, her body trembling in sympathy with his. He doesn't try to kiss her mouth or touch her, he merely clings to her as though the strength and sincerity he feels in her embrace is enough for him. Then the elevator door slides open and Alice wiggles out, singing tunelessly to herself. Rebecca moves quickly away from Nathan, giving the blonde a rather guilty smile.

'Hey, Rebecca, hi there.'

'I'd better be going,' Rebecca says.

'No, don't go on accounta me. Come on into the room. I ain't going no place.'

'No, really, I have to. But if you both have nothing to do this evening why don't you, Nathan and the professor join Eliot and I for drinks upstairs after dinner?'

'Wow, sure, that's a great idea. What d'yer say, Nathan, huh?'

Nathan looks at Rebecca and says nothing.

'Please,' she says inclining her head.

He gives her a kind of smile, a nearly smile, his narrow, wrinkled eyes as sad as sad can be.

CHAPTER SEVEN

Here I am.
    But it's not *right*.
If just living can do this,
Living is more dangerous than anything:

It is terrible to be alive.

Randall Jarrell, 1914–1972. *The Face*

Forty-six floors up in the hotel nightclub Rebecca and Eliot share an intimate candle-lit dinner. The aerial view from their table is truly magnificent. Below the black sky lights are on all over the city, and in the distance the headlights of the vehicles travelling across the Golden Gate Bridge appear as illuminated raindrops glistening and shimmering on the window. Rebecca is so affected by the sight and her thoughts of Nathan Roth that a lump of emotion becomes lodged in her throat.

'Rebecca, you're very quiet tonight,' Eliot observes with a smile. He is not so quiet, he had a very successful day persuading this man Klein to invest in his picture and his mood is one of high spirits and self-congratulation. Understandably he wants Rebecca to respond but she can barely concentrate on what he is telling her.

'I'm sorry,' she murmurs, placing her hand over his on the table. 'I seem to be feeling a little sad this evening.' She smiles suddenly. 'Never mind, I'm sure Alice will cheer me up.'

'And I can't?'

'You always cheer me up, Eliot.'

He looks at her. There is something indefinably formal about her attitude this evening, as though, ridiculous as it may sound, this were only their third or fourth date, as though their relationship were still at the stage where both feel the need to play psychological chess. Rebecca glances up in surprise as a member of the hotel staff appears at their table, an enormous bouquet of flowers in his arms.

'Miss Farrell?' She nods wordlessly. 'These were just delivered for you.' Eliot gives him a generous tip.

'Who would send you flowers?' he asks innocently.

'I . . . I don't know.' Rebecca laughs expectantly, her fingers unusually clumsy as she removes the small card from the envelope pinned to the cellophane. It reads: 'To the most beautiful woman in the world. Thank you for being here with me. Love always, Eliot.' Tears spring into her eyes. For one crazy, irrational moment she had thought the flowers had come from him, from Nathan Roth, and now so great is her disappointment that she finds it difficult to breathe or speak.

'Hey, what's so bad you have to cry?' Eliot asks, watching the change come over her face. 'Don't you like them?'

'They're beautiful.' The smile which has become frozen to her lips thaws slightly allowing her to speak numbly. She draws her finger along beneath her eyes. 'You're very thoughtful.' She squeezes his hand fondly.

The small band is playing an old romantic standard and an attractive blonde is singing on the stage.

'Would you like to dance?' Eliot asks, unwillingly adopting Rebecca's distant tone. He holds her in his arms, cheek to cheek, enjoying the soft warmth of her body, the perfume of her hair.

'I'm pleased you like those flowers, Rebecca,' he says softly. 'You know something, you're the only person in the world who makes me feel human, who makes me realize there is more to life than making pictures.' They turn slowly so that his back is to the entrance and when she is again facing the archway leading onto the dance floor Nathan Roth is standing there staring at them with those tragic, intensely sad eyes. He is wearing new jeans, a new sweater, both of which are too large. He has shaved and combed his wayward hair, he looks scrubbed and young and frightened. He looks like a man about to run away.

'They're here.'

'What?'

'Nathan and the others.' She gives the professor a brief wave as he and Alice are shown to the correct table. Eliot looks at her, her face is glowing, her eyes are enlarged, the smile on her full lips is coming from somewhere deep and secret inside her soul. He releases her from his embrace, staring from Roth to her and back again, his eyes narrowing until his dark brows have dipped to a frown. He walks from the dance floor in one direction and she in the other to greet Nathan.

'I knew you would come,' she says softly. 'Don't be afraid.'

He acknowledges her words with a blink of his eyes, giving that smile of his, not really a smile but a facade created by the shaping of his lips. She knows that he is afraid but not the extent of his fear.

'Let's join the others.'

'How beautiful you look!' the professor tells Rebecca. Her crepe de chine jump suit is the same shade as her eyes.

'Thank you, professor. Good evening, Alice.'

'Hi there, Rebecca.'

When everyone is seated, Alice and Nathan on one side of the table, Rebecca and Eliot on the other, with a fifth chair for the professor at the head, Eliot orders a bottle of the hotel's best champagne.

'I'll have a scotch and ice,' Nathan tells the waiter.

'Hey, come on, live a little,' Eliot says, twisting his mouth contemptuously.

'Scotch and ice,' Nathan reiterates quietly.

Alice is wearing a white dress, stretched to capacity over her ample curves and white plastic triangles dangle from her ear lobes. Eliot's gaze dips to her impressive cleavage.

'That's a nice dress you're nearly wearing,' he says facetiously.

Alice collapses with laughter.

'You're a real card, Eliot,' she informs him with an ambiguous and suggestive smile. 'Ain't he, Rebecca?'

'Yes, he's the joker in the pack.'

Another explosion of laughter all but dislodges Alice's breasts from the bodice of her dress. She eases the shoulder strap up with a minimum of fuss, as someone who is well accustomed to having her clothes fall off in public. The waiter serves the champagne. To Nathan he gives scotch and ice.

'You sure you won't join us, poet?' Eliot says.

'To our friendship!' Adler toasts, raising his glass.

'To our friendship!' Alice echoes, giggling.

Rebecca looks at Nathan over the rim of her glass as she brings it to her lips. Why do you never smile, Nathan, even at me? There is such a deep darkness in you, a darkness of solitude that makes me wonder if you will ever find your way back to the light. The vocalist is singing 'You Are the Sunshine of My Life' and a handsome black couple are dancing alone in the centre of the floor. Alice and Adler watch. Nathan's trembling hand lifts his glass. His eyes meet Eliot's and the two men stare at each other. Nathan is the first to drop his gaze, ill at ease with the other man's unremitting stare. He puts his glass onto the table and looks away, blinking rapidly. When he ventures to look again Eliot is still watching him, his lips jerking up at the edges in a cruel and critical smile. Nathan searches in his pockets for his cigarettes, badly wanting something to do with his hands. A nerve begins to jerk in his left cheek.

'New jeans, Mr Roth? What a pity they didn't stock your size.'

Nathan locates his cigarettes and they drop to the floor. Rebecca bends down and picks them up from under the table. She passes them across.

'And you took a shave. We are honoured.'

'Leave him alone,' Rebecca says intensely, her voice not rising above a whisper.

Eliot looks at her in astonishment.

'Do you think the Chinese New Year here in San Francisco is more exotic than that celebrated in New York?' Adler enquires generally.

'I don't know about you,' Alice says, 'but I'd love to dance.'

Eliot gets to his feet. Nathan looks up at him, all six foot three inches of him, in a beige suit, white shirt and thickly knotted, boldly striped neck tie.

'Alice, it would be my pleasure.'

'I thought you'd never ask,' she says with a flirtatious giggle. 'Is it okay with you, Rebecca?'

'Please, go ahead,' Rebecca agrees readily.

Alice holds his arm proudly as they walk onto the floor. Adler looks at Nathan and then at Rebecca. They are staring at each other.

'Will you excuse me a moment?' He touches Nathan's shoulder in a fatherly gesture before going off and pretending to search for the men's room.

'Did he buy you the flowers?' Nathan's sad, dark eyes hold hers. 'I didn't know you like flowers. I didn't know what would please you. I'll buy you flowers.'

'You please me by being here tonight. By just being you.'

He touches his chin.

'I guess I'm not the world's best dressed man.'

'You're beautiful.'

He frowns, not understanding this word in relation to himself. He uses both hands to push the hair off his forehead and it comes tumbling back untidily. Rebecca laughs.

'You . . . eh, you look very nice. I mean more than nice.' He swallows. 'You look beautiful.'

Dear, sweet Nathan, she thinks, he is trying desperately to flirt with me, to offer me the intimate, whispered words men have always given to women. If only they could be alone somewhere quietly together, if only they could just be alone and talk.

'He dances well,' he says about Eliot. 'I guess he does everything well.' He rubs his eyes, he looks so tired, so tired and frail.

'Oh wow,' Alice says breathlessly, returning to the table with Eliot, 'that sure was exciting.'

The professor comes out of hiding. Eliot offers Rebecca his hand.

'Dance?'

'Not right now.'

Eliot looks at Nathan. 'What a pity you can't dance, poet, but then there must be a lot of things you can't do.'

Nathan gazes out of the window, swallowing hard. A string of lights twinkle in the distance, a necklace of melting snowflakes that he would like to place around Rebecca's strong, exquisite neck, along with a garland of kisses. But he never will. This world is not his world, this world confuses him with its consistent ability to inflict pain. His laughter has no echo, his body casts no shadow. He does not exist in the true, physical sense of the word.

So the evening wears on with Eliot dominating the conversation, Alice laughing appreciatively at his jokes and Adler trying to revive Rebecca and Nathan's interest in the proceedings. The next time Alice gets up to dance with Eliot Rebecca moves into her seat. She touches Nathan's arm, calling him back across the distance he puts between himself and the world.

'Nathan, don't let Eliot upset you. He is under a lot of pressure at the moment.'

The poet turns his face to hers, it is withdrawn and sad.

'I was thinking about tomorrow,' he says, 'I was thinking about the first time I was at Berkeley.'

'Rebecca,' Adler says, 'I just had a marvellous idea. Why don't you come to Berkeley with us tomorrow afternoon and see Nathan receive his honorary doctorate?'

Rebecca puts her hand over Nathan's on the table. 'Would you like that, Nathan?' she asks him.

'Of course he would.'

Nathan blinks, trying with ever increasing difficulty to break out of his self-imposed trance.

'What would you tell Eliot?' he enquires.

'Let me worry about Eliot. Just say you want me to come.'

'I do.'

'Wonderful!' Adler cries, clapping his hands together. 'The college is sending a car for us at two p.m. We shall meet you in the lobby.'

'It's a date,' Rebecca says, holding Nathan's hand between both of hers then releasing it as Eliot approaches the table.

'Changed seats?' he asks.

'I wanted to watch you and Alice dancing.'

'Can't say I blame you. We certainly showed them how it ought to be done, didn't we, Fifi?'

'You bet, lover,' Alice agrees, flushed with honour.

Eliot holds up the empty champagne bottle most of which he and Alice have consumed between them. He also had two large brandies and half a bottle of red wine with his dinner.

'Waiter!' He clicks his fingers.

'No more,' Rebecca says.

'Nonsense. The party has just begun. Waiter, bring another bottle of bubbly and this time bring a glass for Lord Byron.'

'Who is Lord Byron?' asks Alice, looking around for this royal personage.

'Lord Byron was a poet, just like Mr Roth. And that ain't all they had in common, am I correct, Mr Roth?'

'If you say so,' Nathan says softly.

'It speaks, Jesus, it actually speaks.'

'Don't be cruel to Nathan,' Alice begs plaintively.

'Alice, I am never cruel. I am broadening your mind. Educating you. You wanted to know about Byron, well he was also a cripple.'

'That's enough!' Rebecca says, harshly. 'Don't you know when to stop?'

Eliot pours champagne into a glass and pushes it toward Nathan. 'Drink it,' he orders, his voice tightening and no longer playful, 'come on down here with us mortals for a change.'

'You've had too much to drink,' Rebecca says in a disgusted voice. 'Stop being a bloody boor.'

'Oh but I am a boor. In Hollywood we're all bloody boors. Roth can tell you, we're all Philistines, we don't appreciate the finer things of life.' He drains his glass. 'Tell me, Alice, how did you like your visit to Fisherman's Wharf this morning with Rebecca?'

Alice looks dumbly at Eliot and then at Rebecca, who feels her face flushing guiltily. Nathan lights a cigarette.

'Alice, I asked you a question.'

'Yer, I know, but I ain't sure I know the answer.'

'Did you or did you not enjoy your trip to Fisherman's Wharf with Rebecca?'

'Well . . . sure . . . ' Alice says uncertainly. ' . . . it was . . . it was . . . startling.'

Eliot laughs raucously and slaps the table with the palm of his hand.

'Okay now, which parts did you like best?'

Alice looks at Rebecca for help.

'No cheating,' Eliot warns her, flicking her ear-ring.

'I got a real bad memory, Eliot, anyone will tell yer, see I don't remember nuthin' from one minute to the next. Ain't that true, Nathan?'

Nathan nods.

94

'I guess I liked those ships and things,' Alice tries courageously.

'Dumb but loyal,' Eliot pronounces her.

'Don't you think you've had enough to drink, Mr Vaughan?' the professor says.

'Right. I'm outnumbered. Four to one. A literary agent, a professor, a poet and a stripper against a bloody boor.' He pours himself more champagne. 'Hey, Alice, tell these folks one of your dirty jokes.'

'I don't think I oughta.'

'Oh come on, tell the one you just told me on the dance floor about the two dollar hooker and the monkey.'

Alice laughs nervously. 'I don't think I will.'

'You're no fun.' He dismisses her with a wave of his hand. 'Okay, I'll tell a joke. Have you heard the one about the agent and the cripple?'

'I said that's enough!' Rebecca bursts out. 'Apologize or I'll walk out of here right now.'

Alice and Adler look at Eliot, waiting.

'Okay, I'm sorry,' he says grudgingly. He rubs a hand over his face. 'It was a bad joke anyway.'

The vocalist is singing into her microphone as she circles the floor, pausing at the tables. 'If somebody loves you it's no good unless they love you all the way . . . '

'Gee, that's lovely,' Alice whispers as the young woman approaches their table. 'So romantic.'

' . . . Through the good and lean years and through all the in between years, come what may.' She sings directly to Rebecca and Nathan. 'Who knows where the road will lead us, only a fool will say.' Rebecca draws Nathan's hand onto her lap under the table and entwines her fingers with his. 'But if you let me love you it's for sure I'm gonna love you all the way . . . '

Eliot looks at Rebecca's face and then at Roth's. He joins Alice in rowdy applause as the vocalist takes a bow.

'Gee,' Alice says with a sigh. 'I always wanted to be a classy singer.'

She takes the floor to teach Adler the Bossa Nova. Eliot gives Rebecca's arm a tug.

'Come on,' he says resentfully, 'dance with me.'

'You're making a spectacle of yourself.'

'Roth doesn't mind being left alone. He's composing a new masterpiece.'

Nathan's hand moves involuntarily to his stomach as a grimace of pain flickers across his features.

'Are you satisfied?' Rebecca asks Eliot.

'I didn't make the boy sick,' Eliot says in a tone of slurred indignation, 'all I ever wanted to do was have a good time. It isn't my fault he's always ill.'

'Eliot, for God's sake pull yourself together. I'll order you some black coffee.'

Adler limps off the floor, stiff jointed, shaking his head.

'I hope you young people will excuse me, I'm for bed.' He puts a hand on Nathan's shoulder. 'I wish you would also go to bed, you'll need all your strength tomorrow.'

Nathan glances up at him. 'In a while.'

'Okay, sleep well.' He squeezes his shoulder.

'Hey, professor, why don't you tuck him in and sing him a lullaby?'

'Good night, Rebecca, Alice.'

'Good night, professor,' they say in unison.

Adler walks away from the table without a word to Eliot.

'Hey, Nathan, you coming to bed?'

'No, not yet. You go ahead.'

'Shall I stay with yer, huh?'

'No, Alice, I'll be fine,' his patient voice says.

Eliot pours the last of the champagne into his glass.

'Tell me, Roth, why do your hands shake?'

'You shouldn't oughta be cruel to Nathan,' Alice says, upset. 'I don't like you so much when you're cruel to Nathan.'

'Go to bed, Fifi, you badly need your beauty sleep.'

Alice looks at Rebecca, hurt and pouting.

'Go on,' Rebecca tells her kindly. 'I'm going soon.'

Alice comes around the table and kisses Rebecca's cheek. Then she puts her arms around Nathan's neck and kisses him full on the lips. Rebecca looks away and out of the window, overcome by a great wave of bitter sweet sadness. It is to Alice Nathan will soon go, Alice who could never understand the pain that is this man's burden.

'Hey, how about me? Don't I get a kiss?' Eliot asks, grinning.

'No, not when you're so cruel to Nathan.' She walks away from the table, her shoulders haughty with disapproval.

'Are you sure you're all right?' Rebecca asks the poet, reluctant to leave him alone with his thoughts. 'Nathan . . . ' Rebecca doesn't know what else to say with Eliot listening. But she need not say anything, her expression says it all. Nathan glances up at her, his lidless eyes merely points of shadowy light. Rebecca takes her bag off the chair and walks away from the table, leaving the flowers and Eliot.

Rebecca comes out of the bathroom and climbs into bed. She turns off the light on the night table leaving Eliot sitting on the dressing table stool in the dark.

'How long am I going to be in the doghouse?' he asks, laughing. 'Something gets into me when I see him.' His lighter flares up in the shadows as he smokes a fresh cigarette. 'Something just gets into me. If you don't like the way I treat the guy why keep dragging me along to meet him?' He gets up and walks the length of the room before stopping in front of the bed to look at Rebecca's motionless form. 'Why don't you admit he's a pain in the neck?' He stubs out his cigarette in the ashtray. 'Can't you answer me, Rebecca?'

Silence.

'Am I the only one around here whose neurosis is not

made allowances for? Okay, okay, I lost my cool tonight, I admit it. Can't we forget the whole damn thing?' He gets undressed. After some moments in the bathroom he lifts the sheet and gets into bed. 'I'm sick of hearing about his creative temperament.' He turns onto his side and kisses her bare shoulder. She moves away. 'Okay, I'm jealous, is that what you want to hear? I'm jealous. Me, I'm jealous of him because of the way you look at him. I can't put it into words. Rebecca, why can't you answer me?' He places his hand on her shoulder and she moves to the edge of the bed. 'I think I prefer the kind of woman who hollers.' He lies down, his back to her, and in a while she can hear him breathing noisily in his sleep.

I dreamed about you all that night. I dreamed about you and refused to allow the other man to touch me. The other man who is my lover. I did it for you. In your honour. A gesture. A sacrifice to your pain that my lover and I had to make for you. You stood at the foot of our bed weeping for what you believed you could never possess and for what I was ready to give. So I was unable, unwilling to make love with this other man. It was your arms I saw stretched out to me, your body I sought to embrace, your breathing I strained to hear in the silent darkness. Oh Nathan, Nathan, where does sympathy end and love begin?

CHAPTER EIGHT

My heart like a flame turned upside down.

Guillaume Apollinaire, 1880–1918. *Heart*

The ringing of the telephone wakes them at the same instant. Eliot turns onto his side with a groan and squints at the early morning sunlight flooding through their hotel window. He lifts the receiver.

'Hello? Yes . . . ' His head aches, there is the taste of rusty metal in his mouth. He uses his free hand to rub his half open eyes. 'Who?' He comes suddenly to himself and sits up with a jolt. 'Put him on. Hi, hello, Gerry! Hey, how are you? No, no, you didn't wake me, I've been up hours. You know what they say about the early worm . . . ' Rebecca lies there beside him coming back to wakefulness at a more easy pace. She can intermittently hear Gerry Shapiro's raucous voice, a voice that could so easily dispense with the services of the Bell Telephone Company and still be heard this far down the Pacific coast. 'Gerry, that's no problem. Sure, great, well I know, Klein feels the same way I do. He's behind me on this all the way. Hey, no, it's really no problem. You give my best to your wife and tell her I said she comes first. I'll call the airport right now and get our reservations changed. See you in a couple of hours.'

Rebecca feels a sinking feeling sucking at her stomach. Did he say a couple of hours? Her face gets suddenly warm. She must have misheard, not fully awake, they leave for Hollywood tomorrow not today. Change the reservations? Eliot is staring down at her with that maddeningly self-satisfied smile on his firm lips.

99

'Still not speaking to me?' he asks, running his hand gently over her shoulder.

'I'll speak to you long enough for you to tell me what Shapiro wanted at 6.00 a.m. in the morning.'

'He had a call from Klein last night. They want to set up the deal between them. They want me to make the picture.'

'Oh, Eliot, that's wonderful!' Rebecca cries, throwing her arms around his neck and hugging him. 'Congratulations! That's absolutely wonderful!'

'You mean I'm absolutely wonderful.' He lies back on his pillow with Rebecca's chin on his chest, her eyes laughing at the modesty which is so apparent at times like this. He puts his hand in her hair and draws her face up to his. He kisses her mouth.

'Are you proud of me?'

'You know I am. Except when you behave the way you did last night.'

'Hey, we can't lie here,' he says abruptly, glancing around the room. 'How long will it take you to pack?' He swings his legs out of the bed. 'Shapiro wants me in L.A. as soon as possible and that means now. Some crap about his wedding anniversary tomorrow and his wife threatening to leave him if he doesn't take her away for a vacation. I've got to be back in London by the 22nd so when the man says now it's now.' He pushes his uncombed hair out of his eyes.

'Eliot, just a moment.' She lays her hand on the back of his shoulder as he dials. 'Are you saying we're leaving now instead of tomorrow?' Her shocked voice splits the words into separate sentences.

'That's what I'm saying.'

Rebecca's heart rises into her throat as she hears him speaking into the mouthpiece. She can't leave today, now, within the hour. She made Nathan a promise and she cannot break that promise. She cannot. It is out of the question. Eliot rushes around the room, grabbing items of clothing and talking as he goes.

'Just throw these things into the suitcase, we'll be un-packing again in a couple of hours. You know what we'll do? After everything is settled with Klein I'll give John Tyson a call and see if he'll let us stay at his place on Malibu. How would you like that?'

Without waiting for an answer he disappears into the bathroom. Rebecca puts her hand over her eyes and tries to think. How can she break her promise to Nathan knowing what she does about his past, his marriage? Any other man might understand and accept that circumstance intervened, that fate, for good or evil, took a hand. But not Nathan. He will see it as yet another conspiracy to rob him of any happiness, however fleeting, that might be his. Eliot comes out of the bathroom.

'Hey, Rebecca, you not up yet?'

She gets out of the bed. 'Please, can I speak to you for one moment?'

'Can't it wait until we're on our way to the airport?' He pushes past her and grabs his neck tie off the back of the chair.

'Actually, no, it can't.'

'Shapiro is itching to meet you. You know what I thought? We'll take him and his wife out to dinner this evening. Drink to their health, wish them a happy anniver-sary, even buy them a gift . . . Rebecca, what's the matter?'

She is touching her forehead with trembling hands. 'I'd like to stay here until tomorrow as we planned. You go on without me and I'll catch up with you in L.A.'

'What are you talking about?' he demands, a frown of incomprehension burdening his brow. 'Catch up with me?'

'Yes,' she draws a deep breath, 'I have to stay here one more day.'

'Why?' He thrusts his hands into his trouser pockets. 'What could be so damn important that it prevents you from coming with me now?' His voice turns challenging, suspicious, his frown deepens to a scowl. 'Does it have anything to do with Roth? Is that it? You don't want to leave without saying your goodbyes to that damned . . . '

'Eliot, please, it's something I just cannot explain. I want to remain here for one more day. I will meet you in . . . '

'The hell you will. I want you with me now, today. Write him a note, send him flowers for all I care, but come with me.'

'It's not that simple.'

'It's always that simple. It's people who complicate life. You just find a piece of paper and write goodbye alongside your name.'

'No.'

He turns away and then turns back to her again, his tone calmer, more reasonable.

'Okay, I never ask, I always demand. Well, that is a very bad failing of mine. Now I'm asking you, please, Rebecca, come with me, I'd like you with me. It won't be the same if you're not with me.'

She stares at him a moment before sitting down heavily on the bed. She fights down a spiralling sense of dismay, even mild panic. Eliot's claims on her time and affections have priority, if only because he came into her life six months before Nathan Roth, and yet Nathan has surely been part of her life since the first moment she read his poems.

'Please, Rebecca . . . ' Eliot holds her shoulders and lifts her to her feet, his brows peaking with emotion. ' . . . please.'

'All right,' Rebecca agrees sadly, with a sigh.

'You'll come with me now?'

She nods yes.

In an hour they are ready to leave the room.

'You go ahead,' Rebecca tells Eliot. 'I want to make a call.'

He stares at her. He lights a cigarette and then takes his

briefcase off the chair before following the bellhop out of the room with their luggage. Rebecca dials Nathan's room number. It rings and rings. She redials. Still no answer. She tries the professor's room. No answer. Her insides ache. She sits at the dressing table with some of the hotel notepaper. Three attempts, screwed up balls of paper tossed into the waste basket, and then one final attempt, succinct and totally unsatisfactory.

'Dearest Nathan,

I can't make Berkeley this afternoon. I have to fly unexpectedly to L.A. with Eliot. Please try and understand. When I get to New York I swear I'll make it up to you. Please take care of yourself for me.

Love, Rebecca.'

She rushes across the lobby to the reception desk. The Japanese male receptionist assures her that the note will get to Mr Roth.

'Rebecca, will you come on?' Eliot calls impatiently.

In the back of the cab Eliot lights a cigarette. Rebecca can sense his nervousness, his excitement, and something else, something she can't quite define.

'Did you manage to get hold of your poet?'

'No,' she says softly.

'Too bad.'

How strange, she thinks, that a man who has known as much good fortune and love as Eliot should begrudge the little that Nathan might find buried deep in a forgotten corner of his saddened heart. She glances out of the window as the cab passes a small flower stall close by their hotel. Nathan Roth is standing there holding a bunch of flowers awkwardly in his arms as he counts money into the owner's outstretched hand. Rebecca's eyes fill up with tears. 'Oh no . . . no . . . ' she whispers, ' . . . Nathan . . . Nathan.' Let me explain. It wasn't my fault. I made a choice and morally it had to be Eliot. Please understand. Please forgive.

CHAPTER NINE

... that fabled rock, that ship of life, that swarming,
million-footed, tower-masted, and sky-soaring citadel that
bears the magic name of the Island of Manhattan...

Thomas Wolfe, 1900–1938. *You Can't Go Home Again*

Irving Kauffman's suits are a legend on Park Avenue, his
suits, and his equally famous, animated hairpiece. This particular morning his suit is navy and white stripe and his
hairpiece is more excitable than usual.

'Let's have some iced coffee in here,' he barks into his
intercom with his usual charm.

His secretary's voice comes back patiently. 'Doug Rogers
is on the line for you.'

'Put him through and get those coffees.' He mops his
brow as he lifts the receiver. 'I'll be one second,' he tells
Rebecca who is sitting cross-legged in front of his desk
studying papers in a file. She gets up and goes to the window behind Irving's enormous leather swivel chair. She
gazes with pleasure at the sunlight reflecting off the massive
glass monoliths rising up into the Manhattan skyline.

What a beautiful, stimulating city this is, and how easily
she has settled into the fast pace of life, as though she has
been here for years. Is it really only six weeks since she
arrived? She has already made many new friends, and made
her considerable presence felt among the publishing trade.
One person upon whom she has made a special impact is
Joe Wasserman, a tall, bearded, darkly handsome man in his
mid forties, the widowed Vice President of a publishing
house on Fifth Avenue. She and Joe have spent some very

pleasant evenings together, discovering that their tastes are similar and their love of life equalled only by the seriousness with which they treat it, and each other. And Joe plays squash. In fact it would be fun to arrange a match between him and Eliot next time the latter came to New York to see her. And then of course there are the Adlers. She had written to Bernard back in February on her return from the U.S. explaining her reasons for not accompanying them to Berkeley, asking his forgiveness and for news of Nathan. He had written, most of it concerning the poet, ending with a confident assertion that if she wrote directly to Nathan he would reply. She did, twice, and he didn't. She had gone to meet Joan on her first Sunday afternoon in New York. She and Mrs Adler had hit it off magnificently, much to Bernard's delight. A small, nervously happy woman of about fifty, with short, dark curly hair peppered with grey, shining eyes and a gently optimistic approach to life and its many caprices that had instantly won Rebecca's heart. She and Bernard are devoted to each other, and to Nathan, something which became immediately apparent on stepping into their small living room on West 13th Street. Photographs of the poet at various stages in his life, from shy, gawky sixteen-year-old prodigy to withdrawn thirty-seven-year-old genius, grace the walls and shelves. All his awards, degrees, and diplomas are in Bernard's hands for safekeeping. On subsequent Sundays she has been so occupied with trying to arrange the furniture and her belongings in her new apartment that she had had to decline any further invitations until this Sunday.

'Rebecca!' Irving's insistent, irritable voice penetrates her reveries. 'What the hell do you find so fascinating about this city? To me it's just a giant garbage dump.'

Rebecca walks back to her chair. 'Then why do you stay here?'

'Ever heard of a successful literary agent operating out of Hoboken?'

Rebecca laughs. 'You could retire and start to enjoy life.'

'Sure, and spend twenty-four hours in the company of my wife and her mother. Forget it.' Cigar ash drops onto his hundred dollar shirt as he waves his pudgy fingers in the air. 'Did I mention I was talking to Joe Wasserman the other day?' His calculating eyes fix intently on her face.

'No, you didn't mention it, but you will.'

'You and he are getting very friendly I understand.'

'Did he tell you that?'

'No, but I hear stories. You ain't ashamed are you? That guy can do us, and you, a lot of good.'

'Are you suggesting I cultivate his friendship in order to obtain favours?' Rebecca enquires with mock indignation.

'I ain't suggesting anything. I'm just telling you I approve.'

'Thank you so much.'

His secretary brings in the coffees.

He pulls his seat forward and moves the manuscript lying on the edge of his desk to the centre. He places both hands on the dog-eared pages and looks piercingly at Rebecca. 'Now let's get down to business. I read this over the weekend and I don't like it.' The smile vanishes from Rebecca's face, though his words are nothing more than she expected.

'Please be specific,' she says, bringing out her own factual tone.

'It's controversial, it's a hot potato, it could cause trouble, you'll never find a publisher willing to handle it, it's a financial risk. Just how specific do you want me to be?'

'Maria Hernandez has written a story which ought to be published and read. It's human, optimistic, emotional and deals with life now, not in the 19th or 23rd century.'

'She's a drug addict according to your report.'

'If you'd have read the report properly you would have seen that I said ex-drug addict, she's been off the stuff for two years. Her story would give hope to thousands of people, drug addicts and their families.'

'It's not a subject that ought to be treated in a novel.' He relights his cigar which has gone out in the rush of cool air from Rebecca's words. 'It's sociology or something, how do I know? I'm not happy with trying to sell it to a publisher as a novel.'

'Irving,' Rebecca pushes the hair off her face, 'how many ordinary people, people whose lives will be touched by Maria's story, read sociology or psychology? The novel is the popular human way to reach people. Maria's story is full of hope and humour, it's not a depressing story, it's uplifting. Besides which we could call it semi-autobiographical.'

'I'm not convinced.' He pushes the manuscript toward her across the desk and she pushes it back, saying, 'Then I'll convince you. Read it again, keeping in mind what I've said. I admit the prose needs polishing, the grammar, the punctuation, but I've sold professional novelists' work that has been no better than this, and often a lot worse. Tell me when you've read a more touching, yet unsentimental story?' she challenges. 'The reader is totally involved right from the start. You want Maria and her family to overcome all her problems, and when you close the book you feel that there is hope for people like them.' She stands up, gathering her papers. 'Read it again, I insist.'

'You insist?' Irving's toupee definitely moves in sympathy with its owner's indignation.

'Yes,' she confirms in her warm, aggressive voice.

'Now I'll tell you something,' he gazes at her, his voice becoming heavy with the weight of his words, 'it's the wrong time politically for this kind of book. You don't know the territory yet. Maybe you have to be born here to understand, to judge the temperament of the people. Maybe in a couple of years, who knows . . . '

'Maria can't wait a couple of years,' Rebecca maintains persistently. 'She'll take the manuscript to another agency.'

'I wish her luck,' Irving says, not bothering to disguise his contempt for Maria and her book.

'Irving, I warn you, I won't give up easily on this one. You asked me to join you because you were impressed by my record, you said you trusted my judgement and now when . . .'

'Okay, okay, don't get so excited. It's bad for my ulcer.'

'You don't have an ulcer.'

'If I did you'd be bad for it.' His voice becomes placating. 'Look, why don't I do like you say and read it again? Is that fair?'

She knows by the way his hairpiece is twitching that he is lying through his gleaming false teeth, but she smiles agreeably.

'I want to represent this girl and her book. I want you to know that it means a lot to me.'

'I'll keep that in mind. But you ought to know, Rebecca, that every damn manuscript that comes into this office ain't a personal crusade. Maybe you're in the wrong business after all, maybe you ought to be a social worker?' He laughs so that she knows he is only kidding. She slaps a folder down on his desk.

'I've done a breakdown and analysis with relevant comments based on my visits to four of the biggest book stores on Fifth Avenue over the last month. You will find my observations interesting, and very encouraging, under the circumstances.'

'You remind me of my wife, the only woman I know who can make a request sound like an order.'

'Something is missing,' Rebecca confesses to Eliot over the phone that evening in her apartment. 'Something is wrong. I just can't put my finger on it, but somewhere along the line I'm not getting satisfaction from what I'm doing here.'

'You need me,' Eliot whispers into her ear.

'No, really, I'm serious. It's not just this Maria business, it's everything about my work. I'm selling books that would get sold with or without me. I want to sell a novel that makes me proud to know I've accomplished something worthwhile.'

'Like I said, Rebecca, you're an idealist. New York is the wrong place for you. Why don't you throw a few things into a suitcase and join me here?'

'I love New York. It isn't that at all. I'm not quitting yet anyway. It's not in my nature to quit. Maybe it's just Irving.'

'Who can blame the guy, he's not running a charity organization.'

'Oh yes, I forgot, you and he both come from the same hard-nosed school.'

'Hey, don't be so touchy. I wish you'd come out here for a few days. Come on,' he says persuasively.

'Not now, Eliot, I can't, I've got so much to do. But I'm grateful for the offer. I have to go, I'm off to a concert this evening.'

'Rebecca . . .'

'Yes?'

'Nothing. It doesn't matter. I'll call you tomorrow evening. Have a good time.'

'Thank you. Take care.'

CHAPTER TEN

Yet let me now be careful
Not to give too much
To one so shy and fearful
For like a gun is touch.

Delmore Schwartz, 1913–1966. *What is to be Given*

Nathan Roth glances with increasing curiosity at the professor who is comparing the hour on his wristwatch with that on the clock in his living room. That makes the third time now and twice he has asked Joan to check her own wristwatch with his.

'Bernard, relax,' Joan says, smiling at him indulgently, but herself displaying a certain inability to remain seated in one spot for more than five seconds at one go. She fluffs up the cushions on the small couch on which Nathan is seated, removes a spot of imaginary dust from the armrest and combs Nathan's hair with her fingers.

'Look who is telling me to relax?' Bernard says with a gesture of his hand toward Joan. Joan looks at him as if to say 'Be careful now, you don't want him to become suspicious do you?'

Nathan looks from one to the other. There was something very insistent about Bernard's invitation to spend Sunday evening with them, an insistence that went beyond the normal bounds of Adler hospitality. No formal summons was ever needed before. He knows he can come and go as he pleases, unannounced, just as a son might do. But today, well today Joan and Bernard are behaving like hosts and he feels decidedly uncomfortable.

The front door bell rings and the expression of relief that comes over Bernard's face is almost that of a man removing tight shoes at the end of a tiring day.

'I'll go,' Joan says. 'Please.' She shakes her head with a frown toward Nathan.

'Are you expecting anyone?' the poet asks. He turns slowly, using his cane to steady himself, and he needs to steady himself because when Joan comes into the room Rebecca is just behind her.

'Nathan?' she says, obviously as astonished to see him as he is to see her. A deep glow of warmth enters her chest. The same Nathan, in faded blue jeans, washed out sweat shirt, sneakers and no socks. She laughs her throaty, husky laughter. 'Oh, Nathan, it's so good to see you again.' Bernard beams with happiness.

'Well say hello to Rebecca,' Joan urges the younger man.

His moist eyes travel unsmilingly over her wide suntanned face and strong dark body inside a white sleeveless dress. He turns his gaze onto Adler, his glower demanding an explanation.

'I do not apologize for this little deception,' the professor informs him defiantly. 'You wanted to see Rebecca again and you are too stubborn to answer her letters or return her calls. Rebecca wanted to see you. Is it so unforgivable that we arranged for you to see each other?'

'No, of course it isn't,' Joan answers her husband, slipping one arm through Rebecca's and the other through Nathan's, 'and you can blame me too, it was just as much my idea.'

'I'm not going to blame anyone,' Rebecca says, her smile taking in all three of them. She leans forward and presses a kiss to Nathan's cheek.

He nods, his melancholy eyes watching her accusingly from under his untidy hair.

Joan looks at Bernard. 'Give Rebecca a drink and then come and help me in the kitchen.'

111

Rebecca sips Joan's homemade lemonade, enjoying the slightly tangy bitterness on her tongue. Bernard closes the door behind him with a pleading glance at Rebecca. She watches the poet's gaunt face for a second, touched by the beauty of his haunted eyes, staring at something only he can see.

'I'm very sorry about what happened in San Francisco. But the least you could have done was answer my letters.' Her voice trails off. Is he even listening? He hasn't moved since she came into the room but now he sits down and lifts the packet of crushed cigarettes from the couch. Several are broken, and he stares at them as though wondering how they got that way. He puts one between his finely curved lips and smokes, his eyes distant and remote. He looks tired and drawn, but when has he ever looked anything else? The strain of his expression, the anguish of his thoughts makes the skin taut over the bridge of his nose, exaggerating the bump. That wonderful, Jewish, pugilist's nose, yet did anyone ever look less like a fighter?

'How have you been?' she asks gently.

'Okay.' He draws smoke deep into his lungs.

'Nathan, can't we be friends?'

'Friends?' He looks directly at her. 'Such an emotive word with so many different meanings.'

'Much more than friends,' she says, hoping that her tone leaves him in no doubt as to her particular definition, at least where he is concerned.

'I'm surprised you don't get angry with Bernard, an independent woman like you, pushed into a situation.'

'Bernard isn't pushing me into any situation I don't want or can't handle.'

He gives an odd, neutral smile, that mouth making the shape but there is no emotion behind it.

'What's funny?'

'You always sound so sure of yourself.'

'Do I?' she says as though this is an implied criticism.

'Perhaps it's because I'm accustomed to making my own decisions, relying on my own judgements.'

His next words drift out on a cloud of smoke as he leans forward to stub out his cigarette. 'Why didn't you go to Hollywood with Eliot?'

'Because I wanted to come to New York. I wanted to see you again.'

He laughs humourlessly.

'You expect me to believe you came to live in New York just to be near me?'

'Poor Nathan,' she says mockingly, 'does that frighten you so much?'

He gets up and limps to the half bottle of scotch on the table in the corner and pours some into a glass. He drinks it straight down. Rebecca watches his entire, frail body give a momentous shudder as the liquid passes into his stomach. He turns around and stares at her. Her long legs are crossed, the hem of her cotton dress reaching to just below the knee. She has beautiful legs, not only shapely, but strong. Since the accident strong legs are something he has come to admire and envy. His eyes move to her hands clutching her glass. He remembers her hands from the first time they met, trustworthy hands that would not let you fall nor fail. He once loved Madeline's hands, so delicate and white, with their exquisitely manicured and varnished nails, long and sharp. But now he hates them and hates his own body for withstanding the cruelty those hands could inflict by merely refusing to touch him. He looks at Rebecca from a different angle, moving to the other side of the room. She carries her beauty with a nonchalance that serves only to make her more beautiful, more desirable. Desire? A word not usually in his vocabulary. Not since Madeline.

'It would have taken most people years to pull up roots and start all over again somewhere else,' he says eventually.

'Admiration?' she enquires, her eyes focusing teasingly on

his face. 'I'm a nomad, remember, I have no roots. I'm happiest when I'm on the move.'

'How long do you plan to stay in New York?'

'That depends on how stimulating I find my work, and on you.'

Nathan makes a sound like a grunt and limps to the far side of the room. He stands with his back to her.

'It's a good thing this room isn't any larger, I'd get weary just watching you. Why don't you just sit down?'

He moves his head from side to side and then lowers it.

'I'm still here,' Rebecca says airily.

'Do you know what I think, Rebecca?'

'I love the way you say my name. I love your New York Jewish accent when you say it.'

'I think you truly appreciate my poetry and that you are mixing your feelings of pity for me with your admiration for the poet.'

'You are the poet and the man. The two can never be separated, just as you are what you write. Don't you believe that, Nathan?' she asks in surprise.

'The man no longer exists.'

Rebecca crosses the room and speaks to his bowed head. She puts her hand on his cheek.

'Admit you feel nothing when I touch you and I will admit that the man no longer exists.'

He removes her hand.

'I'm not afraid to die. It might be the perfect existence we all dream about.'

'Why die when you can live? Life can be the perfect existence, if you give it a chance. I know how dreadfully she hurt you . . .' She stops because his face has contorted with pain. She takes his hand and kisses the knuckles. 'I would never hurt you, Nathan. I know what you are, who you are, the precious frailty of your existence, the vulnerability of your soul. I know how fortunate mankind is just to have men and women such as you walking this earth.'

'No,' he says.

'No, what? Do my words embarrass you? Does the depth of my feelings for you and your poems scare you so much?'

'If I wasn't a poet, if I was just me, a cripple, a man without a shadow to cast, would you still want to help me?'

'You wouldn't need me. You would be a different person. How can I answer that question? I want to help you, the man I know as Nathan Roth.'

'You . . . can't help me.' His lips turn down with the bitterness of his words. 'I owe her . . .' He turns his head away. 'I owe Madeline.'

'What do you owe her? That you suffer the rest of your life? That you die without ever knowing how it feels to be loved by a woman?'

'The debt has to be paid,' he says, emphasizing each word equally.

'What debt? I don't understand. The pain is yours. She owes you.'

'Leave it, just leave it.'

'Are you still in love with her?' She takes his arm. 'Are you?'

'No,' he says without hesitation. 'God, no.'

Her gaze skims his face. He is telling the truth. She knows it. She feels it. 'In that case, Nathan,' she says in a calm, assertive voice, a voice without desperation or fear, 'I won't allow you to pay the debt. I will never allow you or anyone else to extinguish a flame that must burn bright for all eternity.'

He meets her steady gaze, his eyes narrowing as he says in passive amazement, 'You mean it.'

'Did you ever doubt it?'

Delicious cold meat salads, slightly salted butter spread thickly on slices of wholemeal bread. A light, crisp white wine bought extravagantly in Rebecca's honour. The glasses are hardly empty before Bernard is refilling them, and Joan must be assured at every moment that her culinary efforts are unrivalled.

'How is the bread?'

'Wonderful,' Rebecca says.

'Joan bakes it herself,' Nathan says. She looks at him and his lips are shiny with butter. She laughs and he becomes suddenly self-conscious.

'Eat,' she tells him.

Joan looks at Rebecca. 'How is your work?'

She gives a rueful smile.

'All I can say is, I'm not as dedicated as I thought I was. Most of the time I'm fighting with Irving. He wants to play safe, take on the same kind of books. I can't really blame him, it's his agency, his money. I'm a new girl at the office, but just for once I wish I could place a book with a publisher that wasn't about a "modern" woman obsessed with her own physical and spiritual ills or a square jawed hero in leather breeches raping every willing woman in sight.'

Bernard laughs and Joan says, 'Oh my goodness,' in a voice of mixed sympathy and shock.

'It's that bad,' Rebecca says with fierce contempt. 'At the moment I have this manuscript written by a Puerto Rican girl.' She goes on to tell them about her difference of opinion with Irving and finishes by saying with uncharacteristic resignation, 'I'm beginning to wonder if it's worth all the blood.'

'So long as it's Irving's blood you're shedding,' Bernard quips, blotting his lips with the napkin. 'But seriously, my dear, it's not like you to sound so ready to give up. I would think of you as ready to fight for what you believe in.'

'Lately I'm thinking more and more about what I do believe in. Nathan will tell you, I'm not someone who can stick to one job or one place very long before I feel ready to tackle something new or different.'

'You lack a vocation,' Bernard says with conviction. 'You need someone . . . '

'Bernard!' Joan interrupts sharply, up until then only following the conversation in silence.

'May I be permitted to finish my sentence, please?'

'Go on,' Joan says unwillingly.

'Thank you. I was about to say that Rebecca needs someone or something,' he looks at Joan as if to say, satisfied? 'to whom she can feel committed. To a warm, loving woman a job, making money for others, is not enough. Am I right, Rebecca?'

'Bernard, I think sometimes you go too far.'

'I don't mind,' Rebecca assures Joan with a smile. 'Besides which he is most probably right. You see my mother left Patrick, my brother, and I a large sum of money each. I used some of that money to furnish my apartment and the rest I invested. Patrick used his to start a small aviation business with a friend in Montreal. My problem is,' she pauses with a smile, 'well it's not so much a problem, it's that I don't actually need to work to earn a salary.'

'A woman of means,' Nathan says, making his first contribution to the subject.

'Look out,' Joan warns Rebecca, 'this boy is a fortune hunter.'

'Why don't you start up a business of your own?' Bernard asks, pouring the last of the wine equally.

'I did have an idea to start up my own literary agency but now I'm not so sure.' She looks at Nathan. 'So much for your opinion of me always being so sure of myself.' She drinks some wine, while she reflects. 'I suppose I lack motivation.'

Bernard looks at Nathan.

'That's why I envy Eliot so much,' Rebecca says, 'he knows exactly what he wants, he's known since he was a child.' She puts her napkin on the table by her plate. 'Anyway, before I forget, you're all invited to my apartment for a house warming party when I'm settled.'

'When?' Bernard says eagerly, sitting forward.

'Very soon.'

'Some of us can't wait,' he says looking at Nathan.

They finish the meal and Rebecca tries to insist that she be allowed to clear away the dishes but Joan is equally adamant that they should all relax and ignore the washing up for now. Nathan lowers himself to the small couch and Rebecca props his cane up against the armrest.

'Can you reach it there?'

'Thank you,' he says, swallowing thickly.

Bernard and Joan exchange another of those meaningful looks.

'At least let me make the coffee,' Rebecca says.

'Sit.' Joan makes her face as belligerent as those kindly features will allow. She and Bernard look so young and so fresh this afternoon, she in her pretty flower patterned dress, and he in his beige linen suit. How easy it would be to grow to love these people who have opened their hearts and home to her. How easy it would be to think of Bernard as the father she never had, and Joan as the mother she never really understood. She sits beside Nathan. Bernard goes to the hi fi system; an extravagant gift to the Adlers from Nathan when he could still afford to make such gestures, Bernard had told her bitterly, before that woman used his money to feed her own base desires, and soon Mahler's Eighth Symphony is drifting quietly from the turntable.

'Nathan's favourite composer,' Bernard remarks, returning to his armchair. 'Do you like Mahler, Rebecca?'

'Very much. We ought to find out when they have Mahler on the programme at Carnegie Hall or the Lincoln Centre,' she tells Nathan. 'We could go together.'

'Mahler was a mystic like Nathan,' the professor says with a grave countenance, 'a man of eternal questings, seeking, and searching, a man obsessed with the meaning of life.'

Rebecca gazes at Nathan whose head is lying back on the couch and whose eyes are closed as he listens to the music, apparently deaf to all else in the room, including Bernard's words.

'I don't know anything about Mahler's life,' Rebecca says, 'but I know something of Nathan's and it seems to me he is obsessed with the meaning of death.'

Bernard removes his spectacles and begins to clean them. 'When have true mystics not been concerned with death?' he asks, avoiding her gaze.

'Must it always be every poet's destiny to die in tragic circumstances? Is it impossible for a mystic to find some peace on earth? Life is the meaning of death.'

Bernard raises his eyes to her face and they are brimming with tears.

'I pray,' he says haltingly.

Joan enters the room with a tray of chocolate ice cream and coffee. Bernard gets up hastily and wipes his eyes on the back of his hands before replacing his spectacles. He takes the tray. Joan studies his face. She looks at Rebecca and at Nathan's face in deep repose.

'You must have some of this ice cream, Rebecca,' Bernard says with forced cheer. 'They come from all over the world to sample Joan's very own recipe for chocolate ice cream.'

'Fool,' Joan says, kissing his bearded chin. 'What would you do with such a man?'

'Love him,' Rebecca says sincerely. She takes a bowl of ice cream off the tray and gently wakes Nathan from his communion with the music. He murmurs a shy thank you.

'Have just a little milk in your coffee, Nathan, huh?' Joan pleads.

'Black, please.'

'Milk and sugar for Nathan,' Rebecca tells Joan with an authority that makes all three of them look at her. Bernard and Joan sit in their armchairs with their coffee and ice cream.

'What do you think of this heat?' Bernard asks Rebecca, breathing out loudly and fanning himself with a magazine.

'Take off your jacket, Bernard, Rebecca doesn't mind, she is one of the family now.'

Rebecca flushes with pleasure. It is a long time since anyone used that warm, embracing word in connection with her. She smiles gratefully at Joan.

'Well so you are,' Bernard says, removing his jacket.

Nathan touches his chest just above the waistline and winces slightly, stopping when he sees Joan watching him with sudden apprehension.

'Do you have a pain, Nathan?'

'Leave him alone,' Bernard says flippantly. 'Who doesn't suffer from indigestion these days? Rush, rush, rush. No wonder they call it the human race.'

'Nathan, why don't you take one of those pills I got for you?'

'Joan, he doesn't need pills. I could tell you what he needs, and it isn't pills.'

'Nathan and I are going to a concert one evening,' Rebecca says, to ease the tension. 'Isn't that right, Nathan?'

'It's a long time since I've been to a concert,' the poet reflects, his eyes and voice not so much distressed as remote, 'not since before . . . ' His sentence remains incomplete.

'By the way, Rebecca, how is that young man, Joe, is that his name?'

Bernard stares at both women fixedly, as though to censor them with his eyes. Nathan looks at Rebecca.

'He's very well,' Rebecca answers, at a loss to know why Joan would bring up the subject in front of Nathan who is watching her with those pain-filled eyes, eyes that no longer accuse so much as question her with silent despair.

'You see, Nathan, you are not the only man in Rebecca's life,' Joan says.

Nathan puts his cup and saucer and his bowl of ice cream, untouched, on the table. He presses his chest and swallows.

'I'm going to do the washing up,' Joan says. She bites down on her lower lip, obviously distressed.

'I'll help you,' Rebecca says, gathering the plates.

Joan is leaning over the sink, her eyes closed, moisture seeping from beneath the lids. Rebecca shuts the door. She puts her arms around the woman and rests her cheek against the back of her shoulder.

'How good you feel to lean on,' Joan says in a faltering voice, 'the young women today are so strong and healthy.' She sniffs, takes a lace handkerchief from the pocket of her apron, blows her nose and wipes her eyes. 'I'm better now. You mustn't fuss.' She slips her hands into a pair of rubber gloves and plunges them into the hot, soapy water.

'Joan, is he very sick?' Rebecca asks softly, in a taut voice.

'I don't know,' she shrugs. 'I don't know.' There are still tears in her eyes and her expression is bewildered. 'How can I know what is emotional and what is physical? Suffering is suffering. Pain is pain.' She begins to clean the dishes with a small mop. 'It is though something inside him has been removed, cut out, and only bitterness put in its place. Do you know how close to the edge a man like him comes every day of his life?' She puts a plate on the rack to drain and Rebecca lifts it with the tea towel. She wonders if Bernard told Joan about the hospital in San Francisco wanting to do tests. Probably not, knowing Bernard's insistence on making light of the whole matter. He was reluctant to talk to her then and nothing has changed. Joan says, 'The pains are getting worse. He is losing weight. Look at his face, his eyes, haunted.' She shoves a stray hair impatiently from her forehead with a weary sigh. She seems about to add something more but then only shrugs again meaninglessly.

'We have to make him visit a doctor,' Rebecca says.

'You think I haven't tried? I've made a dozen appointments. He doesn't go. Bernard encourages him. He is so frightened that it might be serious he has blocked the whole thing from his mind, which of course suits our suicidal Nathan.' She starts to cry. Rebecca holds her close, stroking her hair, her eyes soft with sensitive understanding. 'Killing himself by self-deprivation. He is destroying himself, Rebecca, and he will avoid any treatment that offers hope of success.'

'He can't avoid me,' Rebecca says confidently. 'One day I'll earn his trust. He'll realize that not all women are like Madeline Boucher.'

'Nathan and women,' Joan says giving an inverted smile, 'that boy is so young in his attitude toward the opposite sex.'

'Aren't all men?' Rebecca says with a superior lift of her left eyebrow. 'When it comes to relationships they are all children compared to us.'

'Help him, Rebecca,' her look is intense and pleading, 'he needs someone like you, someone who won't take no for an answer. He has always been so insecure and that woman wiped out the little confidence he had. Help him, I beg you.'

'We'll all help him,' Rebecca says, lifting Joan's face by the chin, 'we'll bring him back to life with our love.'

In the last hour before they leave the Adlers' apartment Nathan reads to them from his last book of poems. They listen, enthralled, to his gentle, hesitating, muted baritone voice, speaking his own words with the mysterious inner rhythm of a religious man reciting from the *Kabbalah*; a Jewish prophet offering illumination to those blessed with the awareness to listen and understand. In the silence that follows his last reading Rebecca reaches for his hand and holds it tightly in her lap. He does not resist. Joan and Bernard look at each other and Joan puts her hand to her mouth to stop herself from crying again.

Rebecca hugs Bernard, Nathan kisses Joan and finally they

are installed in the back of the same cab. Joan and Bernard wave to them from the door.

'Well they may have arrived separately,' Bernard observes, 'but they left together. Do you still think I'm too pushy?'

Joan takes his arm, not wishing to prolong her suddenly melancholy mood. 'I think you're a romantic old fool.'

In the back of the cab she asks, 'Would you like to come up and see the apartment?'

His eyes move rapidly over her face. 'Now?'

He glances around her apartment. Every piece of furniture has been carefully chosen by the occupant and is stamped with her strong personality. Smoked glass and chrome, stainless steel, darkly stained wood, bottle green leather corner couch, chocolate brown fitted carpet, fitted wall unit for her collection of books and an impressive stereo unit. On the coffee table are scattered a selection of literary supplements and last Sunday's *New York Times*. The air smells warm and exotic, it smells of Rebecca, despite the air conditioning. A comfortable room, yet something is missing. The room has not yet been taken over and lived in. That's it, he decides, trying to pin down this feeling, the room has yet to be lived in rather than merely occupied. As Rebecca takes a bottle of wine from the refrigerator in the kitchen she can hear him moving restlessly about, a caged animal searching for an exit that will release, not his physical being, but his tortured spirit. When she joins him with the bottle and glasses he is sitting on the corner couch smoking a cigarette and staring into the distance.

'Are you still in pain?'

He takes the proffered glass from her hand. 'Indigestion.'

'You might be able to play that game with Bernard but not with me.' She pours the wine. 'I'm not even sure I should be allowing you to drink this stuff.' She half fills the glass.

'I thought you were against alcohol?'

'Not in moderation. I just don't happen to like the taste of most alcoholic drinks. Besides wine isn't alcohol. I take the occasional glass and I keep it here for guests.'

'Such as Joe?'

She laughs briefly. 'And when Joan was talking about Joe I thought you weren't even listening.'

'Does Eliot know?'

'Of course. Eliot doesn't expect me to sit home every night. We're not promised to each other for eternity or anything, you know.' She laughs again at her own little joke and stops at once because Nathan isn't even smiling. 'Even now Eliot is very likely sharing his jacuzzi with a Hollywood nymphet.'

'Can I have some more wine, please?' He holds out his glass.

'No. You've had enough, and I've had enough of watching you wince. I'll make you a cup of milky coffee if you like?'

He shakes his head. Rebecca leaves the armchair and sits beside him on the corner unit. He moves slightly to give her room.

'How is Alice?' She keeps her voice inflectionless. 'I like Alice. Honest personalities are rare nowadays.'

'You say you like Alice as though the discovery amazes you.'

'Why do I always end up adopting a defensive attitude to you?' Her smile becomes amused, but her voice is tense. She must not allow him to bait her. 'Do you approve of the apartment?'

'It's fine,' he says, purposely noncommittal.

'I still have some work to do on it.'

She leans forward and removes a long, grey hair that had been lying across his right eyelid, obviously irritating him.

He reaches for his stick and hauls himself awkwardly to his feet.

'I'd better go. It's getting late.' He limps across the room and takes his jacket off the chair.

'Stay here with me tonight,' Rebecca says softly.

No answer.

'Nathan, I'm asking you to spend the night with me.'

He moves a few steps to the left and then stops. He transfers his cane from one hand to the other and then back again. He looks like a man unable to decide what to do about his body, his arms, his legs, a man wishing the floor would open and swallow him before he must answer.

'Nathan?'

'I heard you,' he says in a hoarse voice, smiling slightly, 'but I'd disappoint you and shame myself.' He swallows hard and stares at the floor.

'No shame, no disappointment, only affection.'

'I'm grateful.'

'You think my asking you to stay is an act of charity?'

Rudely, bluntly, he laughs. 'Isn't it?'

Rebecca's voice and face harden as she stands up to confront him.

'I do not make love to men out of pity.' She looks at his passive face. 'You don't even realize you've insulted me.'

'As far as I'm concerned I've spared you a harrowing experience.'

'Was that meant to be funny?'

There is a brief, embarrassed silence before he says, 'Look at it this way. You won't be compromising yourself. What would Eliot have to say if he walked in and found us together in your bed?'

She rounds on him, her cheeks ablaze.

'Are you presuming to judge me? That bed in there is mine, not Eliot's, not any man's. I paid for it, I sleep in it, and I decide who shares it with me. If you don't have the decency or grace to . . . ' She cannot go on, he is looking at her with those strange, brooding eyes, the eyes of a holy man beaten but not broken, a man still ready to believe in his own salvation, if only the light glimmering in the tunnel of his soul's darkness can grow bright enough to show him the way.

She walks slowly to him and stands before him, her eyes looking into his with a tenderness he has never known before. She lifts his hand and kisses the cold white knuckles. She holds the hand to her soft face and kisses it again while her eyes hold his.

'Are you frightened of me, Nathan?' she whispers.

'I'm frightened of what I can't give you, of what I know you deserve. I wouldn't want to compete with Eliot or Joe, if you know what I mean.'

'Lovemaking isn't a competition. You never have to compare yourself to another man. We'll just lie together. I'll hold you while you sleep. You'll wake in my arms in the morning. You'll come back to life.'

'Don't . . .' he begs, tears welling up into his eyes. '. . . for Christ's sake don't torment me . . .'

She lifts her hands and sinks her fingers into his hair. 'Hold me, Nathan, put your arms around me and hold me tightly. Allow me to share my strength with you.'

His shadowed, tormented gaze moves over her sensual features. She moves close to him, close so that her breasts are touching his chest and the throb of life in her loins makes his body vibrate. She holds him tight and kisses him fully, deeply, passionately, keeping back nothing of herself, her longing for him. How long has she dreamed of the moment when she can embrace the frail body of this man, holding him against her own vibrant, life-inspiring self? She runs her fingers through his hair, over his shoulders, across his narrow back. A sound, muted, pained, a moan of sheer ecstasy breaks from his lips that have become warm beneath hers. He returns her kiss, touch for touch, thrust for thrust. Deep and lamented inside himself he feels the first stirrings of an emotion he believed he could never again know in the arms of a woman. He shivers with desire, making her body tremble in answering pleasure. He uses his left hand to caress her, to feel the contours of her glorious body. His soul seems to have become too full of joy to remain caged in a world of darkness, without summer, without love. He speaks her name over and over, a chant, a living poem to her beauty. The smell of her body perfume fills his nostrils, drugs him with a promise of what ecstasy can be his for the asking. He lifts his right hand to her face, inadvertently dropping his walking stick on the carpet between them.

'Leave it . . .' she tells him, trying to keep him in her embrace. ' . . . it doesn't matter.'

'It does to me,' he says in a hollow voice, hardly opening his mouth to release the words.

He waits as she picks up the stick and he takes it from her hand. His eyes have lost that glow of passion and have turned once more remote, staring into a world she cannot know or even enter. A world of secret pain. His eyes have grown moist, he had forgotten for a moment that he was a cripple, and how he became a cripple, but now he remembers, now the exotic, womanly smell of this woman and her soft cushioning lips cannot affect him.

'Nathan . . .' she says in a soft, pleading voice. She lifts her hand to his face and he wards it off, shaking his head. 'If you could only know how I feel about you. I want you, Nathan, I want you to make love to me.'

He lowers his gaze.

'Does my frankness embarrass you, Nathan? It shouldn't, it should make you proud. No man has ever affected me the way you do.'

'Could . . . I have a glass of water?' he asks without raising his eyes.

'Do you want ice?' she calls from the kitchen, where her shaking hand holds the glass under the rush of water. She goes to the kitchen door. 'Do you want . . .' She stops. The front door is open. She runs outside. He has already gone.

CHAPTER ELEVEN

Once
Near the half of the night, the winter night,
I awoke and gazed through the shadows;
He who loved me lay on my bed and slept.
His breath was the roar of sea shells in silence.
I listened . . .

Gertrud Kolmar, 1894–1943? *Paris*

In Rebecca's office one week later, her boss, and an American feminist writer of impressive reputation (and sales figures, as Irving is so often reminding Rebecca) are discussing the reasons this novelist wishes to change agencies and possibly choose Irving's organization as her literary representative. She is a woman who insists that all her business dealings will be with other women. She believes that women in positions of authority and responsibility ought to give other women 'a boost up the ladder'.

'Reach down and haul them up after you, huh?' Kauffman suggests, smiling broadly at what he considers a clever pun on her metaphor.

She ignores him, not for the first time since arriving.

'Positive discrimination,' Rebecca states forcefully, keeping her face straight, and trying not to laugh at Irving's discomfort.

'Exactly,' the novelist cries, slapping the arm of her chair. 'Men are stupid. They can never comprehend the problems faced in a world run by males.'

Irving waits in vain for her to look his way and say, present company excepted. Instead she continues to behave as though he is invisible. But he has to admire Rebecca, her ability to adopt a manner that appears to complement her client's attitude and yet retain her own strong personality. She is no feminist, not in the sense she would have this novelist believe, and yet anyone listening to their conversation would not suspect it.

'If I were faced with interviewing three applicants for the position of my assistant,' Rebecca begins, offering the other woman a cigarette from the box on her desk and lighting it for her, something she would not allow Kauffman to do earlier, 'and one was a woman, I would unhesitatingly discriminate in that woman's favour.'

'Bravo!' The novelist looks at Kauffman who shifts uncomfortably in his chair, tugging at his collar and his neon-lit neck tie. 'That's the only way we can infiltrate their ranks.' She leans over and tips her cigarette ash into the tray which Rebecca holds out to her. 'I can see I'm going to be very happy with Rebecca Farrell looking after my interests.'

That she was finally going to decide on Kauffman's agency was far from certain until this moment, so he beams at Rebecca as though she is a baby and he is a politician at a vote-catching rally.

Rebecca looks at her watch. 'We ought to be going to lunch now. I booked a table for 12.45. I thought we would have drinks in the bar first.'

'She is a wonderful organizer,' Kauffman says, standing up, 'just as reliable as any man.' Before the words have even left his lips he knows it was the wrong thing to say.

'And why the hell shouldn't she be?'

Kauffman reddens and his small, alert eyes blink rapidly.

'Patronizing son of a bitch,' the novelist says, throwing her bag over her shoulder. 'Ready, Rebecca?'

The phone rings.

'Excuse me a moment,' Rebecca says. She puts the receiver to her ear. 'I can't speak to anyone now, Diane, I'm about to have lunch with a client.'

'Rebecca, I'm sorry to interrupt but it's that same man, the one who rang you last week and hung up before I could put him through.'

'Rebecca, we're waiting,' Irving calls impatiently from the door. 'What's holding you up?'

'I'll be one second. Do you mind?' she asks the novelist with just the right degree of deference.

'Go right ahead,' but neither she nor Kauffman make a move to leave her office.

'Put him on,' Rebecca tells the receptionist.

'Rebecca?' Nathan Roth's voice has a pronounced slur.

Last week, last night, every night she dreams about him. He is never very far from her thoughts.

'Is it possible that we could meet?' She tries to convey by her tone that it is difficult for her to talk.

'No. I don't want us to meet. I only wanted to hear your voice again.' The plaintive, strange finality of this statement gives her a cold feeling in her spine. She suppresses it by looking over to the door and telling the waiting novelist and Kauffman, 'I'll meet you at the elevator.'

Irving steers the woman out of the office and turns to look at Rebecca. He makes a throat cutting gesture before banging the door behind him.

'Nathan?' She sits down. 'Are you still there? I spoke to Bernard and Joan yesterday. Why are you drinking so much? What the hell are you trying to do?'

'Last night I wrote a poem about your eyes. Did I ever tell you what your eyes do to my soul?'

'Oh, Nathan, please listen to me. Why must you be the only man in New York City without a phone?' She listens to the beating of her own heart, and covers her anguish with annoyance. 'Did you get my letter?'

'Letter?'

'I can't talk to you now. I have a client waiting outside. Please try to understand. I also sent you a telegram. Didn't you get that either?' Her voice becomes exasperated. 'Come up to the apartment this evening, I'll cook dinner and we'll talk.'

Click.

'Nathan? Hello?' Dialling tone.

Kauffman puts his head around the door, his beady eyes glistening with belligerence.

'I'm coming,' she says, dropping the receiver into the cradle. 'I'm coming . . . ' She almost adds keep your hair on, but it is doubtful, under the circumstances, if Irving would appreciate that slice of cockney humour.

Evening and no Nathan. She surveys the dinner table set with cutlery, chilled wine and flowers. Well, she didn't really expect him to show up. If he said he wasn't coming then he might have come. As it was he said nothing, so one guess is as good as another. One thing is certain, the situation cannot continue this way.

Always the same dream now. A pale, lifeless man beneath a white sheet on a trolley in an empty corridor. Then the sound of running feet. The rattling of the trolley. The chalk-white face beneath the sheet and she wakes, trembling. He falls across her thoughts like a shadow, drifting into her vision as she sleeps like night creeping under closed lids. Oh Nathan, Nathan, the past can be lost somewhere in the labyrinth that is my body, without memory, without ever being able to haunt you again. Without me, Nathan, your soul cannot regain its power to breathe.

Two days later Rebecca and Irving are in conference.

' . . . this kid has been in prison ten out of her twenty-five years, and you want us to represent her?'

'As literary agents, not attorneys.'

'You're funny, Rebecca, you know that? I'll laugh all the way to the poor house.' He lights a cigar.

'Can we stick to the point, Irving, I have an appointment at three.'

'Sure. The point is I'm saying no. She's illiterate.'

'Rubbish. How could she have written such a wonderful story if that were so? All she needs is someone who'll work with her on the manuscript.'

'You, I suppose?'

'No, an editor.'

The phone rings.

'What do you want?' Irving barks into the mouthpiece.

'For you.' He thrusts the receiver at her. 'Make it short.'

'Hello?'

'Dear God, help me.'

Not a dream, but reality. A voice reaching out of the impenetrable, silent darkness.

'Nathan? Where are you? Are you sick?' A coldness grips her heart. 'Shall I come to you? Where are you?'

'I want what I do not want. I embrace that which seals my soul and I am tortured by the fear of the fear of wanting you.' Click.

Rebecca pushes the hair slowly off her forehead and then touches her temples with hesitant fingers.

'What's the matter?' Irving asks, studying the lighted end of his cigar.

'Nothing . . .' she controls her voice, forcing it back to normal, willing herself to concentrate on the manuscript before her, ' . . . nothing.'

'Good. Then tell me about this editor.'

'Editor?' She tries to concentrate. 'Oh yes, I found an editor, someone you know and admire, who is willing to make this manuscript work for publication.'

'I don't believe you,' Irving says frankly.

Anger, that's the thing now, anger makes her concentrate, helps her polarize her thoughts. She stands up. Her features tighten. The anger she feels toward Nathan will have its outlet in Irving.

'All right, now we have two alternatives; either I meet with this editor and introduce her to Maria or I write my letter of resignation. Which is it to be?'

'Don't blackmail me,' Irving warns her, although shocked by her outburst, 'no one is indispensable, especially a female who comes in here and after three lousy successes ...'

'Four lousy successes. Milton Krammer called this morning. He wants *Tree of Life* for the Fortune Autumn fiction list, at my price.'

'How much did you ask?' Irving demands, his eyes popping. She tells him. His hairpiece moves slightly to the fore as though acknowledging the admiration that its owner cannot bear to put into words.

'I'll go draft that letter. You'll have it in an hour.'

'Okay, okay,' Irving agrees grudgingly, 'if it means that much to you go waste the agency's time ... and Rebecca.'

'Yes?'

'Congratulations on the Fortune deal. Krammer is a bastard.' She looks directly at him only so that Irving might observe and loathe the smile of satisfaction on her face.

She leaves her office at 6.30, hails a yellow cab and gives the driver Nathan's address. In a while they are moving through a less affluent part of town, past all-night liquor stores, their windows piled high with a hundred different brands of beer, past black kids, white kids, kids like Maria, crouching or sitting on the pavement, their hopeless expressions illuminated by the interior of the store. Winos sleep in the doorways of closed shops, a sudden moan emanating from a slack, wet mouth, a vital supply of inexpensive oblivion concealed in a small brown paper bag. Prostitutes in tight hot-pants and grotesque thigh-high boots, strolling arm in arm as they wave to a friend or chat with a prospective client. A police siren cuts through the slowly falling darkness, then the accompanying cry of the ambulance speeding through the dangerous streets to save the life of some miserable junkie or rescue a broken body from the wreckage of a mangled car. That damn noise, how it haunts her, will she ever get used to it? Like something demented, a reminder of the vulnerability of the human body and its immortal spirit in an environment of its own tragic creation. Such an airless night. The cab windows are soldered closed. No one drives in this neighbourhood with their car windows open. The atmosphere is tense, electric, as though before a violent storm, or is that merely how she views her meeting with Nathan? She stares out of the window. This is a part of New York City she has never been to before and it does not fit in with her image of the Big Apple.

'Is it much further?'

'A couple a blocks. You from London, lady?' The driver's grizzled features beneath a battered cap break up into a grin of appreciation. 'I'm gonna go there someday.'

The cab pulls up at a narrow entrance sandwiched between a Chinese laundry and a ladies' hosiery shop. The entire building is criss-crossed with that familiar New York sight, the fire escape. Rebecca pays the fare.

'You want I should wait?'

'No, I'm fine.'

'Hey, listen, lady, you shouldn't hang around here too long, know what I mean? How you gonna get home?'

'Cab?'

'Not round here you won't. What say I pick you up in an hour, that be convenient?'

An hour? Yes, that should be plenty of time.

'Take care now.'

She walks quickly into the building, stepping over rotting garbage. Somewhere a cat howls in shocked pain. She squints into the darkness, no light in the hall. Just ahead is a door which she pushes open before climbing the littered stairs. No light on the stairs either. The heat is unbearable, making her suddenly feel sick. Nathan lives here? A drunken, gruff voice calls out to her from a bunch of ragged clothes lying in a corner of the landing. There is a scuffling noise as something runs over her feet and down the stairs. She runs up the next flight, pausing only to catch her breath when she has reached the top. Empty bottles, crushed cigarette packets, a broken hypodermic syringe, all lying at her feet. At the sound of a woman's scream she freezes, holding onto the banister rail as her heart races. The sound of glass breaking. Voices raised in heated argument. Familiar curses. Spanish? Words Maria uses in times of stress. A radio or T.V. is blaring out a popular tune. She has reached Nathan's door, splintered, peeling green paint. Rebecca knocks loudly and urgently, eager to be admitted. After a few seconds the door is opened by Alice in a red satinized dressing gown. Her protuberant eyes show alarmed surprise. After a few embarrassing seconds she pulls herself together sufficiently to bring out one of her disconcertingly friendly, if hesitant, smiles.

'Hey, Rebecca, how are yer?' She runs a hand self-consciously over her uncombed hair. Her face, without make-up, is pale, yet not unattractive; the face of Alice Kowaski, rather than Fifi Laverne. She makes no move to allow Rebecca into the apartment.

'I'm sorry for not warning you I was coming. You're not on the phone are you? Is Nathan in?'

The television is on and a middle-aged lady with a strained expression is selling a product to keep dentures in place.

'Er . . . well, no, as a matter a fact he ain't home. I ain't seen him all day. Shall I tell him you came round?'

'Can I come in for a moment?'

Alice looks unsettled, undecided. She pulls the folds of her dressing gown tighter around her waist.

'Well okay, but I gotta go to work soon.' She admits the other woman. 'This is home. You wanna make yourself comfortable? I was watching T.V. You like Bugs Bunny?'

Rebecca can advance no further than a yard or two beyond the front door. Her jaw drops and her mouth opens. The room looks as though it hasn't been cleaned for a year. Only one word can describe it, chaos. Magazines and clothing piled on the couch, soiled cups and plates stacked by the chairs, empty beer cans discarded and left where they have rolled. The wallpaper is peeling and to hide the damp patches, posters of movie stars have been taped to the walls, no doubt by Alice. There is no carpet, only a rope mat placed in front of the armchair upon which Alice is lounging with a can of beer. On the floor by her feet is an empty take-away pizza box and a pack of chewing gum. The ashtray on the arm of the chair is overflowing with cigarette butts. The room smells of stale food and stale perfume, not to mention stale cigarette smoke. On a small table in one corner is a long black wig on a stand with an enormous jar of cold cream and a pile of used Kleenex. There is nowhere to sit that is not cluttered with every conceivable item of a woman's apparel, from odd shoes to bottles of nail varnish, otherwise Rebecca would sit down and try to assimilate what she has seen. She closes her mouth, and swallows. Only Alice's sudden yelp of laughter brings her back to herself with a jolt.

'Alice,' she manages slowly.

'Yer? Hey, wanna can a beer or sumpin'?'

She gets up and slouches barefoot into the kitchenette, a narrow alcove with a stove and a refrigerator from which she takes another can of beer and offers it to Rebecca who shakes her head dumbly. Alice goes back to the T.V. with a shrug, saying defensively, 'I'm gonna fix this place up one a these days.' Then the conversation has to be temporarily terminated because Bugs Bunny and friends are occupying the screen. Rebecca goes into the cooking area. There is no door, no curtain, nothing to prevent the cooking smells from invading the rest of the apartment. Dishes are stacked high in the sink, the garbage can is overflowing with empty fast food cartons. The cupboard shelves are empty except for two cartons of cigarettes and a bottle of scotch. A noisy giggle emanates from Alice as Daffy Duck takes the stage to sing 'You Oughta Be In Pictures'. She accompanies him with predictable enthusiasm.

'Alice ... do you ever clean this place up?'

Another burst of mindless laughter from Alice. Rebecca rushes into the living room and switches off the television, rounding angrily on Alice.

'Hey, what'd yer do that for, huh?'

'I asked you a question. Do you ever clean this place?'

'Sure, sure I do. I'm always cleaning up.' She flushes with indignation. 'I knew you were gonna say that, that's why I didn't want yer to come in.'

'It's disgusting,' Rebecca says, shaking her head in dismay.

'It's okay for you, but I work nights and sleep days. When do I get to clear up? I gotta take care of myself.'

'I also work. But I still manage to find time to keep my apartment clean and cook for myself. When was the last time you prepared Nathan a nourishing meal?'

'Hey, look, Rebecca, you can't come into my home and talk to me that way. I bet you ain't got an apartment like this, huh? I bet your apartment is all nice and full of expensive furniture and stuff. If you lived in a place like this you wouldn't give a shit about cleaning.'

She puts a fresh piece of gum into her mouth. Rebecca remains silent, accepting the partial truth of this accusation. What woman could be houseproud about this particular house? She clears a space for herself on the couch and sits down to think.

'Okay, so I ain't the greatest housekeeper in the world,' Alice admits, an expression of guilt coming into her eyes. She adopts a comically dignified expression with her plucked eyebrows. 'I'm a career woman.' She lifts her chin. 'But that don't mean I ain't got feelings for Nathan. I don't love him, not that way, not the way you love him.'

Rebecca feels the blood rush to her face. She keeps her features set rigid as Alice continues, ' . . . maybe I ought not to have said that, straight out, that way. I ain't a bad person, Nathan will tell you that. Like one time when I was calling his wife a bitch he said to me that nobody is all good or all bad. You ain't all good, and I ain't all bad. You oughta remember that.'

'If I seem hard on you, Alice, it is because I care about Nathan. I can't bear the thought that he lives in a place like this.'

'I also live here, me and millions of other people.'

'I never did thank you for helping me out that evening in San Francisco. Eliot didn't believe either of us, of course, but thank you anyway.'

'Hey, that's okay,' Alice says, not too indignant to enjoy Rebecca's gratitude. 'I know how yer was feeling for Nathan even then. I wanted to . . . '

'Where does Nathan work?' Rebecca interrupts, uneasy with the turn the conversation has taken.

'In the bedroom. Through there,' she points.

'Do you mind if I have a look?'

'Sure, help yourself, but I ain't so sure Nathan wouldn't kick up a fuss.'

'He'll never know.'

Alice goes back to *Looney Tunes* and Rebecca opens the bedroom door. By now she is fully prepared for what meets her eyes. Again, just bare floorboards. The bed is unmade, a tangle of sheets and blankets. A yellowing net curtain hangs listlessly from a length of string and the view from the dust-encrusted window is of a trash can and a rotting fence covered in political graffiti. One leg of the dressing table is propped up by an out of date Manhattan telephone directory. Scattered across the top are lipsticks, hair curlers, more cold cream, bottles of half used perfume and a book on how to win friends and influence people, among many other sundry items. Just visible beneath the bed is a large cardboard box.

Rebecca folds the sweater which is draped around her neck and uses it to kneel on as she drags the box from under the sagging mattress. She rests on her haunches and stares at the contents of the box. Notebooks, loose papers, papers held together with rubber bands, scraps of paper, all covered in the poet's slanting, almost feminine handwriting. She rests both hands on the side of the box, her heart beating so fast she feels weak. Two years' work. The results of two years' lonely, tortuous journey into a man's soul. She cannot breathe. It is as though she has stumbled onto a sacred place, the centre of the poet's universe, the holy of holies.

She experiences a strange sensation, an almost religious feeling, as though she ought to say a prayer, or speak softly. A mixture of elation and apprehension rises in her throat. Wonderful and heartbreaking. Glorious and tragic. How can she simply push this treasure back where she found it and pretend it doesn't exist? She owes it to the world, to Nathan, to the people who have waited so long to hear and know the words of the mystic. She cannot, will not close her eyes and walk away. Bernard, if Bernard were here now, would urge her, beg her to do something. But what? Wait for Nathan and insist he put these papers in a safe place? No, he would never listen to her. She runs her hand reverentially over the writing, knowing suddenly what she must do.

She opens the door and goes back for the box. In ten minutes the cab will be back to collect her. Alice looks at her from her chair.

'Hey, what you got there?'

'Alice, I want you to give Nathan a message from me.'

Alice gets up.

'Ain't that Nathan's poems and things? Where are you

taking those? Nathan ain't gonna like you moving his things.'

'You let me worry about that. You just tell Nathan that if he wants his papers back he knows where I live.'

'Oh, gee, Rebecca, he's gonna go crazy when I tell him. I ain't sure I should let you . . . '

'You don't have any choice,' Rebecca interrupts, tucking the box protectively under her arm, 'tell him I forced you, tell him what you like, but I'm taking it with me.'

Rebecca sits in the back of the cab with her precious cargo on her lap. It shouldn't be too long before Nathan Roth turns up on her doorstep, and she isn't above a little friendly blackmail.

CHAPTER TWELVE

I have so fiercely dreamed of you
And walked so far and spoken of you so,
Loved a shade of you so hard
That now I've no more left of you.
I'm left to be a shade among shades
A hundred times more shade than shade
To be shade cast time and time again
     into your sun-transfigured life.

Robert Desnos, 1900–1945. *Last Poem*

I call to you as in a dream. But the dream is yours, and my voice cries out in the night, wanting you so badly that I have nowhere left to hide or run.

He moves through the dark streets like a hunted animal, the fire of pain in his stomach, as though acid were eating away at his flesh. Can he even remember where she lives? Only her words: 'I can save you. I can awaken you.' Can you awaken the dead? What is there of his mortal self left to save? Love is a poem. He can sing the words in a voice so pure that the angels would weep by his coffin, but the actions elude him. They always have. He is an ancient mystic and a child of his own repressions. What was the price paid for solitary confinement? The giving birth of a poem in the prison cell of his chosen way? The desperation of loneliness, the decay of a body that burns with the need to be embraced, a soul dancing on the edge of the abyss. Just for once he would like to win, he would like to be declared a winner in this game called living. She can show him how, she can teach the prophet, the mystic, how to write his own fate and have him shed tears of joy, not despair. If he can remember where she lives. A few drinks in a bar downtown. Must keep a clear head. For a while the alcohol deadens the pain and then it returns more fiercely than before. The cab took them to her apartment that night, he was too sick with pain and love to know where. But he must remember. Every day that passes, every second that he loses brings him closer to defeat. He must find her now, tonight, and beg for salvation, for a renewal of his faith.

'I really don't know how it's going to turn out,' Rebecca says modestly, serving Joe Wasserman Chicken Maryland at her dinner table. She sits down opposite and watches with bated breath as he samples the smooth pieces of chicken breast.

'Delicious, really, I swear.' His broad, white-toothed smile appears in the centre of his black-bearded face.

'My first try,' she admits.

'And you needed a guinea pig.'

Rebecca laughs. She pours more wine.

'You were telling me about this writer whose manuscripts you stole,' Joe reminds her, picking up the conversation where they left off before she served their main course.

'Yes, he's a poet, a very famous poet. I expected him to come around here and claim his property. I had this complicated scheme of blackmail worked out. But it's a week now and no word from him. I hope I haven't gone too far.'

'Do you have any reason to be concerned?'

'He's unpredictable,' she says grimly.

'Maybe he just doesn't care.'

'Oh, he cares. He lives only for his work.'

'Do you take such a special interest in all your clients?'

'No, not exactly. He's more than a client.'

'I see.'

'You don't, because even I don't see. He doesn't only

143

need a literary agent, he needs a nursemaid, a secretary, a confidante, an accountant and a strong right arm.'

Rebecca blushes, Joe is watching her with his perceptive brown eyes and she is suddenly aware of leaving off the most important qualification on that list, perhaps intentionally although she hasn't fooled either of them.

'May I know your client's name?' Joe asks carefully.

'Nathan Roth.'

'Roth?' He is surprised. 'Didn't his wife die in an accident a couple of years back?' Joe remembers, frowning as he searches through his considerable store of knowledge on contemporary writers and their fates. 'He stopped writing and disappeared, in a literary sense.'

Rebecca rests her fork against her plate and goes to the cabinet beneath the hi fi. She takes a key from the drawer and unlocks it, throwing back the doors for Joe to see.

'Well I never . . . ' Joe says softly, his eyes opening wide on the cardboard box and its treasures. 'That,' he gestures toward it, 'that's what you took from his apartment?'

'Correct.' She relocks the doors before sitting down.

Joe wipes his mouth on his napkin, speechless. Rebecca tells him about her visit to Nathan's squalid apartment, her removal of the box, and about its contents. 'He has letters from writers as famous and well respected as himself, unanswered, simply pushed into that box beneath piles of other letters, statements.' She pauses to gather her breath before launching forth again with renewed vigour and outrage. 'Do you know I came across a stack of statements from the bank and from his publisher? The royalties had been paid into his account and never used. There were letters from the bank complaining, complaining,' she repeats with ironic emphasis, 'that he was not using the facilities made available to him. He wasn't writing cheques, using the money, can you imagine that?'

Joe laughs, struck by the obvious depth of her involvement with this poet and his apparent lack of interest in the world of commerce.

'I haven't had a chance actually to make an audit of his earnings but I can tell you they're high, and he lives like a pauper, while that money sits in the bank gathering dust. There are enough poems in that box to fill a dozen new books, and hundreds more on which he has been working over the years. There is something else, something far more important. The man is very sick. I don't know what it is, he suffers from stomach pains, very severe on occasion. Do you think I'm crazy to be so concerned?'

'Absolutely not,' he hastens to assure her, touching her hand affectionately. 'In fact you don't have to look very far for a publisher for Mr Roth's work.' He gives her a meaningful smile. 'I'd be honoured to publish his first collection for three years.'

'Honoured,' Rebecca repeats quietly, her expression turning reflective.

'Rebecca, you sound disillusioned. What's troubling you?' He holds her hand between both of his. 'Is it Irving?'

'Partly. At least at Greaves I had some chance of taking on a book that wasn't commercial, provided it was well written. Here, well, I have to fight tooth and nail just to get a fair hearing.'

'You're not afraid to fight,' Joe says faithfully.

'No, I'm just afraid that I'm using my energy and strength on the wrong crusade.'

'All writers need someone like you to fight on their behalf. You're not wasting your talent, believe me.'

Rebecca remains silent, thinking about his words.

Joe asks, 'Did you give any thought to my proposition?'

'Oh, Joe, I've had so much on my mind, give me some more time, will you?'

'If anything is worth having, it's worth waiting for, I always say. But consider this, Rebecca, as an editor working for me you would have almost total control over what you publish. You'd be in a position to really help those writers whose cause you've taken up. You'd be the buyer, not the seller, and I'd back all your editorial decisions one hundred per cent. Maria Hernandez and her story could be the first of many such successes.'

'It's very tempting, I admit.'

'Then why not give me a definite yes?'

The entry phone buzzes.

'Excuse me.'

'I'll be drafting out the contract in my head,' Joe says as she gets up from the table. She takes the receiver off the wall. 'Hello?'

'Rebecca, it's me, can I come up?'

Her breath catches in her throat at the unexpected sound of his soft, plaintive voice.

'Nathan . . . ' she says at last, ' . . . come up.' She goes back into the dining room. 'Joe.'

He looks up. 'What's the matter?'

'Nathan Roth is here. He's coming up.'

'Is he angry? Did he threaten you?' He throws his napkin on the table, ready to do battle on her behalf like any medieval knight errant.

'No, it's nothing like that.' There is a sudden awkward silence as Joe comprehends the reason for her dismay.

'He's going to be jealous, right?'

'Just promise me whatever happens you will view the proceedings with your usual tolerance.'

He laughs uncertainly, not quite knowing what to make of Rebecca's words. The doorbell rings.

'He had to choose this evening,' Rebecca murmurs, crossing the hall. She opens the door. He stares at her. The beauty and smell of her makes him forget everything he had thought of saying, every word, every gesture, has been wiped clean away, as with an amnesiac.

'You look terrible,' Rebecca says, closing her eyes momentarily and compressing her lips. 'Come in.'

He limps inside, using his free hand to tug off his battered tweed cap, the same cap worn summer and winter and all seasons between.

'I came to tell you something.' He takes his cigarettes from his pocket, his hands shake.

'Come into the dining room.'

He follows her and Joe Wasserman stands up slowly, very evidently startled, if not shocked, by Nathan Roth's physical appearance. Seeing him Nathan's eyelids begin to flutter, that nerve starts up in his cheek. The match he has just lit burns down and singes his fingers. He drops it.

'Nathan, this is Joe Wasserman. You heard Joan mention him the other evening. Joe, Nathan Roth.'

Joe comes toward him, his steady, darkly tanned hand outstretched, his expression full of respect. He is honoured, a sensitive man in the presence of a genius.

'Mr Roth, you don't remember me. I was at New World Publishing when they brought out your first collection of poems. It's a great pleasure to meet you again.'

Nathan nods slowly, the suspicion and resentment in his eyes trickling down to his lips, making them thin and pale.

'Joe is Vice President at Swallow now, Nathan,' Rebecca says.

Nathan is looking at Joe; taller than him, broader, but not athletic, not like Eliot, and undoubtedly Jewish, with gentle brown eyes and full, sensual lips. Immaculately groomed, but casual, and smelling of expensive cologne.

'Will you join us for a glass of wine?' the publisher asks hopefully. 'We've had our dinner.'

Nathan shakes his head almost imperceptibly.

'I . . . made a mistake.' He backs away. 'A mistake.' His emotional eyes move over the discarded plates on the table, the intimacy of a tête-à-tête dinner interrupted by his ghostly arrival on the scene. A visitation. An unwelcome intruder. He avoids Rebecca's hand as she tries to halt his progress backward to the door.

'Nathan, please.'

'You're all the same.' His haunted eyes are lost in his thin, shadowy face. Rebecca follows him, gesturing to Joe to remain in the dining room.

'Nathan, wait.' She takes his hand, cradles his palm and strokes the back of his fingers. He watches her as though in a trance. 'I've been expecting you every evening for the past week. I sent you another telegram. I wanted to come and see you but I knew I would just get so angry at the state of your apartment.'

'How many men do you have?' he asks with honest curiosity.

'One. You. If that's what you want.' As she looks at him her eyes fill up with tears. Can he possibly have lost weight since she last saw him? Soon he will be a collection of bones rattling around inside a pair of jeans. 'Joe is a friend, a good friend. He can help you, we both can.'

'Have you slept with him?'

'You have no right to ask that question.'

'That means you have.' He removes his hand from hers and takes the cap from his pocket. He puts it far down over his forehead and although his eyes are heavy with pain his voice is inflectionless. 'Were you going to spend tonight with him?'

'Nathan . . . you have no . . . right . . . ' Her voice becomes hoarse.

'It doesn't matter,' he says listlessly, 'nothing matters. I made a mistake.' He laughs in self-contempt. 'You'd think I'd learn my lesson.'

'Nathan, you don't own me, damn you. You expect too much.'

'You said it. I don't own you. I don't even like you. In fact I hate you.' He opens the door and slams it hard behind him.

Rebecca sits down on the couch with a heartfelt groan.

'I see what you mean about him being unpredictable,' Joe comments, giving her her wine, 'he's changed since I last saw him. He looks much older.'

'I told you, he's sick.'

Joe holds her resentful stare for a moment before saying apologetically, 'Yes, that was insensitive of me.'

'I'm sorry, I shouldn't have barked at you.' She draws in a deep breath, letting it go as a frustrated sigh and muttered curse. She lifts the hair off her face and rests her head in her hand, elbow on her knee. 'That man,' she glances up at Joe who is watching her with intense curiosity and interest, 'that man makes me want to scream. I've got no idea what he'll do now. He could jump out of a window or run in front of a truck.'

'Let's not exaggerate,' Joe says to console her, 'he'll get drunk and then sleep it off. In the morning he'll have forgotten all about it.'

'What am I supposed to do? Run after him?'

'Do you want to?'

'Yes,' she says unhesitatingly and then laughs at herself. She stands up and walks the length of the room and back, drawing her lower lip between her teeth.

'Did you see that cap he was wearing?'

'My father had one,' Joe says with a reminiscent smile, 'everyone's father had one in those days. It was like a Jewish trademark, a symbol of the ghetto, the European immigrant.'

'He looks good in it, don't you think? It suits him.'

'Yes.'

'Why are you looking at me like that?'

'It's ironic. I thought my main competition for your attentions was far away in Los Angeles and now I find he's right here in New York. Looks like Eliot and I both lose.'

'I'm sorry, Joe, I've spoiled your evening.'

He puts his arms around her and kisses her mouth lightly, her answering smile is remote and preoccupied.

I made a mistake that's all. A mistake. I am a mistake. My entire existence is one of God's more reprehensible mistakes. He intended me to be drowned at birth. But God in His infinite regret has tried so often to rectify the mistake. I'm a slippery customer. He casts the net called oblivion and I, by some chance of fate, ill fortune, escape. I must try harder. I must be ready for Him and then I can lie in wait and leap into the net, become enmeshed, wallow in death. I thought ... What did I think? That she would welcome me with open arms? A freak, a neurotic cripple. Here I am, Rebecca, I've changed my mind, I want you to make love to me. I truly want to find heaven in this bitter hell. I want you to teach me how to kiss you, how to seal your lips with my own. These palest of lips, without blood or feeling. I want you to penetrate this bleakness that is my everlasting misery, and light up the chasm that is my life. Why can't I speak those words to her? Why did he have to be there? Why?

After four drinks I think of two strong, dark bodies coupling in a frenzy of passion, mingling in the name of lust, and united in a cry of indescribable agony. My agony. With each fresh, intimidating thought I must take another drink until the fire in my stomach rages, blistering my flesh, consuming my visions, yet leaving me more sober than before. To hell with Rebecca. And Joe. And Eliot. And all the other whole, perfect men with whom she shares her bed and her body. Alice the whore, the stripper, has more decency in her little, bitten-down fingernail than Rebecca, the Lady, has in her entire soul. I hate her. So it's true, love is akin to hate? Where are they now, those two unclothed bodies? Twisting and writhing in the dark, finding each other and through each other themselves. While I am lost, and will remain lost. An outcast.

She sits next to Joe on the couch, preoccupied with her painful and ominous thoughts.

'Isn't there anyone you can call?' Joe asks, changing direction in mid sentence.

'What?' She stares at him rudely without meaning to.

He repeats his question, adding by way of elucidation, 'Someone Nathan might go and see, a drinking buddy, perhaps, or a member of his family.'

'There are the Adlers, but I doubt if he would go there. They would only ask him about me.'

'Do you want to look for him?'

'Would you mind?' Her voice is so full of hope that he hasn't the heart to say he would rather stay here alone with her than search the bars for a lost poet.

'I have my car downstairs. If it would make you feel better we'll try and find him.'

'There are hundreds of bars he might have gone to,' the practical side of her nature points out, wanting to be persuaded it is not a futile exercise.

'It's your decision, Rebecca.'

'Then I'd like to try.'

I remember when she caressed me in London . . . in San Francisco . . . here in New York . . . I remember the smell of her flesh, her hair; the glow of her skin. I can recall all these things as though she were here with me now, seated beside me, fondling me.

'Has he passed out?'

Joe lifts his head off the table.

'Gently,' Rebecca instructs, frowning her anxiety. She rests the palm of her hand against his forehead.

As though she were here with me now . . . caressing me . . .

'My God, he's burning up.'

Joe gets him onto his feet. Rebecca holds his cane, his arm. His head flops forward and his feet drag as they half carry him from a bar on 49th Street. No one stares, everybody here is in the same, pitiful condition. After a dozen such places, searching a dozen such gloomy, smoke-filled interiors they have finally found him. A miracle. Who says God is not on his side? It depends on your way of looking at it. If he didn't want to be found then God has sided with his enemies. Joe tucks him carefully onto the back seat of his car. Rebecca lowers his head to her shoulder and caresses his hair, his cheek, his ear. 'As ... though she were here ... with me now ...' Nathan's drink-thickened voice says suddenly. 'I have ... no objection to him ... in fact I approve ... at least he is of the faith.'

Joe laughs. He looks at Rebecca through the rear view mirror and says ruefully, 'He sounds like my mother.'

Rebecca can only manage an answering smile, brief and sad. The car moves through the night on its way back to her apartment. Joe didn't ask, he didn't need to, he knew where she would want to take this mad, drunken poet. This sick fool. This unfunny clown. This shadow.

'Her fingers ... her lips ... I am helpless when ... she touches me ...'

'Nathan, shut up.' She puts her hand over his mouth. After a moment he stops trying to remove it and is promptly sick on the floor of the car.

'Oh Joe, I'm so sorry.'

'Don't worry,' he says, but she can judge from his restrained tone that he is angry, and justifiably so.

Oh Nathan, Nathan, it never had to be this way. She wipes his mouth and chin with a handkerchief. He sits there breathing heavily, sweating profusely. His eyes engulf her with unspeakable pain, the ache of pure pain, and the agony of love. She shakes her head, her disapproval only token, for Joe's benefit. She has to let him believe this total disruption of their evening is something she can never forgive. But she has already forgiven. An amused smile is tucked in at the edges of Nathan's aesthetically moulded lips. Even now he is mocking her. A sudden spasm of abdominal pain grips his body, making every muscle in his face contort.

Yes, punish me. Degrade me before her. I deserve no less. She holds him tight, caressing his forehead, her eyes wet with sympathy. His pain is her pain.

'Maybe we ought to take him to a hospital?' Joe suggests.

'No . . . no hospital . . . Rebecca . . . tell him . . . no hospital.' His fingers grip her arms. 'Rebecca . . . I beg of you . . . if you care about me . . . don't let him take me . . . to a hospital . . .'

If I care about you . . . Joe makes the decision for her. They are only a couple of blocks from her apartment. Nathan relaxes in her arms, breathing easier, shivering on a hot, airless night. Don't mock me, Nathan, don't force me to help you destroy yourself with that lowest of low tricks, emotional blackmail. If I care about you . . . if I care . . . I promised Joan I would make you see a doctor . . . I promised . . . His grey head rests against her breasts.

'You take care of me . . .' he whispers, drunk on pain.

Joe carries him up to the apartment over his shoulder. His tolerance, even after everything that has happened, astounds Rebecca. A vision of Eliot's belligerent features pushes into her mind. Under the same circumstances he would have laid Nathan in the road and driven over him.

'Will you allow me to wash the floor of your car?' she asks lamely in the elevator.

'Don't be ridiculous. I'll take it to a car wash.'

He lies there in the bed, his eyes closed, his face skull-like, bone white, two bright patches of fever high on his prominent cheek bones, and he mutters ceaselessly, a jumble of incoherent words, punctuated by the only sound that makes any sense, her name.

'I think we should have taken him to a hospital,' Joe observes standing at the foot of the bed as Rebecca bathes the poet's face with a damp flannel.

'No. He would only have discharged himself in the morning and gone back to that apartment. At least this way he is comfortable and I can keep an eye on him.'

'Where are you going to sleep tonight?'

'On the couch,' she says matter-of-factly, self-pity not being one of her faults. 'It's a large couch.' She smiles at Joe and he smiles back, wondering.

'Do you want me to give you the name of a specialist I know? If he won't go to a hospital maybe he'll see a doctor?'

'Thank you, yes.' She rests her hand on Nathan's forehead and looks up at Joe. Something flickers in his eyes, his expression turns reflective. He begins to understand the importance of this ghost-like cripple in this woman's life. The reason why, on the one occasion they had spent the night together she had seemed to give her body to him and yet hold her spirit back. Her senses had enjoyed him but her heart, it now appears, had been with another man. This man.

'I'd better go.'

She follows him to the front door, although he protests. 'Can I call you?'

'I wish you would. I'm sorry about this evening.'

He kisses her cheek. She kisses his mouth.

Back in the bedroom Nathan is sleeping peacefully. She draws the sheet to his chin and brushes his forehead with her soft lips.

In the morning she leaves a note pinned to his pillow.

'This is the deal. If you're not here when I get home after work, around 6.30, you'll never see your papers again. Have a nice day!

Rebecca'

Nathan, lying in bed, her bed, reads the note three times and three times he kisses the signature.

The sheets smell of you, Rebecca. It is like sleeping in a fragrant summer garden after the rain.

CHAPTER THIRTEEN

Lift up these shreds of being and mix me with
This wind, this darkness.
I'll strive once more.

Isaac Rosenberg, 1890–1918. *The Unicorn*

Rebecca lets herself into the apartment at 6.45, listening carefully for signs of life in her lounge. Her half-hearted attempt at blackmail would mean nothing to Nathan. If he wants to leave her apartment he will, knowing full well that she would be the last person on earth to harm his work in any way. She enters the lounge quietly. He is asleep on the couch, his head fallen back, a book from her shelf open on his lap. She closes the book and places a cushion beneath his head. She knows he suffers from insomnia, yet when he does sleep it is the sleep of the dead. She looks at his naked feet, his bony hands, his sinewy arms and thin neck. Sometimes his face is astonishingly beautiful. Other times ugly, gaunt, old. The pain does that to him. The pain in his stomach and the other one in his soul. They are equally pernicious, equally unbearable. They are both feeding off the poet's death wish. She'll need all the strength and cunning at her disposal to rout such ruthless enemies.

In the shower she washes the grime and heat of Manhattan from her skin, singing softly to herself. She turns off the water, and as she steps naked from the cubicle the bathroom door opens. Nathan enters and stops, immobilized, stunned by the unexpected sight of Rebecca's magnificent body, dripping with water, turned slightly away from him as she reaches unhurriedly for her robe.

'Hi,' she says, in a tone that implies no embarrassment or indignation at his continued presence or hypnotized gaze. 'I hope my singing didn't wake you.'

'I . . . I . . . didn't realize . . . you were home,' he stammers, unable to remove his eyes from the smooth, round, dark skinned beauty of her buttocks and thighs, at the just visible blackness of her pubic bush, or her high thrusting breasts with their large roseate nipples. She wraps her robe around her and belts it in one easy flowing movement. She wipes the perspiration from her face, and releases her hair from the knot on top of her head. It falls, heavy, damp, loose on her shoulders. When she smiles at him her teeth gleam white against her skin.

'I never lock the bathroom door; don't worry. How are you feeling? Would you like some dinner?'

For a second she sees in his eyes a look of desire so intense that she feels its burning heat deep in her own loins, but then he stifles it almost at once, with what must be a tremendous effort.

'You . . . you should have locked the door,' he says, backing out, a muscle twitching in his cheek. 'How the hell was I supposed to know?'

'Nathan, wait . . . '

He slams the door.

She sits at the dressing table brushing her hair. He knocks, although the door is wide open.

'I'm sorry,' he says. His hand trembles as he brings his cigarette to his lips.

'For what?' Briskly she draws the brush through the mass of glossy, black hair.

'For acting like a fool.'

'How can you help acting like a fool when you are a fool?' She goes to the drawer for a shirt.

'I . . . eh . . . took a shower. I hope you don't mind. I washed my hair.' He puts his cigarette into his mouth, lets it remain there and pushes the soft hair off his forehead. 'I used some of your shampoo.'

'I'll survive.'

'Rebecca, please.'

She keeps her back to him, her jaw set determinedly. No, Nathan, she thinks, that's not enough, you have to try harder, you have to make a real effort. He looks at her as she bends over to pick something from the floor. She has strong calves, strong ankles. Her feet are perhaps too large, the toes long, curled into the carpet, gripping the surface upon which she stands, totally certain of her right to belong in this room, this apartment, this city, this world. Such a firm, confident foothold on life, on reality, on the future. He stares at her proud head set on a strong neck, and broad, commanding shoulders. Oh how he envies her, envies and resents her. She is strong with a mysterious strength, a strength which renews itself over and over from some hidden source. She turns suddenly, catching his expression off guard.

'Nathan,' she says in a quietly astonished voice, 'you really do hate me, don't you?'

He lowers his eyes, his words barely audible.

'I hate you as death hates life. I hate you because I am death and you are life.' His face is sweating. He wipes at it with the back of his trembling hand. He stands there, a slight colour rising in his cadaverous cheeks, his uncombed hair tumbling into his deeply wounded eyes. 'I'm sorry,' he says, the intensity of his gaze deepening to an obscure shame. 'All I want is to write my poetry and die when the time comes.'

Rebecca sits down heavily on the edge of the bed, her jeans held limply in her hands, her face turned upward to him, her eyes full of questions.

'Why hasten death? Do you want to write and die in a swamp? Or later, if you go on this way, in a mental institution, a home for the incurably sick? If you are so keen to die, Nathan, why don't you do it quickly?' she asks with an attentive sadness.

'I don't know . . .' he admits with a troubled, confused frown. 'I've existed in a place that is neither life nor death for so long that I just don't know anymore.'

'Stop living in her shadow, Nathan, it's your only chance of survival. She tormented you while she was here and now she crucifies you in her death. Don't you see how happy it would make her to know she still has power over you?'

'What do you want me to do?'

'I want you to live!' she comes back quickly, forcefully. 'I want you to taste the sweetness of life, not starve on the bitterness of death.'

'You should be a poetess.'

'Words, Nathan, you just want to hear words. You ignore their meaning.'

'I don't doubt your sincerity.'

'It's not enough. It's not nearly enough. Just now in the bathroom, I saw it in your eyes, the pain of a man unable, unwilling to accept his own feelings.'

He says nothing.

'I'll make us some dinner.'

He sits across the dining table staring at her.

'Rebecca.'

'No, I don't want to discuss it anymore.'

'I'm grateful to you.'

'Nathan, if you say that to me one more time I'll slap you so hard you'll spin for a week.'

He laughs, a noise like a door opening on rusty hinges.

She gathers the plates together, noting, without comment, that he ate most of his meal. He takes his cigarettes from his pocket and she takes them from his hand.

'You've just eaten, at least give the food time to settle before you poison it with smoke.'

'I'll help you wash up.'

'No need. Go into the lounge, I'll bring coffee.'

He stands up, watching her, uncertain what to do next. She goes into the kitchen. He follows, getting under her feet as she moves from one side of the room to the other, reminding her of a child who knows he has done wrong and wants to make it up.

'Nathan, go into the lounge.'

He limps away, his head down. She carries the coffee through.

'I want to explain something to you,' he says.

'No more explanations. Drink your coffee.'

He presses his lips tightly together, drops his head and studies his long, thin fingers.

'That night, after we left Joan and Bernard, I tried to explain then . . . I tried to tell you something about me.' He rubs his eyes as though this will help him think. 'The fact is . . . ' He moistens his lips and swallows. 'The fact is I'm no good . . . no good . . . ' His voice sounds as though it is caught on something in his throat. ' . . . no good at sex.'

Rebecca puts her cup and saucer on the table, and slowly sits back in her chair.

'No good at sex,' he repeats with painstaking slowness so that there will be no further misunderstandings.

'I understood what you were trying to tell me that evening,' Rebecca says in a compassionate voice, 'and in my experience gentleness is the first requirement of any good lover.'

'Oh, Rebecca . . . '

'Let me finish, please.' She holds up a pre-empting hand. 'If that is so, and I believe it is, then you would make a perfect lover because you are the most gentle person I've ever known.'

'Rebecca . . . I'm as much use to you as . . . '

'Use?' Rebecca butts in, pouncing wrathfully on that word. She looks at him with exaggerated contempt. 'Is that how you think of a man and woman in bed together? Making *use* of each other?'

'No . . . I don't know . . . you confuse me.' He shakes his head. Why does he have so many words at his command when he writes verse and so few when he tries to tell this woman who and what he is? His eyes are so dreadfully sad that for a moment she thinks he will cry.

'Nathan, let's talk about it, let's discuss it like two adults.' She sits next to him on the couch, feeling her hatred of that dead woman rising fast and furious like an undammable tide. But she must not let it drown him. 'Tell me about Madeline.'

'I can't . . . ' he says helplessly in a whisper.

Rebecca takes his hand, playing with his fingers, asking sympathetically, 'Did she tell you you were no good as a lover?'

He wipes his face. She looks into his eyes, all darkness, all tragedy. She looks at his furrowed brow with the faint, permanent lines that give him a perpetually quizzical expression, the expression of a scholar whose distracted gaze is constantly searching for the answers. She can literally smell the eagerness of his love for her, the contained intensity of passion within him, mingled with the odour of fresh perspiration. The sweat of panic.

'Nathan, I want you to answer me, please.' She stares at him, the universe condensing into a few inches of space occupied by his pained eyes. 'Nathan, did she tell you you are not a good lover?' Her voice is insistent. He tries to dodge her direct gaze. She feels his hand. A stiff nod of his head. The tension in his face becomes almost more than she can bear. She looks away, close to tears. Tears of hatred for that woman and tears of love for this man. With the aid of his stick he levers himself to his feet. He looks at her and in a voice of maniacally restrained feeling he says, 'I will never make love to you, Rebecca.'

The woman's beautiful lips grow thin with the utter certainty of her next words.

'You will, Nathan, because you know I'm the only person who can give you the peace you so desperately desire.'

Is she superhuman, he thinks, staring at her, does nothing shake her confidence, her belief? Does she never need to be comforted, reassured, soothed, or does her strength of purpose and unfaltering view of her own destiny come directly from God? He is beginning to believe it does, and for some irrational reason the thought enrages him. Suddenly, with a roar of bitterness and self-disgust torn from the very depths of his narrow, heaving chest he throws his cane across the room where it collides with the bookcase and falls to the carpet. He stands there swaying, his meagre weight shifted to his good leg, his long, thin face an unhealthy, livid white.

'Feel better now?' she asks calmly.

He breathes loudly through his nose, staring at her hatefully.

'Damn you, Rebecca, damn you to hell.'

'I'll be damned if I don't help you.'

'Through sex?' He laughs in contempt. 'I'm dead. Even you can't take a ghost to your bed.'

'Not sex. Love.'

'You're laughable, you know that, don't you? Once I respected you, admired you, but now, now I think you're laughable.'

'Then why are you crying?'

He wipes his eyes negligently.

'I'm tired. I want to go to sleep. I'll use the couch.'

'No, Nathan, you take the bed again tonight. I have some manuscripts to look at.'

He is shaking uncontrollably.

'I'll get out of here tomorrow. Stay out of my life. You understand me? Stay out of my life.'

Rebecca opens the bedroom door and moves quietly to the

side of the bed. He is lying in the shadowed darkness, his eyes open, staring into nothing, swallowed up by the void. A wetness glistens on his lashes, a trail of moisture on his gaunt cheeks. She unties her bathrobe and lets it fall to the carpet. She lifts the sheet and climbs in beside him. She holds his frail, wasted body against her warm, life-giving nakedness, looking into his eyes which are hot with tears. She kisses his forehead, his mouth, his throat, slowly, gently, whispering words of love between the most tender of kisses. Her tongue moistens the edges of his lips, drawing them into her soft mouth and enfolding them with her own lips. She kisses his shoulders and the mass of grey hair across his chest, massaging the kisses into his flesh with her hands and her lips, and when she does this a strange, warm, darkness, like wine, flows through his body to his loins, lifting and hardening him beneath her. She presses herself to him . . . Can you feel the strength and love I possess flowing into you, Nathan? Feel the life-force, Nathan, feel it taking hold of you, lifting you, celebrating you.

He watches her through dazed, half closed eyes, smelling the sap of her fruit, knowing the pressure of her finger tips and tongue. The breath rushes from his throat as he returns her kisses, fierce and hard at first because of his terrible uncertainty, and then more gently, taking the rhythm from her body, her tongue. She presses kisses to his stomach, his prominent hip bones. She licks the insides of his thighs. Oh Rebecca . . . Rebecca . . . my body and soul sing with a thousand voices . . . my heart bursts open and a thousand white doves take flight. Your very breath heals me. Your fingers close the wounds, your kisses anoint my flesh. Rebecca . . . Rebecca . . .

She touches the tip of him with the very edge of her tongue and his body trembles, heartbreakingly frail. She arouses him with hands, lips, body, tongue, making him cry out from the shadowy area where his grey head lies deep and trance-like with ecstasy. The poet redeemed, the mystic snatched from darkness to transcend his own death. A thousand strokes of her tongue echo through the labyrinth that is his body, sending forth a burning column of fire that rolls on and on to the very soles of his feet. Somewhere a river is flowing, the sound of water lapping at his limbs, rain falling? Oh yes, yes, let me be for you like the sound of falling rain, the glow of sunset, the first snow on a winter's day. Let me be for you a past, a present, a future. The day of your birth, your death, your resurrection. There are dark, penetrating shapes on the horizon of his consciousness. His face glows in the dark. His eyes are intense points of light. His body is experiencing a rebirth. The lullaby of her hands rocks him, the heartbeat in her lips makes his flesh undulate like the ebbing of the sea. Loving him is a miracle of tenderness. She must count the beats of his heart, time her strokes to the movements of his eyes flickering against the moonlight.

His chest rises and falls, he is a brittle leaf left too long in the dark forest, in the neglected garden where only agony grows. The quickening of his blood must be regulated, the hoarse cries that issue from his lined throat must be gathered and used as a pillow to bolster his grey head. No part of him must be overlooked. Her tongue melts his pain with a heat that does not burn. There is no irony in her mouth, no mockery in her offer of salvation, no pity in her gift of redemption. She is life without compromise, love without contradiction, eternity without death.

Soon her jade gate is wide open and she guides him into her centre, tight and wet and buried deep in the very deepest heart of her. There. The life-force. Know it. Feel it. Experience it. Her eyes shine with intense devotion as she chants a song of life to his nearly illuminated soul. Come, press deeper, plunge into me. Far into me. Oh yes, yes, yes, into me. Can you feel yourself becoming stronger? Is there now light where only darkness prevailed? She runs her hands over his hot, perspiring back. Let me feed you tears and smiles, let me show you how to reach and drink from the wellspring of my body. There. Feel it come. Yes. Yes. Ah. Wait now, wait. With a quiver of his open mouth the current leaps between them. He trembles, coming, trembles in her embrace as though close to death, as though death itself were close enough to touch, to defy. His face darkens with blood, his eyelids flutter helplessly, his head drops to her shoulder, his body becomes rigid, twitching in the last moments of his orgasmic dance. Then he is still.

She listens to his breathing become gradually calmer, softer. The incense of her cave perfume spirals up, up, drugging him, making him drift, a formless being, perfect and divine, caught in the tendrils of invisible hair. She kisses the corners of his mouth, his closed, wet eyelids. He lies heavy in her arms. She speaks with her lips against his ear. Sleep, my darling, sleep. She smiles, lit from within by a fierce flame of devotion, a bright glow of passion, the heat of eternal love.

As she rises from the bed he touches her backside.

'Where are you going, Rebecca?'

'It's morning, my darling, I have to get up, I have to go to the office.'

'Do you love me, Rebecca?' A pleading tone has entered his voice.

'Didn't I prove that I love you last night, and again this morning?'

'Yes, yes, you proved it, but say it, I want to hear you say it.'

'I love you. I love you. I love you.'

His face glows like a child's. She laughs loudly, throatily. She touches his tousled hair and goes to move away from the bed.

'No, wait, please . . . ' His worshipful eyes move over her statuesque nakedness. 'I can't believe . . . '

She moves close to the bed and he kisses the thick bush

164

of her pubis, rubbing his cheek against the black fur, nuzzling his nose beneath, inhaling the aroma of her sex and skin. She rests her hands on the top of his head. He holds her around the thighs, kissing her, kissing her.

'Rebecca . . . I . . . ' he pauses to moisten his lips and because the pause is too long he begins again. 'Rebecca, I want you to show me how to please you . . . how to make it good for you. Please, Rebecca.'

She climbs back into the bed.

CHAPTER FOURTEEN

– Muses: Whose worship I may never leave
but for this pensive woman, now I dare,
teach me her praise! with my praise receive.–

John Berryman, 1914–1972. *Canto Amor*

*All day at the office, whatever I am doing or saying, I think
of you. I remember how it feels when you are inside me and I
want to sing. I recall your face, your pale, questioning face,
transfixed, like a man in the grip of a religious enlightenment,
a man who has beheld a vision of the everlasting salvation, a
man who has had revealed to him the meaning of the mystery
of life, and I want to shout with joy because of the joy I give
you.*

How was your day, gentle poet, my lover? Today I wrote
two poems, the one here on this page, the other between
your thighs. I do not know which is more pleasing. I only
know that words are only words. But your thighs are col-
umns that give me the strength of Samson. What have I
learned from you? I have learned that paradise does exist
and its name is woman. I have learned that the man whose
soul is illuminated from within has a woman, a love so
strong that pain fades, that memories can be wiped from the
brow by the touch of a cool, soothing hand. I have learned
all this in one week, though I seem to have been born
knowing it and just forgot for a while.

My lover is the Jewish poet, the poet with the anxious,
melancholy smile, a man both old and young, sad and
happy. A Jewish poet who asks, why do I always cry when

we make love? I love the taste of your tears. Lie still and I'll dry them with my tongue.

One Friday evening he produces two tickets for the fights at the Felt Forum in Madison Square Garden. Once, he used to go regularly, with a friend, another poet, but that was in another life. Before he was born. Her initial reluctance to watch this 'sport' is slowly dispelled and gives way to surprise. No pain, no blood, no real violence, except among the excitable spectators. The ethnic majority at the rear of the auditorium cheer and scream louder than the white minority at ringside. Nathan jumps around on his seat, shouting, shadow boxing, calling advice to the fighters, his face suffused by an enchanting, boyish smile. Yes, her gentle lover, the Jewish poet, is a fight fan.

During the interval he points out a well built coloured boxer in the cordoned-off area beside the ring. Floyd Patterson, he tells her, but it means nothing to her, though Nathan's voice is thick with awe. A magician? He laughs, remembering. No, no, once heavyweight boxing champion of the world. He shakes his grey head, speechless with admiration. Would you like me to get you his autograph? she asks, joking. Would you? She stares at him. She slips out of their third row seats and waves her programme under Mr Patterson's famous nose. When she returns to her seat with the fighter's signature Nathan nearly crushes her to death with his gratitude. What did he say to you? he keeps asking. I wish I could have spoken to him, I wish I'd had the nerve to speak to him.

He gets into conversation with a friendly, middle-aged man sitting behind them, discussing the old fighters, and talking so much they miss a clean knock-out and Rebecca has to describe what happened. She has never seen him looking so flushed with happiness, so animated, and he keeps squeezing her hand as though unable to believe she is actually there with him, sharing his life.

All in all it is a night she will never forget ... In the cool dark bedroom he persuades her body into a dream-like stupor, fingering the nerve ends lovingly, wanting only to please her, to make her love him more, draw her ever closer. She sits astride his neck with her sex over his mouth and he moves his tongue, the way she has taught him, moving it until the petals flutter gently open to admit the full, wet, warmth of his tongue. Her voice rises in passion, her heartbeats accelerate, his hands grip her buttocks tightly as she comes, dropping pearls of moisture upon his lips and down his throat. Did you know that the Chinese believe that when a man drinks of a woman's Yin essence he becomes strong and enjoys a very long life? You will rival Methuselah, my darling, you will know the strength of a dozen Samsons. He kisses and caresses her greedily with a hunger he never knew he still possessed. His face shines with the kind of joy he doesn't have to put into words.

When Joan and Bernard come for dinner one evening Nathan's laughter echoes around the apartment. He cannot stop touching her body, her hair, her hands. He listens to her words of love as though to remember them until he can write them down. He rushes to show Bernard books she has bought him, music for him to play while he works. Joan cries. She can't help herself, she leaves the room. Alone in the kitchen Rebecca asks her, 'How does he look? Does he look better?'

'Bernard was right, you are his guardian angel.'

Later he has her sit down on the bed, lifts her skirt and parts her thighs. He goes down on his knees and buries his face there, kneeling as though before an altar. He uses the tip of his tongue to follow the furrow of her sexual lips, inserting the full length of his tongue, timing his strokes to her breathing, waiting until she falls back across the bed, her eyes closing as she begins to drift off into that half sleep his tongue weaves about her senses. He sucks and kisses her with his lips and when she is almost there he lifts her legs onto the bed and enters her with himself, exerting a slight pressure until the first cries break from her swollen lips. He opens the buttons of her shirt and makes love to her breasts, fondling, kissing, suckling upon her nipples. Then he lifts her to him, her arms around his neck, helping him, pushing into him, pressing him deeper. Red and white lights flash before her closed eyes, she is suffused with a burning red-heat, a mounting, boiling heat that extends from the tips of her fingers to the soles of her feet. From her swollen nipples to the soft swollen petals of her sex and back again to form a cross-current of ecstasy that is electrifying in its intensity.

I taught you how to make love to a woman in a way any man would envy.

Shopping for some new clothes at Bloomingdale's he has no idea of his size or height and embarrassed he stares at the salesman as though at a mortal enemy. The changing room is claustrophobic, and only Rebecca is allowed to take his measurements. When he pays he counts the bills one at a time into the man's hand, like a child unused to money and waiting to be told when to stop. Outside on Lexington the rain is falling in torrents. They walk across the road to a diner and eat doughnuts and coffee near the window so they can watch the rain.

'Do you like your new jeans, Nathan?'

'They're fine.' Not for him this new phenomenon known as designer jeans. To him jeans are blue denim things which cover his legs and prevent him from getting arrested for indecency. Rebecca takes one of his new sweat shirts from the bag, holds it to his face, smiling; blue suits him, which is just as well because it was the first and only colour he would look at.

'You're going to look very handsome on Sunday.'

On Sunday they meet Joan and Bernard and spend a day at the beach.

'We have to get you a pair of sunglasses.'

'I hope it rains on Sunday.'

'Why?' she asks, shocked.

'We can stay in the apartment. Be alone. Be together.'

She puts her arm around his shoulders. 'We'll always be together, whether it rains or not. The sun will always shine on you if I have anything to do with it.'

He looks at her, at her mouth, close enough to kiss. Still he can't believe her mouth is his, his to kiss, to feel against his flesh. How can one man, one simple, crippled fool be that fortunate? The world isn't like that, or at least he never thought it was. But now . . .

'My parents used to fight all the time. They screamed at each other in a language I couldn't understand, and it always ended up with my father running out of the house and my mother crying. I used to sit up in my room and watch the rain, just like this, watch it run down the window pane.'

Rebecca holds his hand, runs her finger along the curve of his ear, has him lean against her as though she were a rock.

'Mostly I wanted my father to love me, admire me, respect me. He had a shop, he sold women's clothes. He didn't want a poet for a son.'

'Bernard told me you were never very close to your brother or sister.'

'They were never very close to me,' he corrects significantly, 'there was too great a gap in our ages. My parents were well into middle age when they had me. I was never close to anyone except Joan and Bernard.'

'And me.' She kisses his sugary lips, runs her finger down the curve of his nose. 'How did it get that way, your nose?'

'I used to fight a lot at school. I used to get beaten up a lot too. My nose got in the way. It got broken.'

'I can't imagine you fighting.'

'You know how it is, the weaker you are physically, the

170

more you have to prove yourself, especially if you're a Jew. I grew out of that. I saw the trap. I saw that the weakness was their's, not mine.'

'My poor, darling Nathan. I love your nose. It's an heroic nose. I'm very proud of it.'

He touches the window pane with the tips of his thin fingers. Her hand grasps his and their eyes lock.

'We don't need anyone else, do we, Rebecca? Let's just keep it with the two of us, always.' His lips are curved in a smile of worship, his eyes reflect the living force of love. 'Do you love me, Rebecca? How much do you love me? Are you happy with me? Do I please you? I can't believe you're mine. I can't believe I'm that lucky.'

The sudden, manic whirring of an ambulance siren beyond the walls, snarled in the heavy traffic in the rain sodden streets. He stares at her and shivers, a fearful darkness in his frightened eyes.

'It's nothing, my darling, it's far off in another world, another time, another life. I'm here now and the pain is forgotten.'

They hold each other and watch the rain.

Love me. Love no one else. Love nothing else. Love only me. Love me. Love me. A desperate chant forever issuing from his lips. The need to convince him with words and actions that she loves him, idolizes him, becomes ever more intense. They cannot get enough of each other. She washes his hair for him but before it is dry they are making love on the floor. The more they love the more profound becomes the pain, the need to give, to take, to exchange.

In a rare moment of solitude she writes her monthly letter to Patrick.

' . . . I love him, Patrick. Have you ever known me use that word before about a man? For the first time in my life I know how our mother felt and how you feel about Sally. I can't wait for you to meet him, but please, don't have any preconceived notions, he isn't like any of the other men in my life. I'm enclosing a copy of his last published book of poems so that you'll know him when you meet him. You can learn a lot about him from his work. I'm also enclosing a photograph of us taken at the beach this weekend by Joan. It was such a wonderful day! Bernard and Joan send their love to you, Sally and the children.

Have you noticed? Our family is growing all the time. Now there are eight of us. The Adlers are so happy about Nathan and I that sometimes we become a little embarrassed in their company.

Tell me, have you ever stood on Brooklyn Bridge at night? Nathan and I were there last night. I still have stars in my eyes. We walked from Manhattan to Brooklyn, crossing the bridge on the pedestrian walkway. Are you shaking your head disapprovingly and saying dangerous? So is crossing Oxford Street in the rush hour. We stood on Brooklyn Promenade; it was dusk and the lights of Manhattan were shimmering across the East River. The towers of the World Trade Centre rose before us and to our right the Brooklyn Bridge spanned the river. Do I sound like a guide book? Nathan says I do. I must apologize for the unruly form of this letter, darting from one subject to another but I have so very little time to rearrange it coherently. I'm just setting down my thoughts and news as they occur to me.

We're going to a ball game next week and I shall, of course, be rooting for the Yankees, while I eat hot dogs and drink coke from our seat in the bleachers. See how easily your English sister picks up the jargon? Oh to be in New York now that summer's here! I'm going to buy a car and take Nathan for long drives. I want him to try surf bathing, or even a little swimming. I'm a strong swimmer so I can take care of him. He wants to go fishing! I can just see him wearing that battered cap of his over his eyes, dozing in the sun while he waits for a catch. Though knowing Nathan if he actually caught anything he would apologize and throw it back.

Does that tell you anything about him? The kindest, most gentle and shy man I have ever known. He steps over ants! What a lesson to me – I go after insects with an aerosol, cackling to myself as they fall to the floor, dead at my feet. I've written Eliot a long letter . . . How are Tracy's braces? Is James doing well at school? Tell Sally I tried her recipe for apple pie and Nathan adored it . . . '

. . . A poet lives, suffers, dreams and loves. There are moments in a man's life when he knows everything . . .

He strokes her body and face, slowly, experimentally, as though he is blind and has sensors fitted to the tips of his fingers. He explores her body as though touching, kissing, knowing a naked woman for the first time. Her movements are of total abandon to his gentle, worshipping hands and mouth. Absolute obedience to the breath of his fingers as they seek out every secret place in a body that yields to his touch like snow flakes melting in a warm human palm. I am a flower. I am a bird. I am yesterday, today, tomorrow. My lover is a genius. My lover is King David writing his Psalms, Elijah the Prophet. My lover has the wisdom of Solomon. I am timeless. I am whatever you want me to be, whatever you need me to be. I am inexplicable anguish and overwhelming joy. I am night and day, life and life. I am never the other thing. The woman of your painful memories. The woman of your always devouring nightmares. See how my body fits exactly to the shape of your body, your lips, your hands? Can you doubt that the light is near? Can you doubt that your pleasure is a reflection of my love for you? I turn and turn again and am made into a recognizable vessel filled with love like clay on a potter's wheel. The faces of other men I have known become blurred, the outlines of their bodies dissolve beside the shadow of your pale skin. You are burned and grey. You are like a pile of ashes and a light breeze could blow you out of existence. But I gather every ounce of dust with my mouth and give birth to you through my womb. I swallow you, but only so that you might live again. Live again.

In the hot afternoon sun they walk along the Esplanade along the East River by the United Nations Building and watch the tugs in the murky water hung over with a grey heat haze.

'Nathan, I envy your sense of identity,' Rebecca says, continuing the conversation they have been having over lunch. 'A Jewish American, an American Jew. It stands for something. It means something. Me, I never felt particularly Jewish or Irish. My father told Patrick and I stories about Ireland of course, but they were fanciful imaginings full of "the little people", the kind of Irish folklore you see in Hollywood movies.'

They sit down on a stone bench and Rebecca continues. 'My mother told us about her own childhood. She missed the Jewish customs, I think; the Jewish way of life.' She puts her arm through his and looks into his face. 'Teach me about being a Jewess. I want to be truly part of your religion. I want to belong.'

'I'm not an Orthodox Jew, Rebecca, I don't even keep the holy days. Why don't you ask Bernard, he would be pleased to tell you how it is to be a Jew.'

'I want you to tell me. Please, Nathan, tell me how it is to be a Jewish child in a Jewish home.'

'You said your mother told you.'

'I can't remember. It wasn't so important to me in those days. I don't want to end up like my father, wandering from place to place and never feeling that I belong. Don't you see, meeting you, a Jew, has helped me to choose a way of life. I'll be a Jewess.'

'Just like that?' he says, laughing.

'I can be anything I set my mind to.' She narrows her eyes, looking at him, searching his face for some hint of encouragement. 'If I feel Jewish, doesn't that make me half-way there?'

'More than halfway. If you feel Jewish, then you are Jewish.'

'An American Jewess.'

'Pleased to meet you.'

'Then tell me about the Sabbath, is that what we call it? Tell me about the Sabbath in your home.'

He passes his hands through his tousled hair, his thoughts wandering off into the distance, beyond adult pain, beyond the other woman and back to his childhood, remembered with all the usual mixture of sadness and joy.

'As soon as it grew dark, sunset, in fact,' his voice becomes more than normally quiet, so much so that Rebecca has to strain to hear his whispered words, 'we knew the Sabbath was coming in. I would come home from school. The table was set with red wine, matzos, and a special twisted and golden brown bread.'

He repeats the name of the bread for her benefit and she mouths the word with her soft lips.

'Very good.' He touches her hair. 'Two candles were lit by my mother, and she would say a prayer. Then we would wait for my father to come home from the store. It was the best meal of the week. Something we all looked forward to, from Saturday to Friday.'

'What did you eat? Describe it to me.'

'My mother would be in the kitchen all day preparing each course. To begin we had chopped fish balls, or some-times chopped liver.'

'Like we had in the delicatessen yesterday?'

'Like that, only much, much better. Made with my mother's own loving hands. Next we had chicken soup con-taining *locshen* and *kniedalach*, which we ate with the matzos. Then came the boiled chicken, so soft it would melt in your mouth. There were little extras on the table, you know the sort of thing, dill pickles, horseradish with beetroot sauce. We followed all this with fresh fruit.'

'Apples, pears? What sort of fresh fruit?'

'Rebecca, I can't remember, it was so long ago.' He stands up and limps to the parapet, staring at, but not really seeing, a steamer chugging its way up the Hudson. Rebecca follows.

'Have I made you unhappy with my questions? I only wanted to feel part of you, part of your heritage.'

'No, not unhappy. It's just so long ago. I feel like an old man.'

She puts her arm protectively around his waist and rests her head against his shoulder.

'You are an old man, Nathan. Old and young, wise and innocent. You are a poet. All poets feel old. They were there at the birth of our universe. Is it surprising that you feel old and tired? That's the reason you should seek peace now, even if it's only for a few hours at a time.'

'I've found peace, Rebecca, every moment that I am with you brings me peace.'

She knocks on the door of his study, her spare room converted, furnished with a large leather chair, a wide oak desk, a reading lamp, a small bookcase for his own personal books, pens, paper, fresh flowers always in a vase on his desk. She carries a tray with a plate of small sandwiches, a glass of cold milk, a bar of his favourite chocolate. He is bent over the page, his features tense, the expression in his eyes not of this world. She puts the tray down quietly and tiptoes out.

A conversation with Joan on the telephone one evening. 'You mean to tell me you have never visited the Statue of

Liberty? Bernard, Rebecca says she has never visited the Statue of Liberty. We'll have to put that right.'

The *Liberty Ferry* is crowded with tourists, those from other states, and those, like Rebecca, from other continents. Bernard and Nathan talk together at the guard rail, watching for a first sighting of the famous landmark. The women sit on a bench, intent on their own conversation.

'He's putting on weight,' Joan declares, 'he is most definitely putting on weight. I can see it in his face.'

'Should we make him very fat?' Rebecca asks, taking the older woman's arm conspiratorially.

'Yes, Rebecca, I'd like that very much.' She touches her cheek lovingly. 'My beautiful daughter, Rebecca.'

Tears form in Rebecca's eyes.

'Joan, please, will you teach me how to prepare a Sabbath meal? It would be our little secret. I want to surprise Nathan.'

'Come quickly, look, look!' Bernard calls. The Statue is in sight.

Joan rises. Rebecca grips her arm.

'Will you teach me, Joan?'

'Try and stop me.'

People stare at a beautiful woman and a man with a walking stick. They stare, perhaps without meaning to. Is it so difficult to accept a woman such as her, loving a man like him? If she were asked, she would say the privilege is hers.

He takes her to places she never dreamed existed. At 75½ Bedford Street between Sixth Avenue and Hudson he shows her the house in which Edna St Vincent Millay once lived, and it is only nine feet wide. At the White Horse Tavern they drink a toast to Dylan Thomas whose photograph is over the bar. At 7 Washington Square is the home of Edith

Wharton; the Chelsea Hotel where Thomas Wolfe once stayed; Edgar Allan Poe's cottage in the Bronx.

Over dinner in the evenings she tells him about her day. Irving's foul moods, the temporary secretary who can't spell, and whose answer to Rebecca's suggestion she use a dictionary was: If I can't spell the word how can I look it up? Maria's novel, soon to be in print, and the modest nagging worry, would I have sold it to Swallow if I didn't know Joe so well? Of course, you could sell anything. You can do anything.

After dinner they sit together in the lounge and try to make some sense of the contents of his box. He must begin, once more, to publish his work.

Every day Joe calls her, asking for news; when will you have something for me I can send to the printers?

Nathan needs no editor, no agent, no typist. She is all these things. Her energy, enthusiasm and talent for organization astound him. She has filed all his correspondence, autobiographical notes, poems, everything is in order. But he need not concern himself with anything, from the smallest detail to the most worrying of problems. He can depend upon her for everything.

Then she takes him to their bed to embrace and expose the absolute sorrow beneath his flesh, and exchange it for ecstasy. She plays him with fingers of shadow like light on a keyboard. He changes substance, no longer heavy with melancholy he becomes light with pure emotion, following the avenue of dreams into the garden of bliss. There the eternal moment is his to know, the marriage of sorrow that was and ecstasy that is, the immortal death in infinite life. The rebirth.

The pulse of me is only where your mouth burns. It beats only when your tongue beats. Is this not a miracle?

CHAPTER FIFTEEN

Time held me green and dying
Though I sang in my chains like the sea.

Dylan Thomas, 1914–1953. *Fern Hill*

The more love she bestows upon him, the more profound becomes his need, the greater becomes his desire to take what she gives, to isolate her from the world. He paces the rooms when she is at the office, smells her clothes, touches her hairbrush, cries into her pillow. He calls her up just to hear her voice, just to convince himself she is really there, really his. He writes her name on sheets of paper, above the title of the poem, below the last line, kissing the words, trembling with emotion, speaking it aloud, loving the tremor it brings to his lips and loins. Rebecca. Rebecca. Rebecca. He listens to Mahler and he weeps, helpless, hopeless in his devotion. The sad, haunting music reminds him of death. Sometimes alone, he sees Madeline, the dead woman, and she laughs at his despair, his ridiculous all-consuming love, the belief that he can avoid his fate. She tells him he will never keep any woman, he is crippled, sick, neurotic, unlovable, and he searches for a way to end the misery, free the woman he loves. But Rebecca returns to the apartment, unhappy about his voice on the phone, anxious. They make love and the other woman fades, her laughter turning bitter, her taunting words destroyed by the fire of devotion in Rebecca's womb. She, Rebecca, loves him, and he becomes a god. He believes himself immortal.

One Friday she stays home from work and he is forbidden

to enter the kitchen. At sunset she begins to set the table and as she goes back and forth from the dining room to the kitchen he stands there in speechless astonishment. Two candles lit, their tapering flames throwing shadows into the corners of the otherwise darkened room, the knotted, golden brown bread, matzos, red wine, spread upon a snow-white tablecloth.

'Sit,' she says, unconsciously imitating Joan. 'I didn't know which you like best, chopped fish balls or chopped liver so I made both.'

'Rebecca...'

She turns.

'I...I don't know...what to say...' Tears overflow his lashes and slip silently down his cheeks.

'Oh no, no, you mustn't cry, my darling. I wanted to make you happy.' She holds his head to her breasts. 'I don't know any Jewish prayers, but I'm sure God wouldn't mind if I speak what is in my heart. Nathan, thank you for turning my apartment into a home. I love you in a way I never thought it was possible for me to love anyone, and I pray to God that you will live forever.'

There is so much love in her eyes and voice that he is overwhelmed. He rests his arms on the table, rests his head in his arms and weeps. Only you have ever opened me, spread me like the rush of fire in a dry, dead place.

He gives her a diary, an intimate chronicle of his life, a relentlessly honest examination of his childhood, youth, early success, feelings for the dead woman, disillusionment, pain, anger, loneliness, asking her to read it, to know him better, as a man and a poet. He will begin it again.

Page One. The day I was born. The day I met Rebecca.

Saturday afternoon in Central Park. It begins to rain and they are stuck by the lake where there is no shelter and people start to run, those on roller skates slipping on the mud, children cry, radios go silent. But they remain behind because he loves the rain. He stands there getting drenched to the skin, laughing like a crazy man, a maniac, his laughter finally dying down to a breathless vibration in his body as she holds him against her, kissing him, there, in the rain, two solitary figures framed against the Manhattan skyline glistening so proudly in the distance.

'The world has changed. Why does the world look so different?'

'It's not the world that has changed, Nathan, it's you. You've come back to life.'

My God, what rain! A monsoon. Great gusts that flood the roads, swish beneath the tyres of cars, run like rivers in the gutters. Take cover, you idiot, you mad, Jewish poet! He limps away from her, turning, waving his stick in the air, yelling on top of his voice, words of love to the rain that falls upon his face, into his hair, reminding her of an animated scarecrow. They walk through the deserted park together, holding hands, pausing only to look at each other suddenly, earnestly, admiringly, grinning, touching. Hand in hand, laughing, they take shelter under the awning of the Plaza Hotel. She wipes his face with a handkerchief, smooths his hair down with her hands. You'll catch a chill, you're wet through. I'll have to wring you out when we get home. He basks in her loving, warm gaze, his blue veined hands touching her wet face in reverence.

'What would you like to do now?' she asks.

'Kiss your body while it is still wet from the rain.'

In the apartment they remove each other's clothes. He drinks from the bowl of her loins and becomes strong. He rubs his cheek and lips against all the parts of her body. He explores her and looks at her and when he enters her she goes soft, blending with him, with the universe, absolutely at peace. During orgasm he shudders in her arms, shudders as though he will break into a million pieces, crumble to dust, he shudders as though he is reliving the gigantic explosion at the beginning of time, the explosion which gave this universe its form. She holds him then, afraid, fearing that so much joy after such pain is too much for his lean, raw, hungry body. But she breathes the mysterious breath of love into his spent body and he sleeps, whole and indivisible.

He bursts into the kitchen, his face a mask of distress.

'I ... I thought ... you had left me.' He grabs her and presses his face to the side of her hair, breathing loudly. 'I must have ... been dreaming ...'

She holds his face between her hands. A vein stands out on his forehead, zig-zagging to his left eyebrow. She kisses it. His face retains that distracted look.

'I would never leave you, Nathan, you know that.'

'Do we have to go out this afternoon? Can't you call up Joan and tell her I'm sick?'

'And worry her? Certainly not.'

He is trembling in her embrace, still held in the clutches of his nightmare. She looks at his frightened face, her gentle eyes turning apprehensive.

'What's the matter, Nathan, are you sick?'

'No ... no, I'm not sick. I just don't want to share you with anyone. You have so many friends. The phone rings all the time. People asking for you. They have no right to expect you to ... to ...' Suddenly he is shaken by a violent sob, on the verge of tears. He cannot complete his sentence. She holds him and combs his hair with her fingers.

'You mustn't be frightened, I'll never leave you. Those other people, they are just friends, but you, you are my lover, my life.'

My life ...

Her womb is a refuge where no pain can invade.

'Better now?' She turns her head on the pillow to look at him, moving slightly to kiss his naked shoulder.

He does not answer. He is lost in thought. What memory is he reliving in his mind? Which nightmare? She turns onto her stomach and leans over him, her heavy hair falling over his chest and face. She kisses his mouth inside the darkness, sways her head so that her hair strokes his shoulders.

'When I was a small boy my father used to send me to *Seder* classes to learn Hebrew. There were about fifteen of us and we were taught by a giant of a man with great bushy eyebrows and a tangled beard that lay on his stained waistcoat. He ruled us with a rod of iron, with terror. We would have these classes in his home and around five p.m. when the third boy was about to recite his letters the teacher's wife would enter with his tea. He ate black bread, which he cut in front of us, with butter and salt, a salty herring, and lemon tea. Crumbs from the bread would fall into his beard and lie there, enmeshed in the tangles. I was spellbound, we all were, and when it came to my turn to read I was too hypnotized to locate the place. He would point a finger and bellow: "You! Start to read." '

Rebecca laughs sympathetically, running her finger across his forehead as he speaks.

'Consequently I never learned one word of Hebrew.'

'Proving that learning by terror just doesn't work.'

'If I ever had a child, a son, I would never force him to learn. I would only want him to be happy.'

Rebecca's soothing fingers continue to smooth his hair. 'Do you like children, Nathan?'

'I would have liked a son.'

'Chauvinist,' she accuses, only humorously.

'Someone to take my name into another generation. It's sad for a man who has no sons to say *Kaddish* for him.'

'*Kaddish?* What's that?'

'Prayers for the dead. A son says them for his father.'

'Can't a daughter, a woman, say them?'

'The Jewish faith is notoriously biased toward men.'

183

'Except in the kitchen,' Rebecca points out, with a lift of her eyebrow. 'I know that much about being a Jewess.'

He turns his face into her neck.

'Yes, I would have liked a son or a daughter. I would have liked to have known the feeling that comes from being a father. It is an important feeling for a Jew.'

It is later that night that Rebecca empties her contraceptive pills into the bathroom sink and watches the water from the tap washing them down the drain. She has done it slowly and purposefully, without having to consider her reasons or argue with herself. There is no decision to be taken. It is simply, factually, something she has to do. Conceiving Nathan's child would present him with yet one more motivation to live. And God knows, he needs plenty.

The phone rings. Nathan answers it. Listens. From the bedroom where she is dressing Rebecca calls out, wanting to know who it is. Wrong number. Wrong apartment. Wrong city. Go away, leave us alone. Stay out of her life. She belongs to me. The phone rings again. Nathan lifts the receiver, afraid that if he ignores it Rebecca will answer it instead. The man on the other end abuses him, swears at him, knows what he is trying to do. Long distance? Cut off, operator? Can you understand the pain that you cause me? Strange, how many wrong numbers we've had lately, Rebecca observes, quite unaware. Yes, strange. I am like a man fallen from a high cliff, so high that I am taking forever to reach the stony ground. I float in darkness, turning and twisting, first one way up and then the other, arms and legs outspread like one of those free-fall parachutists, only I have no chute to open when the time comes. Is it in waking or sleeping that I feel so weightless? Is it during orgasm? Or otherwise? How long can I go on this way?

Sometimes when the phone rings and Rebecca gets there first he stands to one side trembling, his face waxen, his eyes small and dark with dread, his lips thin with terror. Please, please, don't let it be him. Please let me fall a little while longer, please let me spin and float until I lose consciousness forever. It is a colleague of Rebecca's from the office asking if she and Nathan would like to join her and her husband for dinner at a new restaurant. Nathan refuses to go. Not relieved, but angry, indignant, why should they try to take her away from him? Why? He begs her to say no, to remain alone with him in the apartment, to love only him, to need only him, and she stares at his pale face, smiling agreement, making her excuse to her colleague, despite the lump of sorrow that has become lodged in her throat. He buries his face between her thighs. She closes her eyes in ecstasy. He is happy. Only then does he feel she truly belongs to him.

When Bernard and Joan suggest they leave the stifling heat of the city on Sunday, the four of them, Nathan lies, Nathan says they have a prior engagement without first consulting Rebecca. When she finds out, when Bernard mentions it, and Joan looks at her with pained eyes, all the love and resentment she feels comes flying into her throat. Their first real quarrel. But it is one-sided. She speaks what is on her mind and he stares at her, saying nothing, a gnarled branch fallen from a tree, ready to be crushed, broken, ground underfoot. Later that day he is dreadfully sick and retches into the bathroom sink. She forgives, hates herself, knowing his pain.

'You must see a doctor.'
'I will. I will.'
'When? You always say you will, but when?'
He cries.
'All right,' she says, consolingly. 'Not today, not tomorrow. When you feel better.'

Sometimes he doesn't tell her when he is sick, he clears it quickly before she comes home but she can smell it on him, smell his frailty, his fear. The smell of death clings. It lingers, stronger than the aroma of her love. No, not that. My love is stronger. My love is the will of God. The other is evil. Evil does not prevail. When she is there and he is unwell she puts him to bed and holds him, nurses him, uses her body as a doctor would use medication, to heal the invisible wound. He always looks so frightened when he is sick, as though destiny might still catch up with him, as though what she cannot prevent might still happen. But, in truth, he is sick less often now, he drinks only a little wine, smokes only when he works, and eats the nutritious food she prepares for him. And her body, her love, is a miracle drug.

A classical music recital at Carnegie Hall. They hold hands throughout the concert, faces ecstatic, joy shared, music and love and life. Watching each other for manifestations of the intense empathy they feel for each other. In the restaurant after the concert there is a strange, happy, faraway look on the poet's face as though he can still hear the music inside his head. But then a man looks at her, how can he help but look, and Nathan looks away, lowering his head, eyes withdrawn into lonely, speculative thought. How long can a frail, neurotic cripple hold onto a beautiful, fun-loving woman, his demons ask. You'll lose her, Nathan. You know all about losing. You could fill a book with what you know about loss. You'll never be happy, not until you've lost your life.

When Irving asks her to take a client out to dinner one evening Nathan locks himself in his study and she cannot go out for fear he will roam the streets looking for her, or do himself some harm. When Nathan answers the phone to an old flame of Rebecca's from Paris, in town for a few nights, she hears him telling the man she doesn't live here anymore. Her mounting rage descends upon him.

186

'Why did you do that, Nathan? Why?'

'I don't want to lose you.'

'You won't lose me, but you have to realize that I've got many friends. I like people. I enjoy their company.'

'Men friends. I've seen the way they stare at you.'

'That's nonsense. I have plenty of women friends. They would all be your friends too, if you would let them.'

'I've got no friends.'

'You're a liar. You have plenty of friends. You've cut yourself off from them. You're a wonderful, gentle person, people want to know you. Why can't you give them a chance?'

'I only want you.'

'Nathan, you must never, never tell anyone I no longer live here. Do you understand?'

'You despise me. I'm like your mother. I can't live without you. I depend on you for everything. You despise that.'

'I never despised my mother, and I'll never despise you for needing me. How could I when I've given everything I am to you? But give me room to breathe, trust me, I'll always be here, I'll always love you.'

He begins to weep, his body shuddering and tears overflowing his lashes. She watches fascinated, appalled.

'No, Nathan, no, my darling.' She holds him and kisses him. She takes him to bed and loves him with a selflessness that leaves her exhausted.

Hold me tight, Rebecca, tighter. Tighter. I am fading. The world is closing in on me. The demons are becoming bolder, staying longer, the darkness is deepening.

Nathan, you are draining me dry. Your eyes are dark shadows that haunt me, and touch the backs of my ankles as I flee.

One lunchtime, unable to work, he goes to her office, waits in the lobby downstairs, walks up and down, smokes, stares nervously at the men, handsome, well dressed, who emerge from the elevators. Every one of them is in love with Rebecca, they would all take her from him if they could. Men with attaché cases and slicked hair, clear eyed and energetic. He catches sight of his own reflection in the glass doors, bent shoulders, a twisted leg, untidy, yes, untidy, whatever he wears, new and expensive, chosen by her, he always looks untidy; clean but laughably untidy, as though such stylish clothes cannot bear to be associated with such an unprepossessing figure. Rebecca and Joe Wasserman step from one of the elevators, laughing, chatting. Nathan's face becomes like a mask, his head like a skull, his eyes burn with obsessive jealousy. So this is what she does when I'm not around to see?

'Nathan?' Rebecca's smile becomes hesitant, afraid. Oh yes, she knows what to expect. She knows what his reaction will be. She rushes toward him, puts both hands on his shoulders. His gaze turns inward, feeding on his own self-hate, inadequacy. 'I'm so pleased you're here. Joe and I were going to discuss the cover of your new book over a large pizza. Please come with us.'

'Of course,' says Joe, joining them, offering his hand.

'I don't want lunch ... I don't want ... a pizza ... ' the words tangle in his throat, his face contorts with helplessness. ' ... I want ... I want ... '

'Why don't I call you this afternoon, Rebecca? We can set up another time to discuss the cover.'

'Nathan, please,' Rebecca's voice is steady, her strong jaw tensing. 'Nathan, I am having lunch with Joe and we are going to discuss your book. I'd like you to join us. If you don't, that's your decision, but it's also my job.'

He limps away with that awkward dragging movement of his leg which can become exaggerated in direct proportion to his mental anguish.

'Shouldn't I go after him?'

'No, leave him,' Rebecca holds Joe back by his arm, 'he has to understand, to realize, love is trust. The only possible

188

way I can help him is by being strong. If I go to him now the same thing will happen again tomorrow, and next week. Leave him.'

He licks the insides of her thighs. Why did you treat me that way lunchtime? Why hurt me? Oh Rebecca, why? His expression is humble, worshipping, fearful darkness haunts his frightened eyes. Does that please you, Rebecca? Yes, very much. Tell me I love you well. You love me well, Nathan. He stimulates the edges of her soft, wet sex with his tongue while his bony, veined hands lift her breasts. He is in love with her body perfume, her dark skin, the sensual tremor of her flesh. Am I good at this now, Rebecca? Oh Nathan . . . He licks the moisture and strokes the furrow with slow, tender sweeps of his tongue. He stands in the flicker of light which crosses her eyelids as the climax approaches. He asks how it feels, how does it feel to climax because of him? It feels, it feels as though my body has exploded in a thick cloud of heat and I am burning, burning . . . it feels as though I am on a merry-go-round which is spinning faster and faster until I black out and am thrown off into space, into a bright, white light that eventually becomes a tiny white dot in the centre of my vision, and instead of me being inside the universe, the universe is inside me. That's how it feels. He presses his tongue to her fragrant skin, wanting to taste the difference before, during and after she has climaxed, smelling and tasting her perspiration, the warm honey smell of her sex, resting his cheek against her breasts, listening to her heart fluttering as she ascends. He stares at her eyes as they become glazed, other world sightless, and her lips, parted, swollen. He is amazed at the beauty of her, the unpredictable duration and intensity of her flight. He watches with dark, brooding, tragic eyes . . .

His hunger and fear are immense. He no longer conceals it.

He no longer hides his desire to enmesh her, stifle her with his insatiable craving to possess.

One day when he has asked too many questions – Who was the man? What did he want? Why are you late? Where have you been? – she walks out of the apartment and doesn't return for hours. To punish him. To punish herself. When she comes home he is lying on the bed in a kind of trance. Not asleep. Not awake. A kind of self-imposed and deadly inertia. Pale and still and silent as the grave which calls to him. When she speaks he doesn't hear. When she lifts his head it is as heavy as a stone. You'll die, she says, in a voice heavy with prophecy, yes, you are killing yourself. She undresses, and lies with him, pressing herself to him, enfolding him, nurturing him. Her kisses are for the tips of his fingers, the centre of his stomach, the top of his head. She takes him deeply into her throat. Miraculously he flickers back to life.

'I try not to hold too tight.'

'I know.'

'It's like a fire consuming my body, turning it to ashes.'

'Yet I've never loved any man the way I love you. I tell you so often. I'm always telling you, showing you. You mean the world to me.'

He weeps, wanting more, taking more. A man to whom all is not enough. He is struggling with himself, she can see it. He is battling with his obsessions, but he is losing the fight. Her legs part, granting him entry, giving him a cave in which to hide. From what? From whom? She no longer needs to ask. The answers are all there in the journal. The consuming pain of one man, her lover. Her sex is his only haven, each day he dies there and is reborn. The smell of her intimate place comforts him, makes him sleep, puts him out like a drug when nothing else helps.

Yet is it enough? Does love heal the cracks in a crumbling

personality or merely conceal the depth of the damage already done?

Lazarus, my Lazarus, how many times must I raise you from the dead? Must you truly, finally die to find everlasting peace?

It has to be enough. She has given all.

CHAPTER SIXTEEN

All which despite our love might not endure:
Because this forewrought evil has prevailed
Shall we mourn love and say that we have failed?

James Agee, 1909–1955. *Sonnet XI*

Late one Saturday morning two months after Nathan's move to Rebecca's apartment, the poet answers the front door. The athletic, muscular bulk of Eliot Vaughan descends upon him without warning. A growl of pent-up anger escapes the big man's throat as he lifts Nathan from the floor by a handful of bathrobe and raises his free hand to strike the poet's unprotected face.

'Stop it!' screams Rebecca, running out of the bedroom and reaching them just in time to grab and hold onto Eliot's arm before it comes crashing down. 'Stop it! Leave him alone. Take your hands off him, Eliot, for God's sake, stop it!' She uses her almost masculine strength and the weight of her body to push between them, to loosen Eliot's grip on the struggling poet. Nathan, suddenly, abruptly, released, falls backward, losing his balance and his cane, and landing heavily on the carpet.

'Nathan, Nathan . . . are you all right? Are you hurt?' Rebecca demands, crouching beside him, helping him into a sitting position, examining his face. He is ashen, his eyes wide with fear.

'The bastard is just scared,' Eliot says vindictively, breathing heavily through his mouth, 'and if I get my hands on him I'll give him good reason to be scared.'

Rebecca strokes the damp hair off Nathan's forehead. He

is staring up at Eliot, the perspiration running down his hollow cheeks.

'Don't worry, my darling, I won't let him hurt you.' She puts her arms around him protectively and he lowers his head to her chest.

She looks up at Eliot, her expression openly hostile.

'How dare you?' she asks, narrowing her eyes. 'How dare you burst into my home and assault my friend? Who do you think you are, one of your macho movie heroes? How dare you?' she demands once more, raising her voice to a shout.

'Roth knows why I tried to hit him. He knows why. You damn well ask him.' Even now Eliot is only barely able to control his temper. 'Ask him, go on!'

Rebecca assists Nathan to his feet. He stands there unsteadily, his chest rising and falling beneath Rebecca's reassuring hand like the tiny heart of a petrified bird.

'Ask him!' Eliot shouts, clenching his fists.

'Shut up.' Rebecca stares into his face. 'Shut up or get out, and I mean it.'

Eliot keeps his rage in check long enough to close the front door and follow Rebecca into the lounge.

'I'm sorry . . .' Nathan keeps repeating, over and over in a dead voice, ' . . . I'm sorry.'

'He will be when I'm finished with him,' Eliot says after a silence.

'I told you to shut up.'

'Ask him about the phone calls, Rebecca, and the letters. Ask him what he did with those letters I sent you. Did he read them?' He takes a threatening step toward the couch, his face warping with rage. 'Tell her, Roth, go on, tell her how you put the phone down on me when I called her. Tell her, you yellow bastard.'

Nathan looks at Rebecca, a flush of abject shame reddening his white cheeks. He blinks rapidly and lowers his gaze, unable to confront her questioning eyes.

'Yellow . . .' Eliot says, twisting his lips disdainfully.

All of a sudden Nathan rises and lifts his balled fists, like a child who knows he has done wrong and is prepared to accept his punishment.

'I'll . . . fight you if that's what you want . . . ' he says, barely getting his lips around the words.

Eliot bursts into contemptuous laughter. Nathan's lips quiver, a kind of helpless, hopeless sob escapes his throat. 'I'll fight you . . . ' he says again, lifting his fists higher, blinking at Eliot who is still laughing.

'Sit down, Nathan, please,' Rebecca says gently, 'sit down.'

Nathan lowers himself slowly to the couch and falls silent, immobile, his eyes like those of a blind man.

'I called you every night for a week after you wrote me that letter,' Eliot says. 'I wrote back to you, but I knew what was happening to my letters.'

'I've known about your phone calls for a long time,' Rebecca lies, resting her hand on Nathan's shoulder so that he will feel less ashamed, feel her forgiveness, 'the phone calls and the letters.'

Eliot lights one of his thin, brown cigarettes, not believing her for a second.

'Let me talk to you alone, Rebecca, you owe me that, at least.'

Nathan raises his grey head and looks searchingly at Rebecca's face. The walls are closing in on him. The tunnel is never ending. The lights have dimmed. A fist seems to be hammering away inside his chest. Eliot could not have hurt him more, caused him more pain than he already feels.

'Rebecca?'

'Yes, all right, I heard you.' She takes Nathan's hand and lifts it to her lips. 'I'd like to talk with Eliot.'

Nathan stands up.

'I'm really sorry . . . '

'Don't worry,' Rebecca says placatingly, 'we're just going

to talk, that's all.' She straightens the collar on his bathrobe, looking into his dazed eyes.

'Yes . . . I'll . . . wait in the bedroom.' He makes a very obvious effort to restrain his alarm, to keep a foothold on reality.

'You mustn't worry.'

'No, Nathan, you mustn't worry,' Eliot says with a snarl. 'Are you going back to Los Angeles with him?' Panic robs his voice of its normal resonance so that he sounds like a frightened child lost in a terrifying nightmare.

'I'm not going anywhere. I'm staying with you, always.'

Eliot makes a noise of disgust and turns his back. Nathan moistens his lips and glances with trepidation at the other man. He limps into the bedroom and they hear the door close. Eliot turns around and with an ironic laugh he says, 'I knew in San Francisco but I didn't believe it. It seemed crazy that you could feel anything but pity for the guy. Tell me it is pity, Rebecca.'

'I love him,' she says simply, honestly.

'Love,' his voice is jagged as broken glass. Incredulity passes over his handsome features. 'Love . . . ' He shakes his head, awaiting a further explanation, a sudden denial.

'Can I get you something to eat?'

'Just coffee.'

He follows her into the kitchen where she fills two cups from the percolator. She puts one into his hand.

'It's fresh. Would you like some toast?'

He makes a negative movement of his head. There is a look of strain around his normally clear eyes and a slight stiffness in his stance as though he is still tensed to strike. He looks at the book on the table; suggested meals for sensitive digestions. He transfers his gaze to Rebecca's face.

'Let's go back into the lounge,' she suggests.

He sits in the armchair. She sits on the couch.

'You look tired, Eliot,' she observes sympathetically. 'Are you working too hard?'

'I haven't been sleeping well.' He puts his cup on the table. 'Not since the letter. It hit me very badly.'

'I'm truly sorry, but it's not as if we were still seeing each other.'

'How could we, with you here and me in L.A.? I begged you to come out and join me.'

'We both know it was a good relationship while it lasted. I, for one, have no regrets. But we both know also that it was over as soon as you left for Hollywood and I left for New York.'

'You knew it, I never did. I would never have accepted that, Rebecca. I saw it, I see it, only as a separation, necessary because we both work in different towns. In my mind you were always the only woman for me.'

'You never said as much. If you had I might have been able to let you down more gently. As it was I did explain.'

'I never said as much because you were always so damn busy telling me how you were never going to get involved, how it destroyed your mother.'

'I don't want to discuss my mother.'

'Fair enough, then we'll discuss Roth. That's why I came here. To make you see reason, to force you to face the truth about him.'

'You're wasting your time. Nothing you can say will change my mind. I'll still love him. I always will.'

'He's a kind of crusade, isn't he, Rebecca?'

'I think I can save him from destroying himself, yes.'

'A man like Roth doesn't want to be saved. He wants to take everyone else down with him. I tried to tell you in London but you wouldn't listen.'

'No, not to gossip.'

'Not gossip, fact!' His voice rises on this last word, and his grey eyes blaze. 'Fact one being that it was no accident Roth's car crashed that night, the night Madeline was killed.'

'You were there?' Rebecca enquires calmly, hoisting an eyebrow.

'No, were you?' he asks with equal sarcasm.

'I've read Nathan's journal. I'm aware of all your so-called facts. I'm not going to discuss Nathan's past with you; it's none of your business.'

'Oh, I see, you know he was trying to kill himself and her?'

'I told you, I'm not going to discuss it.'

'Why? I'm prepared to hear his side of the story.'

'You're not his judge, Eliot. He has suffered enough in the past. He wants to forget his wife and I intend to help him forget.'

'Christ!' Eliot bangs his fist on the side of the chair.

As he lights a cigarette Rebecca says quietly, 'They used him; Madeline, all her friends, they took his money, abused his hospitality, destroyed his peace of mind, all those unfeeling bastards made his life hell. Even if he had intended to take his own life that night, he would not have crashed the car intentionally, not with Madeline beside him.'

'Okay, yes, Madeline was a bitch, no one who knew her would deny that, but does that mean she deserved to die, just because Roth was too much of a coward to live?'

'Don't you think he knows that? He's lived with the guilt of that horrific night for three long years. He wakes screaming, sweating. Every time he reaches for his walking stick or looks at his twisted leg he remembers. But he did not want Madeline dead.' She emphasizes each word equally, intensely, sitting forward on the couch and holding Eliot's unconvinced gaze. 'It was an accident, an accident. He wouldn't harm a fly, let alone a human being. He's been punished enough. He deserves a chance to live, and I'm going to fight for that chance.' Her voice seems to vibrate with the passion and power of her love. She thrusts her chin forward determinedly. 'Nothing you or anyone can say will make me change my mind.'

'Not even if I said I love you?'

'I'm honoured, really I am.' She closes her eyes and covers them with her hands. 'I realize that you must feel some deep emotion for me otherwise you wouldn't have flown all this way to talk to me.'

'Come back to L.A. with me now, today,' he urges, pressing home what he thinks is an advantage. 'We'll get married.'

She looks at him in stunned surprise.

'What's the matter, Rebecca, didn't you know that was what I always wanted for us?'

'I love Nathan. I don't love you, not that way.'

'At least you've never been anything else but honest,' he says with grim satisfaction. 'You're sacrificing your beauty, your talent, your entire future to be with a man like him. He'll bleed you dry. He'll wring every last ounce of sympathy and love from you and leave you reeling with shock, wondering what hit you. He'll grow fat while you grow thin.'

'We're going around in circles. You refuse to understand and that makes me very sad. You were always good to me and I would have liked your blessing.'

Eliot blows out smoke with a sigh of irritation. He smiles humourlessly. 'Maybe I could give the bride away; history repeats itself.'

'Cruel insults do not become you.'

He stubs out his cigarette in the ashtray. Rebecca gets ready to show him to the door, but he hasn't finished yet.

'How is Fifi these days?'

'Quite well, thank you. Unlike you, she understands. She came round here one night and we talked. Nathan is paying the rent on the apartment until she can find someone else to share. She wants to see Nathan happy.'

'The lady is full of compassion.'

'I think you'd better leave now.'

'Okay, Rebecca, let's not kid ourselves. You're a healthy

woman with healthy appetites. We've been lovers for eight months, I know the extent of your physical needs, and I don't believe a man like Roth can fulfil those needs.'

'I want you to leave,' Rebecca says, standing up, hiding her trembling hands in the pockets of her housecoat. She feels hollow, as though he has struck her with his fist and the pain will make her cry out without her consent.

'You'll never get around that particular problem, Rebecca. He might satisfy your urge to comfort the weak but as a lover . . . ' He shakes his head with mock sympathy.

'I'm not going to get angry, Eliot, it's not my style. Did these same people who have no doubt told you that Madeline sought other men because Nathan was an unsatisfactory lover also tell you how many men Madeline had while she was with Michelet?'

Eliot looks away.

'No, I thought not,' Rebecca says, her half smile patronizing. Suddenly she feels strangely calm, calm with the memory of how lovemaking is with Nathan Roth. The beauty, the tenderness, the unselfish mutual and complete satisfaction. 'Will you give your friends a message from me? Will you tell them that among decent people gentleness and sensitivity in lovemaking are more important than being endowed like a gorilla? Will you also tell them that Nathan and I do not need to have sex on a water bed, stimulate our appetite with drugs or alcohol, or hang from the chandeliers.' Her lips tremble around a self-satisfied smile. 'Tell them that it's inspiration that makes all the difference, and I inspire the poet and the man.'

Without raising his head Eliot says softly, 'I love you, Rebecca.'

'Thank you for that; we can never get enough love.'

She walks across the room and out into the hallway, waiting for him to leave. Reluctantly he follows. Outside he says, 'It's my fault, I should have told you how I felt. I tried to many times.'

'It would have made no difference.'

'You know what kind of a neurotic he is, and yet it really doesn't bother you. Don't you care that he's half crazy?'

'Poets are crazy. They have to be, they have no outer skin, nothing to protect them like the rest of us, they are raw. But the world needs men and women like Nathan Roth. Poets, artists, performers, teachers, musicians, prophets of creation, of hope. Without them the world is doomed. They redress the balance, put right the damage done by warmongers, politicians, racial and sexual bigots who seek to destroy our world, our optimism for a peaceful future.'

Eliot leans against the door and runs a hand through his thick hair.

'I came here to reason with you, not to get a lecture on behalf of the Peace Party.'

'Yes, I'm sorry, I didn't mean to lecture you.' She takes his hand. 'How long are you staying in New York? Can we keep in touch?' Her voice fades out because Eliot's shrewd eyes have filled with mock pity.

'Do you honestly think Roth will let you keep in touch with me or any man? He's going to take everything, there'll be nothing left for yourself, let alone for friends. He suffocated Madeline with his possessiveness. When she died she hadn't made a movie for two years. He wouldn't let her. He didn't trust her.' Rebecca releases his hand, her eyes turning cold as he goes on with renewed vigour and malice. 'Roth's neurotic jealousy drove her to hit back at him the only way she knew how and you'll end up the same way.'

Rebecca opens the door.

'You'd better get something straight, Rebecca, as far as I'm concerned nothing is settled. You don't want me, fine; I'm man enough to go away and lick my wounds. But I'm not going to allow you to throw your life away on a freak.'

'Get out,' she says in a voice drained of emotion.

'You gave me a message for Hollywood, now I'm giving

you one for Roth. Tell him I said if he were a man and he genuinely cared about you he would get out of your life now before it's too late, because if he destroys you the way he did Madeline Boucher I'll break his scrawny wrinkled neck.'

She tries to close the door on him and he bars it with his shoulder.

'You'll see me again, soon. Tell him that too.'

She slams the door and turns around.

'Nathan?' He is standing there at the bedroom door, dressed, carrying a small holdall and his new denim jacket.

'Where . . . where are you going?'

He puts down the holdall and gets into his jacket.

'Nathan,' she says in alarm, 'what are you going to do?'

'What I should have done months ago. What I should have done the day after you brought me here. Get out of your life.'

'No,' she says, her voice a whisper, her body numb, cold.

'I heard what he said. He was right about me, I did suffocate Madeline with my possessiveness, my emotional insecurity.' He sits down on the chair, his head in his hands. 'I begged her not to spend her time with anyone else, the way I've begged you these last few months. It's happening all over again and this time I have no reason on God's earth to be jealous.'

Rebecca stands beside him and speaks to his bowed head. 'I don't care about what happened between you and Madeline. That's past. It was a bad marriage. You were wrong for each other. You have to look to the future now.'

'I can't, not with Madeline's ghost haunting my dreams the way I've haunted yours.' He raises despairing eyes to her face. 'I wanted to die but she died instead. I killed her. Maybe I'll kill you one day too.'

'It was an accident. You were sick. You should never have been driving.' She strokes the fringe out of his eyes. 'Did you love Madeline more than you love me?'

201

'No . . .' he says intensely, tears springing to his eyes as he closes and then opens them again. ' . . . I never knew the meaning of the word "love" until I met you.'

'Then why go to her when you can stay with me? By leaving me now you're seeking to rejoin Madeline, because only in your misery can she find you.'

'I want her to find me. I want all my demons to find me. I want finally to confront them, not only through my poems but in reality. If I don't they will always be there, always coming between us.'

'You're doing this because of what Eliot said, aren't you? You're taking his words as a challenge. Those old hoary clichés; stand up and be a man, face life like a man . . . such infantile rubbish. You are a man, more a man than I've ever known.'

'Oh, Rebecca, you know me better than that. Have I ever been anything else than grateful for your strength? Can you honestly say I haven't made impossible demands on your love since I've lived here?'

She says nothing. There is nothing to say. He is right, lately she has felt suffocated, much as Madeline must have done. Everywhere she turns he is there, watching her with those suffering eyes, stunning her into a passivity she has never known before. Even now she can see his manic love for her in his tragic, hollowed-out face. His neurotic need to keep her for himself alone is wearing her out, dragging her into a closed, oppressive world he is making for them. But there has to be another way. They must save what they have. How can such mutual devotion not be enough? Yet even the most ardent of lovers must go on living their separate day-to-day lives, existing outside the confines of their relationship, or that precious emotion, however resilient, will finally perish, stifled to death. After this prolonged period of silence Nathan frowns, his forehead creasing, his eyes dark with the knowledge of what he must find the strength to do.

'You see, you know I'm right.'

She takes his hands and holds them tightly, looking into his sad, dark eyes. 'Please, let's give it more time this way, together. Don't turn your back on my help just to prove something to yourself or to Eliot. All relationships have to be worked at, they're all give and take.'

'I agree, but so far, Rebecca, you've done all the giving and I've done all the taking.'

'That's just not true,' she says, feeling the sharp pain of love for him deep in her chest, 'you've taught me that my mother trusted and loved my father and he betrayed that trust. That it was my father's weakness, not my mother's. But I'll never betray you.'

'Don't you think I know that? But could you ever depend on me? I'd never look at another woman, no, but could you say I've never betrayed you with my weakness? When you need a shoulder to cry on, when you're tired or sick, how will I react then?'

'With love,' she says confidently. 'Could a woman ask more?'

'Yes, Rebecca, yes, she could.' His pale face becomes stubborn, his eyes defiant, his shoulders and back rigid as he feels a surge of determination in his throat. 'Love has to be earned. It can't be begged.' He gives an indescribably painful smile as he looks into her face. 'I'm going away for a while.'

'I won't let you. You're crazy. You'll die without me.' A great weight seems to bear down upon her heart, a sense of panic, as if this is a fight against destiny itself. 'I love you, Nathan. My love can sustain you.'

Nathan needs a couple of seconds to control his voice, to swallow the tears that have tightened his throat muscles.

'A . . . poet . . . must be part of the world . . . in which he lives. Produced by it, affecting it, if he can. Poetry is about life, emotions, people. For too long I've tried to cut myself off from reality. You've given me the courage to go outside my poems, you gave me a reason to live, now I have to find the strength within myself.'

'You're stubborn . . . how can you be so bloody stubborn? Where will you go?' She restrains her voice, forcing herself to accept the fact that Nathan's mind is made up, that nothing she can say will deter him. 'Will you go to Joan and Bernard?'

'Are you trying to humiliate me?'

'No . . . why . . . I only . . . ?' she stammers, before breaking off.

'From one crutch to another. I already have one cane to lean on.' He stands up and limps away from her, out of her reach, not wanting her to touch him, knowing his courage will fail him if she does. 'I'm going to an hotel.'

'An hotel? Which hotel? Tell me. I want to be able to come and see you.'

'No, Rebecca, that's not the idea. Don't you see I'm trying to regain some of my self-respect?'

'I won't let you leave. You're being ridiculous.'

'You have no choice.' The veins bulge on his hands and neck, the neck Eliot threatened to snap like a dry twig. 'I should have gone without telling you. I should have left a note or something. I'm weak, I couldn't even walk out of here without tearing us apart.'

'I'll worry about you constantly. I won't have a moment's peace, worrying, wondering if you're all right.'

'I'll be fine. I'll go on writing. I'll pull myself together. You've given me a start, that was what I needed, a start, a reason.' Please, dear God, let me sound convincing, he prays fervently, let me sound as though I am as strong as I would like to be and not as weak and cowardly as I really am. He is trying so desperately to give her an opportunity to breathe again, to be free, can't she see that and be grateful? Can't she allow him to leave now with the minimum of grief? He must go now, as Eliot said, now, before it is too late.

She tries to embrace him but he finds the strength from somewhere to resist the comfort of her arms, the smell of her skin, her hair, which even now tempts him beyond endurance. He gives a slightly stooping gesture of his shoulders. His back is oddly bent, being so thin he looks young, seems so young, yet he is old, feels old. Feels beaten, crushed. Must go now, must go before she realizes and understands.

'Will you take care of my papers?' he asks humbly and his hands shake, his hands and body as though he is caught in a strong wind.

'How long, Nathan?' saying this a coldness touches her heart. 'How long before I see you again, before I know if you are well? How can I live not knowing?'

'I'll call you. I'll call you very soon.' He smiles, lifting his hand to her cheek.

'Don't do this, Nathan, I beg of you.'

His smile vanishes, his hand drops from her cheek. 'I have to. It has nothing whatsoever to do with being a man and everything to do with being a dignified human being. This is my way of showing a little strength for a change.'

'Your entire personality is a sign of strength. Your quietness, your lack of aggression, your great tenderness toward me, your will to write even when you were suffering the most terrible physical and mental torture. Don't you know, Nathan, don't you really see how strong you are?'

A melancholy smile brushes his lips. 'Thank you.' He lifts the holdall from the carpet.

'Nathan . . .' She shakes her head. ' . . . it will take me all my life to understand you.'

'Perhaps I don't have that long.' He gives a gentle, indefinable smile.

'What . . . what do you mean?'

'Only that I've lived ten years longer than you and it feels like thirty years.' A spasm of pain shoots through his stomach but he forbids himself to touch the place with his hand, to reveal his discomfort and the strain shows on his face. 'As soon as I'm settled somewhere I'll let you know.'

'Tell me now. Tell me the name of the hotel. What shall I do about the doctor's appointment? You gave me your word you would go this time. Four appointments, all broken, Nathan, you gave me your word.'

'I'll go, yes, I will. It's okay.'

'It's okay,' she repeats in a flat voice as someone who knows they are wasting their time trying to argue or persuade, 'you bloody stubborn Jew.' She blinks away the tears on her lashes as he embraces her briefly with an encouraging smile. 'If I'd known that Jews were so stubborn . . . '

'A stiff-necked people.'

'Would you please just kiss me . . . properly?' she says in a breathless whisper. 'It's all I ask.'

Her mouth is soft and wet and warm and he almost doesn't make it to the door.

'Nathan . . . ' Her tender, husky voice calls after him as he limps down the corridor without so much as a glance over his shoulder.

My God. My God. My God. Out of sight at last he puts the holdall on the carpet and leans against the wall, breathing deeply, trying to combat the terrible burning in his stomach. The pain this morning has been unbearable. But he has to bear it because he must, because he cannot go running back to her arms, weeping like a lost child. He wipes the sweat off his face and grips the wall for support as a sharp pain like a knife enters his lower chest. He closes his eyes and clenches his teeth. Tears squeeze out from beneath the lids, tears of pain and grief. I am shattered glass, Rebecca. Shards. Jagged and broken. Yes. The mirror no longer holds my image. A ghost has no reflection. Rebecca, my beautiful Rebecca, I set you free. Let no man say I never loved you. Let no man say I tried to suffocate the thing I loved most.

CHAPTER SEVENTEEN

The heart shuts,
The sea slides back,
The mirrors are sheeted.

Sylvia Plath, 1932–1963. *Contusion*

The summer left with Nathan. It is now early October and
a cold wind blows through the streets of New York City,
and through Rebecca's heart. Two months have gone by
since the poet walked out of her apartment, two months
since she heard his gentle voice or felt his gentle breath on
her body. When it rains she walks without an umbrella,
imagining that somewhere in the city, somewhere in a park,
an avenue, a corner of their world, the same rain is falling
on him, on her Jewish poet.

Every Sunday she visits the Adlers. Often they catch
themselves talking as though Nathan is lost to them forever.
Where could he have gone? Joan will ask in confusion. Why
did he have to go? Bernard will ask, hurt and bewildered.
But Rebecca, ignoring her own despair, will cheer them
with words of hope for the future, a future shared by all
four of them. She works, her routine mechanical, her concentration easily wavering, her commitments of less and less
duration. The selection of poems made by Nathan just
before his departure has been contracted to Joe's publishing
house and is scheduled to appear in the spring. Rebecca is
monitoring its progress every step of the way. It is, after all,
a continuous if somewhat tenuous link to the poet, one that
brings him closer to her in thought and deed.

Where are you, Nathan? Where are you, my lover? Are you in pain? Can you sleep without me? Do you hear me call to you through the long, lonely nights? Or have you yielded to the everlasting darkness called Death? I weep for you, my Nathan. I weep because you would not, or could not, accept the only chance you have for life. Strange, I have come to believe in the Angel of Death, the thousand-eyed, million-tentacled monster who waits, crouching, in everyone's nightmares. I spend my time planning ways to deceive him, to trick and confuse him, to throw him off the scent. Not for me, you understand, for you. People have noticed, Nathan, they have noticed that I am no longer me. I smile but I do not smile. I laugh but there is no sound except sudden gusty winds in a hollow place. I speak but my words are only echoes of last year, yesterday. I am closer now to understanding how my mother suffered. Loved and suffered. I am lonelier now that I have ever been, me, the woman with so many friends ... friends, lovers, admirers. I would trade them all for one glimpse of you, for one brief touch of your hand. For the first time in my life, Nathan, my poet, I know what it is to love.

Toward the middle of the month the dreams begin again. The manic wailing of the ambulance siren. The trolley. The empty corridor. The running feet. The lights in the ceiling which burn her eyes. A motionless body beneath a white sheet.

I saw you in a dream. You had ceased to live but were not yet dead. Why did you always cry? Your tears fell on the garden of my joy and flowers grew in the secret passage. Your footsteps leave no trace, your laughter has no echo, the swell of your breath is lost in the burden of darkness.

Come back, Nathan, come back to me.

'I have a list of every hotel in New York City. I'm going to go through the list, hotel by hotel, until I find him,' she tells Joan and Bernard excitedly.

'What's the point?' Bernard asks with a lethargic shrug. The years that he and Joan had seemed to shed on Rebecca's addition to their family have now returned with a vengeance. The Adlers look old, old and hopeless, especially Bernard who seems to have lost his zest for life.

'The point is, Bernard, I have to do something. I have to try.'

'And suppose he is using another name?'

'Rebecca will find him,' Joan states in a tone that flatly contradicts Bernard's. She at least wants this slender hope to cling to, and resents her husband's terrible pessimism. 'Let me have a page from your list. I'll do the same.'

Hopeless, Nathan. Yes, Bernard is right. You could be calling yourself John Smith, how am I expected to know? We'll never find you this way, but you counted on that didn't you? There was always a vanishing point in your eyes. Strange, I always thought it was me who would run in the end.

'I'm going to hire a private detective,' Rebecca announces, one Saturday two weeks later. 'They know all about finding people who don't want to be found.'

'That's a wonderful idea,' Joan says, once more grasping at straws.

'You both watch too much television,' Bernard says before returning to his own depressing thoughts.

'Do you want him back, Bernard?' Rebecca demands.

'You have to ask me?' The professor's eyes and voice are indignant, mortified.

'Yes, Bernard, I have to ask because lately you are robbing Joan and me of all our hope.'

Bernard gazes from Rebecca to Joan who nods slowly, once. His tired eyes produce tears behind their bifocal lenses and his full lips tremble uncontrollably. Joan rushes to embrace him and together they draw Rebecca into their arms. Come back, Nathan, if not for me, then for these two people who love you as a son.

Every day she calls the detective agency just off Times Square. Every day the same question: Have you found him, my lover, the poet? Every day the same answer: A few leads, some old friends, some sightings. Nothing concrete. It's just a matter of time before we trace him. Time is something he doesn't have. I know. I feel. I dream.

Finally however, it is neither Rebecca's hotel list nor the detective agency that brings news of Nathan, but a quite unexpected source. One evening Rebecca is alone in her apartment reading a manuscript when the phone rings. She answers every call now with a loudly beating heart and an eager, yet tentative voice, wishing to know, yet fearing to hear.

'Hello?'

'Hi Rebecca, it's me, Alice.'

'Alice, how are you?' Disappointment, relief makes her voice lose all inflection.

'I'm really well. They started me on a new routine at the club and . . . '

'Excuse me, Alice, can this wait for another time? I'm very tired.'

'I saw Nathan.'

'When?' She can barely speak, her heart is thumping so madly.

'Last night. We had a drink together for old times' sake.'

'Alice, where was he?' Rebecca almost shouts.

'I'm getting to that, see he made me promise not to tell I'd seen him but I followed him outa the bar and back to his hotel.'

'The name, Alice, the name, please.'

'I got it written down here. Hold on a sec.' The sound of crumpled paper being straightened fills Rebecca's ears. 'Yer, hello, here it is, the Thorburn on East 34th Street. You know it?'

'I'll find it.'

'Hey, Rebecca, did I do wrong breaking my promise? Only he looked real bad. I ain't never seen him look so bad.'

'You did right, Alice. You did wonderfully.'

Half an hour after putting the phone down on Alice, Rebecca is entering the lobby of the Thorburn Hotel, a 'lobby' not much better than the main room of Nathan's old apartment. The manager, a surly character eating a hamburger, drags his bulk off his chair long enough to ring Nathan's room on his ancient switchboard.

'He ain't there, lady, I'll tell him you called.' He slumps into his chair.

'What is his room number?' Rebecca asks, standing her ground.

'I ain't supposed to . . .' His small eyes start greedily from his head as a ten dollar bill appears on the counter top. '309, third floor.'

In five minutes Rebecca returns.

'See, I told you, he ain't there.'

'He doesn't answer but I can hear something. I want you to open the door please.'

The man holds out a grubby hand. Rebecca, less concerned with the morality of the situation than Nathan's health, places another ten dollar bill on the outstretched palm. The manager goes with her to the third floor and uses his pass key. Rebecca pushes past him and rushes inside. Nathan is lying on the floor, his motionless body surrounded by papers and flanked by an overturned chair.

'Call an ambulance!' Rebecca shouts as she kneels down beside him, cradling his head in her lap. 'Please . . . call an ambulance . . . ' She stares at his chest, at the slight movement, desperate to locate some life in him. Suddenly his eyes flutter open and show instant recognition. He tries to speak her name, tries so terribly hard, but his lips barely move.

'Nathan, I'm here now . . . ' she keeps her voice totally calm so as not to frighten him, ' . . . you'll be fine, someone has gone for an ambulance and I'm staying with you. We'll be together, I swear to you . . . '

He hears her as though from a distance, across other voices, other sounds. She holds him, lifts him from the floor and holds him against her, rocking him in her arms, stroking his hair. He feels so light, so weightless, without pain, without fear. Is this death? His eyes close slowly and his head sinks against her chest.

The paramedics who attend his motionless body in the room are young and astonishingly capable. Rebecca sits on the floor a little to the side not wanting to get in their way as they work. Don't die, Nathan, please don't die. One lifts his grey head and covers his nose and mouth with an oxygen mask. The other attaches an intravenous drip to his arm. They talk constantly to each other, rapid, quick fire instructions, but so utterly calm at their life and death task. They wrap the poet in a yellow blanket and lie him carefully on the gurney. As they push it along the corridor the intravenous bag sways drunkenly on its hook. Doors open on both sides of the corridor and curious, sleepy faces peer out, eager to see what is happening or irritated at being woken from their dreams. Rebecca doesn't notice them, she sees only the deathly white, unconscious face above the blanket, half concealed by the oxygen mask. Outside on the street the red and blue lights of the ambulance blink and flash as they turn on the low roofed vehicle. The attendants lift the gurney and Rebecca climbs up alongside it. One medic climbs in with the patient while the other takes his place in the driver's seat. The siren wails. The same siren that had shrilled and wailed through her nights, haunted her sleep, brought that fearful look to Nathan's face.

If I should die, he had once said. No, you won't die. But if I should, keep a memory of me in your heart for as long as you can. You won't die, we'll be together always. There is no one to speak for me. No one to offer prayers. No one of my blood. Automatically Rebecca moves a hand to her stomach, fingers spread wide and curved, as though to protect and conceal a precious mystery.

'How is he?' she asks. It is the first time she has spoken since the paramedics' arrival and her mouth is dry.

'Fine,' comes the noncommittal reply.

Rebecca glances at the young man's face. He is lying. She knows when someone is lying. Her heart forces its way into her throat. She finds Nathan's hand inside the blanket and holds it tightly. It is cold, icy cold. There are beads of sweat on his brow which the medic blots with a wad of tissue. His life, the sacred flame, is flickering out.

At the hospital emergency entrance the doors of the ambulance are opened by a nurse and a doctor. The stretcher is removed and mounted on a trolley. The trolley is wheeled into the emergency room. Rebecca tries to follow but is stopped by another nurse. She looks through the small window in the door as they transfer Nathan from the trolley to the examination table. There are so many people around his prostrate form that she cannot see clearly what is happening, but their anxious, tense faces tell her all she needs to know. She walks to the far wall and leans against it. There is a choked pressure inside her throat and her chest, and her facial muscles are stiff as though she has been exposed to a cold, numbing wind. Please, Dear God, don't let Nathan die. My melancholy poet, my lover, my friend. Her head snaps up as a nurse emerges from the emergency room, harassed, preoccupied.

'Please . . . ' Rebecca runs forward only to be dismissed with a vague smile as the nurse hurries past. 'I'm with the man . . . in there . . . ' She finishes, speaking quietly, to herself, 'I'm with Nathan Roth . . . '

Yes, they are all fighting to keep him alive and there is nothing she can do to help. Helplessness is a new experience for her.

Do you remember the dreams, Rebecca? What has to be, has to be. The circle is closing. No! No, I will never allow the flame to go out. I'll fight. I'll use the breath from my own body if I have to, but I'll never, never let you die.

A tall, handsome, dark-skinned man wearing a white coat over his street suit goes into the emergency room. In a little while he pushes open the door and after a second's hesitation he approaches Rebecca, evidently having been informed that she accompanied the patient. He offers his hand and a smile designed to put her at her ease.

'My name is Jackson.' Briefly Rebecca grasps the slender hand. 'And you are?'

'Rebecca Farrell,' she says quickly. 'How is he? Could I see him? Has he been asking for me?'

'He's still unconscious, Miss Farrell,' the doctor says kindly, but not patronizingly. 'Do you know where we can contact Mr Roth's next of kin? I need their permission to operate.'

Rebecca's anxious gaze flickers over the doctor's regular features.

'When?' she asks finally.

'They're preparing him for surgery right now.'

Rebecca pushes the hair off her face with a hand that will not cease its trembling. She nods once, slowly, so that he will know she understands what he is telling her but cannot yet speak because a shock wave has risen in her chest almost knocking her off her feet. She pulls herself together and her voice emerges, though the words fall from her lips in no particular order.

'I . . . can tell you . . . his sister, he has a sister, a brother and a sister but they live . . . I don't know exactly where

214

they live. Out of state . . . years. He hasn't seen them. New
Jersey I think.' Slowly her cognizance returns. 'There are
people, the Adlers, like parents, but if it's that urgent can't I
sign? I'm closer to Nathan . . . closer than anybody.'

'Why don't you sit down while I get the relevant papers.'

'Yes, yes, I think I will. Thank you.' She smiles and then
doesn't smile, suddenly weak.

In the midst of signing she pauses to ask Dr Jackson, 'Is
Nathan going to be all right?'

Jackson meets her direct, emphatic gaze, judging her to
be a woman who can face the truth of a situation.

'Miss Farrell, I honestly don't know. Of course we'll do
everything possible for him, but Mr Roth has a breach in
the stomach wall, there is a massive haemorrhage.'

Soon they take him from the emergency room and wheel
him down the long corridor to the elevator. The lights in
the ceiling burn Rebecca's eyes, those and the tears she
refuses to cry. Mustn't cry. No tears. Be strong now, he
needs my strength. He needs my confidence to pull through.
I'm not afraid, I know you will live. Nathan beneath the
white sheet is the colour of candle grease, his nostrils
pinched around their flared edges, his cheek bones sharp,
the flesh fallen away. I know you won't die. She remains
close to the trolley holding his hand, while a nurse steadies
the container of blood from which a tube leads under the
blanket. The nurse smiles reassuringly at her. She doesn't
notice. Her eyes are fixed on Nathan's face. As they ascend
in the elevator his tragic eyes open.

'Darling . . . ' Rebecca says softly, leaning over him.
' . . . I love you. I'll pray for you. I'll never leave you.' He is
too dazed with drugs and fear to understand or even hear
her words but the expression of grief and devotion on her
face is more than enough to convey their meaning. Tears
appear in the outer edges of his eyes and roll down into his
grey hair, dislodged by the movement of the trolley as they

leave the elevator. His lips move but no sound emerges. If he could have spoken he would have told her that nothing matters except that he was, is, loved by a woman such as her. She alone made his life worth living. But he has never felt so weak, so broken in body and spirit, so close to death. His eyes close and he floats down into darkness. Rebecca kisses his forehead. It is damp, like flesh in death. The double doors of the operating theatre swallow him up.

She moves automatically to one of the chairs, sitting, lethargic with shock. A breach in the stomach wall. She closes her eyes, takes a deep breath, releases it very slowly. The words echo in her brain, throb in her heart, make her hands sweat. A breach? How can he live with a tear, a hole in his stomach? How is that possible? But he will live. He must live. She could cry now, there is no one around to watch, to mock her weakness, her fear. But when she tries she finds she cannot, her eyes and throat are dry. Her despair is too profound even for tears. She presses trembling fingers to her forehead. She must call Joan and Bernard. In all the confusion, the urgency, she had forgotten. But she ought to ring them, and she will soon, in a while. She can't face speaking to them right now, explaining, comforting. But they have a right to know. The man is like their son. And their son is dying. No, not dying, please Dear God, no.

The telephones are located next to the coffee machine, sound proofed by perspex bubbles. She presses the appropriate numbers on the dial and waits, her stomach churning with apprehension, her jaw muscles tightening as she rehearses what she will say, the kindest and briefest way to say it.

'Hello?' comes Joan's gentle voice anxiously.

'It's Rebecca, I'm sorry to call you so late . . . '

'Bernard, it's Rebecca.'

Bernard's voice rises excitedly in the background. 'Has she found Nathan?'

'Joan, please listen. I'm calling from Bellevue Hospital. Nathan was admitted about an hour ago.' She has to speak quickly before her voice deserts her. 'He's in the operating theatre on the third floor. Please come.'

'Oh ... God ... no ...'

The receiver is put down clumsily in Rebecca's ear and the silence of the machinery intensifies.

Thirty minutes later the Adlers arrive, Joan slightly ahead of her husband, too anxious to wait for him, yet not wanting to leave him entirely alone. Rebecca goes to meet them, taking Joan into her arms.

'What ... what happened?' the older woman asks, bemused, her red-rimmed eyes searching Rebecca's face for answers. 'How did it happen? When?'

Very briefly Rebecca tells her about Alice and the hotel.

'Please,' Joan says, suddenly remembering her husband, 'please comfort Bernard. I just want to sit down for a moment.'

Rebecca walks her to a chair before returning to Bernard who is standing in the centre of the corridor staring at the doors of the operating theatre like a man who believes he can see through a solid object with his naked eyes. Rebecca holds him around the waist.

'Bernard,' her voice is infinitely gentle. She knows what he is going through, her own grief can match him tear for tear, agony for agony. 'Please, come and sit down beside Joan. She needs you. We both do. They won't be much longer and then we can all see Nathan.'

Bernard obeys her, heavy and slow, a shuffling old man with dark pouches beneath his eyes, eyes that have lost all hope, eyes that have lost all light. Rebecca sits beside him holding his hand.

'He'll get well again, Bernard,' she says with staunch conviction. 'We'll all be one happy family again, you'll see.'

217

She looks from Bernard to Joan. 'Isn't that right, Joan? Tell him and he'll believe you.'

'Nathan will get well again,' Joan says in an emotionless voice, as though responding only to a heartfelt prayer shared by them all. 'He will get well again.'

'He knows how much we love him, he wouldn't leave us.'

Bernard seems lost in thought, placated by her comforting words but then he says with sudden anger, 'He left us. He chose to be on his own, to suffer.' He turns to Rebecca, his eyes awash with tears behind his half lenses. 'Wasn't I right about you and him, Rebecca? Didn't I guess how you felt about him?'

'Yes, Bernard,' she lifts his hand to her cheek, 'you knew I loved him. You alone guessed how I felt.'

At 12.10 Dr Jackson emerges from the operating theatre still wearing the drab green surgical clothing, with a mask still hanging limply around his neck. He removes his cap and with a weary sigh rubs it over his tightly kinked hair. Rebecca rises, but only with a tremendous effort. Her body had never felt so burdened, so clumsy and her legs are made of rubber. Jackson acknowledges the Adlers, guessing their identity. He indicates with his head that he would like to speak with Rebecca out of their hearing. She joins him some way down the corridor and looks into his tired, slightly bloodshot eyes.

'He's alive, Rebecca,' he begins in a restrained voice, 'but I don't know what to tell you except that we've done everything we can.'

Rebecca turns her back on Joan and Bernard and stares at the wall as the doctor continues. 'I wish I could offer more hope. I'm sorry.'

Unable to hold back her tears Rebecca covers her face with her hands, but despite the pressure they escape from beneath her eyelids. Jackson puts his hand on her shoulder. She rubs the tears away suddenly, angrily, forcing back her grief by will-power alone. She cannot give herself up to the despair she feels, who would then be left to give Nathan the strength to renew his slipping hold on life? She takes a handkerchief from her pocket and wipes her nose.

'Is it possible . . . ' she stops to clear her throat of uncried tears, ' . . . is it possible for me to stay with him?'

'Of course. They'll be taking him to the Intensive Care Unit. We'll go together.'

Rebecca looks over at Joan and Bernard. The truth can wait for them, they will know soon enough.

Wheeled from surgery he looks ravaged. A ghastly grey, bloodless face above a white sheet. The ghostly, weightless look of something floating just beneath the surface of a lake. Undulating, silvery grey hair, skin, bone. A forty-year-old face and body that has aged decades and is in danger of fading totally.

Oh no, oh no, look at you. My darling. What have they done to you? You are drained of life. You are like a shell. A shadow that must flee at dawn. Nathan, listen to me, these things do not matter, we can build you up, make you well again, but the spirit is something you have to attend. Nathan, please, you have to want to live.

Outside a door marked with the letters I.U.C. they wait while Nathan is transferred to a bed with metal-sided safety rails like a child's cot.

'He's dying,' Bernard whispers.

'No, Bernard, that's not true and you mustn't say it. He'll regain consciousness very soon. We'll be able to talk to him, let him know we're here.'

'He is dying,' Bernard repeats in his long-suffering voice, a voice which refutes any denial of the fact, even from his beloved Rebecca.

Joan takes his arm. 'Rebecca won't let him die.'

He rounds on her. 'Who told you that – God?'

'Bernard!' Joan exclaims, shocked and shamefaced. 'How can you blaspheme?'

Dr Jackson rejoins them.

'Do you know who that boy is?' Bernard asks him.

'Nathan Roth, the poet.'

'Do you know what *The New York Reivew of Books* said about Nathan's first collection of poems?'

'No sir, I don't,' Jackson admits with sympathy and respect.

'Not now, Bernard, please,' Joan begs, shaking her head.

'They said, and I quote, "There is an immense intellectual devotion to the soul of poetry in this young man's work."' He pauses, gathering his thoughts as Joan looks helplessly at Rebecca and the doctor. 'They said there is that unmistakable authenticity of a poet speaking from his own depths.'

'That's wonderful, sir,' Jackson says soberly.

'You see, young man,' Bernard removes his spectacles and cleans the lenses on his handkerchief, once more transported back to the classroom where he is lecturing his students on his favourite poet, 'the educated poet who has the words is just a poet, but the man who has the words and the visions from some deep well of tragic consciousness is a genius. That is the difference. Nathan Roth is a genius ... a genius ... ' His voice fades into the enfolding silence.

'Why don't you go home and get some rest?' Dr Jackson suggests, wearing the distressed frown of someone who doesn't know what to say next.

'Yes ... I talk too much ... I always did ... it's a failing of mine ... ask Joan ... '

'Can we see him just for a moment?' Joan asks.

'I'm not sure Mr Adler should ... '

'I'm quite well,' Bernard butts in, raising his head. 'I'm quite myself again. I want to see him. I want to see my son.'

Rebecca and Dr Jackson watch through the window. Inside Joan begins to cry. She presses a tearful kiss to her fingers and puts them to Nathan's lips. Bernard seems to sway on his feet. Joan has to guide him to the door. She leaves him to take refuge in Rebecca's arms.

'He looks so bad . . . he looks so very sick, Rebecca.'

'I'll watch over him, you mustn't worry. I'll stay with him all night. Nathan wouldn't want you to remain in the hospital, he would want you to take Bernard home for a good night's rest and come back in the morning.'

Joan inclines her head uncertainly; she would like to stay, to support Rebecca, to pray for Nathan but she must think of Bernard.

'Let's go home now,' she tells Bernard, breathing out sharply with the effort.

Bernard's gaze is centred on the floor between his feet. He makes a slight nodding motion of his head acknowledging her words, his kindly face distorted with sorrow. Rebecca walks them to the elevator, an arm around each of them. She comes back to Dr Jackson, her smile of gratitude for his patience quivering as it reaches the corners of her mouth. He holds the door open for her.

Nathan is lying flat, his arms by his sides on the sheet, his naked torso the same colour as his hair. A tube leads from the inside of his left arm to a supply of blood on a stand by the bed, and a plastic bar curves around both cheeks from which two short tubes disappear into his nostrils. His eyes are shut, his lips firmly closed. An expression of unconscious sorrow gives his face immobile dignity and grace. The Dying Poet. Death and the Poet. She sits on the chair and puts her arms through the safety bars, gently entwining her fingers with his. She leans over and kisses his lips, trying to warm them with her own, trying to breathe her life into his.

'Are you all right?' Dr Jackson enquires.

She nods, weeping silently, invisibly.

'I'm on call. If I'm needed they know where to find me.'

221

He squeezes her shoulder with a paternal informality. 'Try to get some sleep. He'll receive the best of care, believe me.'

As he leaves, Rebecca's night-long vigil of prayers begins.

CHAPTER EIGHTEEN

But when the self speaks to the self, who is speaking? –
the entombed soul, the spirit driven in, in to the central
catacomb; the self that took the veil and left the world –
a coward perhaps, yet somehow beautiful, as it flits with
its lantern up and down the dark corridors.

Virginia Woolf, 1882–1941. *An Unwritten Novel*

Nathan, do you remember how it was between us? Can I
say you taught me how to love? Never before have I felt
such intense devotion to a man, never before have I loved so
intensely. If you die now, Nathan, you will break my heart.

She gazes up as a nurse enters, not the same one who had
checked on the poet diligently through the long night, but
another, middle aged and plump, in white trousers.

'Your husband, honey?' she enquires, exchanging the near
empty container of blood for a full one.

'No,' Rebecca says softly, regretfully. Her throat is dry.
She spent the night speaking to him, trying to coax him
back to life. But there is no change in his condition, she can
see that just by looki. g at him. There is no flicker of life in
his bluish eyelids, no movement in his body or limbs. She
swallows with difficulty. 'No, not my husband.' Though I
wish he were. I wish I bore his name. I wish you so many
things, my darling, but mostly I wish you life.

The nurse's sympathetic gaze becomes one of concern.
There is a pale, tight tension around Rebecca's normally
soft mouth and her beautiful eyes are dulled by lack of
sleep.

'You been sitting here all night, honey? I didn't know,

I've just come on duty. I'm going to get you a real nice cup of coffee. Make you feel better.'

Tell her what would make me feel better, Nathan. No? Then I shall tell her. I shall tell her that only your recovery can bring a warmth to my heart.

She fans the flame of his breath. She speaks to him of laughter and tears, of the rain which they shared like a kiss. She tells him there is no yesterday that does not include her love for him. The past that he fears, has always feared, is only a greyness, a fog of misunderstanding in the mouths of envious men. Her words of devotion fall like rain on his immobile, suffering body, invoking moments, joys they have known and which no amount of loss or pain can obliterate. The forever times . . . the mornings of waking, face to face, breast to breast, thigh to thigh . . . the instant recognition that love is there, reaching out for them. The second of unearthly silence when neither dare speak lest the serenity of the moment be lost. Those sad, bitter-sweet tears shed across the landscape of their bodies because the time of joining, the total oneness was so brief, so wondrous but so tragically short, a single breath against a quivering flame. Come back to me, Nathan, come back so that we may once more share such joy.

Rebecca leaves Bernard at Nathan's side and takes Joan for coffee in the cafeteria. Like her, the Adlers have been in the hospital all day, waiting, praying for a miracle.

'When Bernard came back from San Francisco after meeting you, do you know what he said to me?'

Rebecca has heard this story so many times, from Joan's lips and from Bernard's, but she doesn't have the heart to spoil Joan's game, to steal this tiny source of comfort. She lifts the woman's hand from the table and holds it tightly.

'What did he say?' she asks with an indulgent smile.

'He said, I met a young woman, a beauty. You've never

seen such beauty except perhaps in those glamour books. But this woman is different, she has brains and wit, she is strong and gentle, and she is in love with our Nathan, he said with that self-satisfied smile of his. You know the one I mean?' There are tears in Joan's eyes, she sniffs and smiles simultaneously.

'A professor's smile,' Rebecca says, 'professors and poets, they think they know everything.'

'You know what else he said?' Joan's eyelids blink and the water escapes, rolling down her cheeks. 'He said . . . you were sent by God . . . to take care of His favourite poet . . . ' She shakes her head to indicate that she cannot go on.

Rebecca comes around to Joan's side of the table and embraces her.

'Joan, try to think about the future, a future where Nathan is well and we're all together. That was something Patrick and I learned when we were young. Instead of concentrating on the painful present you must imagine that it is the future, a time when you can look back on now and say, yes, it was very bad, but we came through and look how happy we are now.'

'What would Bernard and I do without you?'

'I have only one regret, that I did not come into Nathan's life so much sooner.'

Yes, the life is escaping from his body. His soul hovers above his grey head, weeping in silence, tears that will seal his eyelids and lips forever. She prays: Please, Dear God, please, there are words but I don't know them, I am only half Jewish. He is the poet, the Jewish poet. But please, Dear God, don't let him die. Forbid Death the right to embrace his frail body, forbid the shadows to envelop his ghost.

Late afternoon on the following day. Rebecca waits in the corridor as Dr Jackson examines his patient. Finally he appears, his hands in his coat pockets, his expression reflective of his grave words.

'He is in a very deep coma, Rebecca.'

She sits down.

'Yes, I knew he should be conscious by now. I guessed that of course,' she says in a very quiet voice. She pushes the heavy hair off her drawn face. 'It's her . . . ' she whispers under her breath.

'I beg your pardon?'

'A ghost calling to a ghost. The dead seeking retribution.'

Madeline, for too long you have beckoned him into the darkness, tempted him with an obscene promise of oblivion in exchange for his mortal pain. But who gave him such torture? Who buried him in layer upon layer of unjustified guilt? Who dragged him down with you into your coffin and blocked the living sunshine from his agonized soul?

She calls to me, Rebecca. I know, Nathan, but you mustn't go to her, you mustn't even listen to her words. I wanted to die that night, Rebecca. In those days I thought about death all the time. I was obsessed by it. But I never wanted to hurt her, I never wanted her to die. I could have taken pills, I did once before when I was young, but they found me, they found me and pumped me out. So pills were unreliable or, rather, people were. You never knew when they would try to save you, when they would interfere and subvert the course of destiny. But that night I knew I had to find a way. She was laughing at me, she was always laughing at me, taunting me. I had to escape forever. I ran outside to the car, her car. I had never learned to drive properly, too nervous people said, too careful, not with my own life, you understand, but with others. But that night I could only think of one thing, my own death. Then suddenly she was climbing into the car beside me, laughing, taunting, demanding I drive her to Michelet's house. At first I refused, I couldn't let anyone subvert destiny this time, this time I was going to die, and I couldn't die with Madeline beside me in the car. But then it was okay, there was no need to panic, none at all, I could do it after I had left her with her lover, yes, of course, that was more fitting.

The road stretched out ahead of us, an empty landscape disappearing into darkness. She kept on talking, she kept on saying things, bad things, how useless I was in bed, why didn't I find myself a pretty boy, so many in Hollywood, would I be better with a male lover, she kept on asking. Then she started on my driving, I held the steering wheel too tight, I gripped it like I gripped her in bed, like a frightened fool. Why don't I drive faster, coward, coward. I began to cry. I seemed to be swimming in a deep lake of water, drowning, unable to breathe. She laughed at my tears. I could hardly see where I was driving and she grabbed the wheel, turning it to the left as her laughter blossomed up through her white throat. Everything happened so quickly, so quickly. I didn't want her to die, not her. Only me. And not that way, not with her beside me, laughing, so that even in death I was mocked.

There was so much noise, the violent shattering of glass, the angry screeching of tyres, the peculiar dull thudding noise of metal twisted and crushed on impact with the road. Then she wasn't laughing anymore. She was screaming and screaming. She screamed as the car turned over, a football kicked down a steep bank, somersaulting, going on forever. Then suddenly it stopped. She stopped and the car stopped. We were upside down in a ditch and she wasn't screaming or laughing anymore. I was conscious. There was blood in my hair, running down my face into my mouth, and blood on my leg, so much blood on my leg. I moved my eyes so that I could look down at it, my leg, and it did not seem to be part of me. There was no pain. Just silence. In a while, I don't know how long, they came, their sirens cutting through the unreal quiet, their anxious voices drifting around me as though I were in one world and they in another. When they took her from the wreck she was already dead. Her neck was broken. That beautiful, white neck that I had loved and then loathed, but never, never wanted to destroy.

Rebecca, am I dead? Nathan, listen to me, I am your hold on life, your escape into love, into the future. Do you want Madeline's moment of death to be her moment of greatest triumph? Fight, Nathan, fight to live.

There is a trail of spittle at the corner of his mouth. She wipes it away with a tissue and gently kisses the area. She combs his hair, assists as Nurse Kate gives him a sponge bath, her devotion moving the emotional nurse to tears. She passes her hand over the dressing on his stomach as though in benediction, she listens to his breathing, the way the soul flutters in his breast ready to take flight, ready to desert its earthly home. She traps it with her hands, her mouth, her words. She shows him reflections of their joining in the mirrors of his unconscious mind, moment after moment of blending so that he can only escape from life into life, into love. The sound of her voice rocks him as though she were the cradle of his existence. She breathes deliverance on the mask of his face in semi-death. Her words form a bridge across the abyss of his soul.

She calls to me, Rebecca, stop her, stop her, don't let her take me. I wanted to die then but not now, please Dear God not now. Now I want to live. Yet I am dying. That I have lived so long is a miracle.

On the fourth day she wakes with a sudden start. It is late evening and she has snatched a couple of hours' sleep with her head above his on the pillow. Now, without moving her head she stares at his long, thin fingers as they try to spread themselves on the sheet.

'Nathan . . . ' she says in a breathless voice.

The hand rises and falls again immediately. Rebecca looks unbelievingly at his flickering eyelids, opening only very slightly and then closing, to flutter like a delicate butterfly wing.

'Nathan . . . please try . . . please try . . . '

Again his fingers attempt to rise from the sheet, to remain there, hovering a second before Rebecca offers her hand and his fingers curl slowly around hers, trying desperately to form a grip.

'Nathan . . . for me . . . do it for me, I beg you.' His eyelids flutter rapidly, open and then close again. 'Try harder, Nathan, try again, Dear God, try, Nathan, please, for me, look at me, come back to life.'

His eyelids draw up like heavy shutters on a room closed too long against the sunlight. His eyes are unfocused, unseeing, full of pain. Rebecca leans over and puts her face close to his, her tears wetting his cheeks.

'I love you, my darling, I love you. Can you hear me? I love you, please come back to me.'

His fingers tighten around hers, telling her he knows she is there though he cannot follow the movement of her soft lips.

'Nathan, come back to me, I beg you. Fight to live,' she says, shaping each word carefully for him. She wraps her other hand around his and squeezes until her arms ache. 'Feel the strength passing from me into you. Can you feel it, Nathan, can you feel how much I love you?' A tear falls from her eyes onto their entwined fingers and Nathan stares at it in fascination. 'My strength can bring you back to life, my strength and my love, but you have to want to live. Please want to live.' She presses his hand to her mouth. 'Nathan, I need you. I don't think I've ever told you that before, my darling, but I need you. I'm so very frightened without you.'

She kisses his lips as his sleep-dulled eyes watch her unbelievingly. No woman has ever needed him. He is trying to concentrate on what she is saying but the words, those unique words somehow affect him like nothing he has ever heard before.

'Do you remember, Nathan, how I told you I wanted somewhere I could belong, somewhere I could call my home? Well, I found that place, I found it not in a town or a city but in your heart. Wherever you are, Nathan, is my home. So you see I do need you, without you I would be homeless again.'

His eyes close and moisture seeps from beneath the reddened eyelids. Rebecca touches it with her lips, her body convulsed with emotion.

At Rebecca's request they transfer him from the Intensive Care Unit to a private room overlooking the hospital gardens, laid out with all the burnished colours of the fall, where he can hear the birds, watch the rain falling down the window pane and be aware, from his more pleasant surroundings, that death is no longer a certainty. Rebecca fills the room with flowers, puts his favourite books where he can see them, along with gifts and get well cards that have come into the hospital from all over the western world. She reads to him against a muted background of Mahler that comes from a small cassette machine on his night table. When he sinks into deep sleep she talks to him, urging him back to consciousness, begging him not to succumb permanently to the darkness.

Around his bed human shadows float, Joan and Bernard, the medical staff, and Rebecca.

Always Rebecca. Day and night. Life and death. Conscious and unconscious. She is always there, fighting for him. She floats in and out of his dreams, her anguished face constantly in his field of vision, pleading with him to come into the light of her love, her salvation. But the other woman is there also, a symbol of his own lifelong will to self-destruction, and this other woman thrusts him into a void, where his arms and legs will not obey him, where his brain will not function. Her fingers on his flesh are icy cold and freeze him so completely that he often believes he is already dead. She lulls him into a sleep of such utter weightlessness that he thinks he will never wake, not in the world of the living. But he does, and more often now, after periods of unconsciousness that are of briefer duration. Am I going to die? his faint voice often asks her plaintively.

Then one day Dr Jackson removes the plastic apparatus from his cheeks, while the tube taped to his arm now has a colourless liquid flowing through. But he still sleeps and wakes, and sleeps again, weak, frail. Sometimes his tragic eyes watch Rebecca's face as she sits with him, holding his hand. Am I still alive? She leaps into his drug-deadened eyes and lights the fires of hope. She crosses the infinite desert of his agony and embraces him as a womb embraces and protects a foetus. After each collision with death she arrests his fall, using her own soul to catch his wasted body. Her soft, husky voice traverses the miles between his feverish waking and his death-like slumber. She scatters memories of their yesterdays on his eyelids like gold dust, she enters his trance with visions of summer days and love-filled winter nights. This could be our future.

Weary and drained she goes for a walk in the hospital grounds. A tree. A blade of grass. A cold wind. All remind her of Nathan. All contain a poem or a poet. Poets are like that, they live in everything, they inhabit whole worlds and tiny grains of sand. They live in everything and for everything. To chop down a tree, to mutilate a branch, to crush a flower is to murder a poet. His words carry on the wind . . . the poem between your thighs . . . Oh Nathan, Nathan, the sky contains you. The earth embraces you. I am desolate. How many times did we make love in the presence of death? She sits on a bench, a book of his poems pressed against her chest.

'Rebecca . . . ' she lifts her gaze, shading her eyes from the watery afternoon sun, ' . . . can I sit down?'

'Eliot,' her shocked voice says quietly. 'What are you doing here?'

He sits, legs crossed, and lights one of his cigarettes.

'I called your office from L.A. They told me about Roth. I flew over. I thought maybe you might need someone.'

Rebecca looks at him obliquely.

'I haven't changed my mind about him,' Eliot says, 'but that doesn't mean I want him to die.'

'He won't die. I won't let him die.' She feels tears gather in her eyes.

'Knowing you, Rebecca, I believe it. How is he?'

Rebecca pushes the mass of black hair off her face with a tired gesture.

'Resting. He sleeps most of the time. He's very weak.' Her lower lip begins to tremble, she bites it and looks away.

Eliot tries to put his arm around her shoulders but she prevents him, shaking her head.

'At least let me comfort you,' the man says, a plea in his voice.

'Only Nathan can comfort me now.'

Eliot crushes the butt of his cigarette under the heel of his shoe. He presses his hand against his forehead as though to pressure the thoughts that lie inside his mind into some kind of order.

'You know he wrote to me after he walked out of your apartment. He told me he was never going to see you again and that he knew you were better off without him. He asked me to go on calling you. He knows how much I love you.'

'Eliot, it's over between us. It's over . . . ' She stands up and Eliot grips her arm, pulling her gently back down again.

232

'Stay awhile.'

'I'm sorry, I've never meant to hurt you.'

'How are things in the office?' he enquires for something to say while he controls his feelings. He studies her face. The effects of strain, grief and exhaustion have left their mark. But she is still the most beautiful woman he has ever seen. 'I guess you stay at the hospital?'

'Irving Kauffman Associates can manage without me, Nathan Roth can't.'

'Have you thought about what will happen if he lives? He'll never be completely well, he'll always be a burden to you.' He stands up and walks behind the seat. 'He'll need nursing day and night. He'll turn you grey before your time, like my mother.'

'Your mother did what she had to do.'

'At least my brother wasn't suicidal. There will always be something in Roth's life to give him an excuse to end it all. You'll smile at another man, come home late one day from the office, and he'll have his excuse. He was neurotic long before he met Madeline. Ask any damn psychologist, a man like him never loses his desire to die.' He puts his hands on her shoulders. 'Get away from here before it's too late, Rebecca. Come out to L.A. with me.'

Rebecca sits on the bench and looks directly at him, raising her eyebrows.

'I don't care that he is neurotic and insecure and all those other failings we all suffer. I really don't care. Can you understand that, Eliot? I love him because he is what he is, a genius, a poet, a man living on the very edge of sanity. I wouldn't want him to change. He would no longer be Nathan Roth. I just want him to know a little peace between each battle that rages in his soul. That's the most either of us can hope for. I know I'll never "cure" him, but then I don't want him to be like other men. I've known a lot of men and I didn't love them, not the way I love him and all his neuroses.'

Eliot gives a nervous fore-shortened laugh.

'What's funny?'

'Nothing.' He stares at the ground. 'I was just thinking, God help me, I envy him.'

'Rebecca . . . ' he whispers faintly, in a hollow, drugged voice.

'Yes, my darling, I'm here. I'll always be here. I'll always be with you.' She strokes the hair off his forehead and kisses the hairline, pressing her soft full lips to his damp flesh.

He looks up into her eyes. 'I can hear the rain.'

'Yes, it's just started.' She goes to the window and pulls back the curtain. Then she moves his head slightly on the pillow so that he can watch the rain drops form translucent patterns on the glass. The hint of a smile forms on his colourless lips. She sits beside the bed, the touch of her fingers on his forehead like a healing balm. In a while he says, 'She still calls to me.'

'I know, but you have to ignore her and she'll go away forever this time.'

'Rebecca . . . ' his tongue comes out slowly to moisten his dry lips, ' . . . thank you . . . thank you for everything.'

Tears edge their way into Rebecca's eyes but she manages a pained, distracted smile.

'You're welcome.'

'Rebecca . . . '

'Yes, my darling?'

'I want to live.'

She brings his hand to her lips and he feels her tears wetting his knuckles, hears her voice speaking his name. The fog clears for an instant and he is able to see clearly her loving face with its dreams of tomorrow. She goes down on her knees beside the bed, her face pressed into his chest. He lifts his hand and brings it to rest on the top of her head in a gesture of comfort, of reassurance. His eyes move to the window where the rain is falling softly in droplets that chase each other down the pane.

'Is it possible, for the first time in my life I really want to live?'

CHAPTER NINETEEN

I have forgotten the word I wanted to say.
A blind swallow returns to the palace of shadows
on clipped wings to flicker among the Transparent Ones.
In oblivion they are singing the night song.

Osip Mandelstam, 1891–1938. *Stone, Poem 113*

One week later Dr Jackson welcomes Rebecca into his office.

'Thank you,' she says with a gratitude no less profound now, for the umpteenth time of saying it, 'thank you for Nathan.'

'As I've told you before, Rebecca, I performed the surgery, you performed the miracle. I assume you got my message and that's why you're here?'

'Yes, one of the nurses said you wanted to see me.'

Jackson indicates the visitor's chair and waits until she is seated, then he too sits down behind his desk. He chooses a folder from the pile to the right of his elbow and places it centre, his elegant, brown hands touching, palm to palm as though praying.

'I have the results of the tests we've been doing on Nathan. Now before you start jumping to conclusions let me finish,' he adds quickly, reading correctly the expression of anxiety on Rebecca's face. 'He seems to be responding well to treatment.'

Rebecca releases a long, drawn-out sigh of abject relief. 'Thank God . . .' she whispers, shaking her head slowly. She puts her fingers to her forehead.

'Rebecca, it's the long term effects of Nathan's condition that concern me now . . . '

'Of course. He knows he can't . . . '

'Rebecca, please allow me to finish,' Jackson says with difficulty, and Rebecca studies his face for a clue to his sudden seriousness. 'I had a long chat with Nathan yesterday and among the things we discussed was the future. What will happen when he leaves this hospital.'

'He'll come home with me, that goes without saying.'

'He's a very sick man, Rebecca.' He lifts the letter opener and passes it from one hand to the other, his gaze on the sharply pointed blade. 'He's been sick a long time and he'll never be well again, not completely well. He's making remarkable progress. I would never have believed a man in his condition the night he was brought in here could have recovered. I never concealed anything from you. You know I thought he would die.'

'Dr Jackson, I know how sick he is, I've always known. It didn't stop me falling in love with him.' She crosses her legs and brushes a hand across her lap nervously as though removing a speck of invisible dust. 'I don't expect him to compete in the Olympic Games if that's what you're trying to tell me. A man who has been through what Nathan has been through can never be the same again. He was never Superman, God knows, but I'm not in love with Superman.'

'Okay,' Jackson stops toying with the letter opener and sits back in his chair, 'cards on the table. For the first year or so he is going to require constant medical attention. He'll have to come back here and see me regularly so that I can monitor his progress. He must stick rigidly to a special diet. He must have freedom from anxiety and stress, mental and physical rest and teach himself a fully developed sense of his own mortality. With the right kind of attention he can live a full and long life. If he goes back to his old lifestyle he will be dead within a year.'

'He wants to live,' Rebecca says with quiet emphasis,

'before he didn't care, it's true, but now he has my love and he wants to live.'

'Do you know what you'd be taking on?' He raises his hand as Rebecca gets ready to interrupt, her mouth becoming indignant. 'No, don't answer, just listen to me. His entire routine has to be reorganized to avoid stress and fatigue. He needs constant nursing. Am I making that clear to you? Not forever, no; but certainly for the first three or four months after he leaves here.'

Rebecca swallows and a kind of clicking sound emerges from her throat before she says with perfect composure, 'He'll come home with me, that goes without saying.'

'Nathan has asked me to hire a private nurse who can attend him.'

Rebecca laughs, although Jackson has said nothing remotely funny. 'What?' she says with a frown.

'Nathan doesn't want to be a burden to you. He doesn't want you confined to the world of a semi-invalid. I can only admire his unselfishness; it almost matches yours.'

'I don't believe you,' Rebecca says in a shocked voice.

'He believes that with a private nurse at the beginning and Mrs Adler's . . .'

'Joan?'

'Yes, Nathan intends to move in with the Adlers for a while and I think it's a good idea.'

'Oh you do?' Rebecca says angrily. 'So between you you've sorted out Nathan's life and there is no place for me, is that it?'

'Rebecca, please, try and see it from Nathan's point of view. He wants only to spare you. That is the depth of his love for you.'

'My God, he must think me the most selfish of women. He could never be a burden to me.' Her eyes blaze with tears of mortification and shock. 'I would willingly devote all my time and energy to making him well again. Doesn't he see that, Doctor?' she asks in amazement.

'I can only admire both of you for the love you so obviously bear each other.'

'But you still think Nathan is right?' She arches an arrogantly interrogative eyebrow. 'I'm not the type to stay at home with an invalid husband?'

'I didn't say that.' Jackson's tone becomes annoyed.

'No, but it's what you think,' she accuses.

'Oh really?' He stands up. 'How can you sit there and suggest such a thing when I've watched you day after day, night after night, at that man's side, holding his hand, talking with him, never complaining, only praying. I've watched you, so don't tell me what type I think you are. I'm tired, you're tired. Why don't we . . .'

'Yes, I'm tired, tired of trying to prove my devotion to a man who appreciates only pain and cruelty. So you go ahead and get him that nurse, I'm not going to stop you, but neither will I stand around while a stranger attends to the needs of a man I love.' She puts her hand over her quivering mouth, unable to go on.

Joan and Bernard sit each side of Nathan's bed. Rebecca stands by the window gazing out, going over and over in her mind Dr Jackson's revelation of that morning. She is still unwilling, unable, to believe his words. How can Nathan even consider allowing someone else, a stranger, to minister to his needs when she, Rebecca, would do anything for him, not out of duty but love?

' . . . and there were several telephone calls from the poetry editor of *The New Yorker* enquiring after your health.'

Bernard stops only to draw breath but Joan takes the opportunity to warn him with only token disapproval, 'You are tiring him, Bernard.' She cannot bring herself to dampen Bernard's spirits, not when Nathan has a slight colour in his cheeks and a second pillow supporting his grey head. The sight of him smiling when they had entered his room just after lunch had brought them unexpected joy.

'I'm not tired,' Nathan says in a soft, frail voice of someone who has been to the very edge of eternity and been drawn back by a force greater than death. 'I like to know what's going on outside these four walls. I only wish Rebecca would get some fresh air while you're here with me. She stays cooped up in here with me for hours.'

'You're right,' Bernard agrees, glancing tenderly toward the subject of their immediate concern whose expression shows she is too deeply involved with her own private thoughts to be listening to the conversation. 'Rebecca, why don't you and Joan go for a walk? It's a lovely day, chilly but sunny.'

'Rebecca?' Joan calls gently when the young woman doesn't answer. 'Rebecca, are you with us?' She laughs.

'What?' Rebecca blinks her way back to the present, turning her head to look blankly at Joan. 'Sorry, did you say something?'

'Bernard suggests you and I take a walk so that he can be free to tire Nathan without my interference.'

Rebecca looks at Nathan. She had been gone for over an hour that morning, seeing Dr Jackson, and when she returned her eyes alone had told him how she felt. Twice he had tried to broach the subject, and twice he had turned coward, closing his eyes and feigning sleep.

'I'd like to go out for a while, yes, but would you be offended if I went alone? I have some thinking to do.'

She takes her coat off the chair and leaves the room without another word, not even glancing in Nathan's direction. Joan looks at the poet who lowers his gaze. Joan goes after Rebecca. She calls to her and the young woman stops.

'Rebecca,' she takes her hand in both of hers, 'I want you to know that the private nurse, moving in with us, is not Bernard's or my idea. Neither of us are happy about it. We want Nathan with us, of course, but only if he were alone. Which he isn't, and he never will be again. What can I say?'

'Nothing. Nathan and I will have to work it out between us. But whatever happens I'll always love you and Bernard.'

Joan closes the door of Nathan's room and sits down beside the bed. She looks at the poet's drawn, tortured face.

'You're hurting her, Nathan. She's shown you only devotion and you're hurting and confusing her. Why?'

'You're making a terrible mistake,' Bernard says, shaking his head slowly, 'you're turning your back on your guardian angel. I can only call that blasphemy.'

Tears appear on Nathan's lashes. 'I owe her my life,' he says, barely able to articulate the words, looking intensely from Joan to Bernard and back. 'The greatest gift I can give her now is her freedom.'

'I read something in a book or a magazine once, I cannot quote it word for word,' Joan pauses to recollect the memory, 'if you give someone their freedom and they fly away they were never yours in the first place . . .'

The elevator door slides open and among the people who step into the corridor is Eliot. He walks in the direction of the vending machines where Rebecca is trying to wrest a cup of coffee from the reluctant clutches of the unreasonable dispenser. He smiles as she kicks it right where she judges its guts would be and the anaemic brown liquid comes gushing forth before the plastic cup has settled in the claws.

'Go to hell!' she says, giving the machine another kick.

'Hey, hey, vandal!' Eliot intones, coming up behind her, 'do you want some more change?' He offers her a handful of coins on his open palm.

'No. I am not giving this perverse monster another cent.'

Eliot looks at her reflectively. 'Why do I get the distinct impression that it's not the machine you'd like to kick so much as something a little more liable to howl with pain?'

'You get that impression because it's true.' She tosses her hair off her face and produces a suddenly cheerful smile.

'How would you like to buy me a cup of coffee and a doughnut, Mr Vaughan?'

'Rebecca, there is nothing I'd like more, but I have a plane to catch. I came up here to say *au revoir*, I'm going back to L.A.'

'Oh,' her smile turns sad at the corners of her mouth. She takes his arm as they walk back together toward the elevator. 'Do you hate me, Eliot?'

'No,' he laughs at the ludicrousness of that question, 'I love you. Come back with me. Marry me, please.'

She smiles up at him regretfully and shakes her head.

'Are you going to marry Roth?'

'Right now I don't know what I'm going to do. Why don't you just hold me tight a moment?'

He embraces her, holding her against his body, unable to prevent his chest from contracting with the pleasure of having her to touch and smell for this one, last time. Then he puts her away from him abruptly, his features that had grown soft suddenly tightening and his grey eyes full of despair.

'Eliot, I'm sorry . . .'

'If you need help with the medical bills or you ever want a shoulder to cry on you know where to find me, but I can't guarantee not to try and start our relationship back up again.'

'I really don't know you at all, do I?' Rebecca wipes the moisture from beneath her eyes.

'Maybe that was our trouble, we really didn't know each other.' He touches her hair briefly. 'Don't let him turn you into a nursemaid.'

'No,' she promises, laughing, and the laughter sounds as though it is caught on something in her throat. 'Don't let Hollywood turn you into a beast with a cash register for a heart.'

'Too late.'

He stands in the elevator and stares at her longingly,

consigning to memory every inch of her beautiful face and strong, voluptuous body.

'God bless you,' Rebecca says softly.

The door slides shut.

Around 3.30 on the following day Rebecca enters Nathan's room with a large gift-wrapped package. The poet is dozing, his eyes closed, two short, sharp lines of shadow at the corners of his mouth. She feels a gathering love for him so immense it threatens to drive her off her feet. She sits down on the edge of the bed. His eyes open.

'Hi,' she says, leaning forward and kissing his thin, tightly shut lips. She strokes his face, his chin, lets her hand drop to his shoulder, his narrow shoulder beneath the unflattering half-sleeved hospital gown tied at the back of his neck with strings. 'Did I disturb you?'

'No.' His voice is hoarse. She holds a glass of milk to his lips. His eyes never leave her face.

'Why are you shutting me out of your life, Nathan?'

He drops his gaze, his face yellow, the muscles in his neck standing out like stretched ropes. Rebecca stands up and removes her coat. She lays it over a chair, goes to the window and stares out at the clouds gathering for a storm. How strangely fitting, she thinks.

'Did you get plenty of rest this morning?' she asks.

'Alice was here for an hour. We chatted. She told me about a new routine they've got her doing at the club.'

'Did she give you a demonstration?'

Nathan says nothing.

'Alice is becoming quite the career woman.'

'Did you have a good morning?'

'Busy. I went to see Irving and then I had lunch with Joe. He wants me to join him as an editor in the New Year.'

'I'm pleased,' Nathan says haltingly. His hands grasp the covers, his skeletal fingers digging into the mattress.

'Are you?' A painful smile pinches the corners of Rebecca's mouth.

'Of course. He recognizes talent when he sees it. You can do much more good as an editor for a writer in whom you believe than as an agent.'

'Yes, that's what Joe said. I'm undecided. I said I'd take a vacation first.'

'A vacation is a wonderful idea.' Please God, give me strength, he prays silently. 'You need a vacation.'

Rebecca walks slowly to the bed, her eyes fixed on his face.

'Is that what I need, Nathan?' her voice is mocking. 'A vacation?'

He stares at her, blinking.

'You have to get away from me,' he says, emphasizing each word equally, and each word is a stone dropping from his lips, 'you have to get away from me before it's too late.'

'Do you love me, Nathan?'

He closes his eyes and lets his head fall back to the pillow.

'I refuse to dignify that question with an answer.'

'Then ask me to marry you,' she instructs softly. 'I'll sit here and you ask me to marry you, take care of you, love you, give you children.' She lifts his hand from the sheet and caresses it before lifting it to her lips. 'Go on, Nathan, ask me.'

His eyes open full to the brim with tears. He shakes his head and the tears go rolling down his gaunt cheeks.

'I can't . . . I can't . . .' he says in a broken voice. 'I love you too much to condemn you to a life with a sick, neurotic cripple.'

'Do you know what today is, Nathan?' Her voice has become very soft, very low, almost as though she is whispering to herself.

'Your birthday?' he guesses.

'Try again.'

244

'My birthday?' he says negligently, blinking in that way he has when he is nervous or afraid. 'I'm bad on dates, I don't know,' he says with his fingers against his temples.

'Well, I'll tell you. Exactly one year ago today you walked into my office in London.' She takes the large package off the chair and places it across his lap. 'Happy anniversary, Nathan.' When he only stares at the package she unpeels the paper for him and gradually the contents are revealed as a box of Magic Tricks. 'It seemed appropriate,' she says, 'because it marks another anniversary in our lives. It was that morning in San Francisco when I discovered I was in love with you.'

Nathan raises eyes that are softened with tears to her face. When he blinks they fall to his chin and then to the box.

'Rebecca . . .' he says in an anguished voice.

'You smile so freely at the nurses, yet I have to work so hard for even a tiny smile. You called Joan the kindest woman in the world and bought Alice a pink rabbit that banged a drum. I don't know exactly what I want to convey by telling you all this, or what I want to tell you that I haven't already shown you in my actions. When you went away I worried about you night and day. When you were in the operating theatre I prayed for you in a way I have never prayed for anyone. When you seemed so close to death I nearly died too. Dr Jackson called your recovery a miracle, my miracle. Well if it was, it was a miracle of love. I don't want any reward,' she puts her fingers to his cheek, to the wetness, 'I just want to know if I've proved my devotion. You see I love the smell of your frail flesh, the dark shadows beneath your tragic eyes, the fine bones beneath your white skin. I know and love every mark, bruise and vein of your body and every wrinkle on your face. I love the way your hands tremble with nervousness. It is as though God entrusted me to take care of you, and I went further, I loved you.' She gives a soft whispering laugh. 'Why do you look so shocked? Did you think me incapable of such total love? So did I. Well, I wanted to tell you I love you, and ask you why I am no longer to be part of your life and here I am making a speech. There is only one question to be asked, Nathan. Do you feel strong enough to make a home with me, or do I get out of your life forever?'

CHAPTER TWENTY

Change, move, dead clock, that this fresh day
May break with dazzling light to those sick eyes.
Burn, glare, old sun, so long unseen,
That time may find its sound again, and cleanse
Whatever it is that a wound remembers
After the healing ends.

Weldon Kees, 1914–1955. *Small Prayer*

All here, all those close to their hearts, all gathered in the visitors' waiting room at the front of the hospital to drink the health of the happy couple. Patrick, Sally and the children, Joan and Bernard, Dr Jackson, Nurse Kate, Irving Kauffman and Joe Wasserman, friends of the poet from his Greenwich Village days, plus a half a dozen young students from New York University who turned up unexpectedly that morning and received not a bulletin on their idol's state of health but an invitation to join the wedding celebrations. What all these people found was not a sick man but a joyous groom.

Someone calls for quiet and gradually a hush falls over the room as all eyes turn to the frail, neatly dressed man in the wheelchair and the tall, beautiful woman by his side, her hand resting on his shoulder. Rebecca smiles indulgently, expecting herself and her husband to be the subject of yet another touching toast. But Irving hands the poet a large manilla envelope from which he removes a set of galley proofs, holding them up for the guests to see. The poet's gaunt face becomes flushed, nervously he clears his throat.

'I . . . eh . . . can't make speeches . . . ' he fidgets with the brake handle on the wheelchair as his old friends' laughter dies down, '...so I'll just say thank you for coming and give this wedding gift to my wife.'

As the applause subsides a bewildered Rebecca is instructed by Joan and Bernard to read the first page, a dedication that will eventually appear on the inside of Nathan's new collection of poems, his first for three years. As Rebecca reads, the few, simple words blur before her tear filled eyes.

'Read it out!' Patrick calls, his small son and daughter joining in.

Rebecca shakes her head slowly, too overcome with emotion to comply with their request. Soon all the guests have taken up the cry and Nathan takes the pages from his wife's trembling hands.

'It says: To Rebecca, who gave me back my life.'

Rebecca has no control over the tears that run down her face. Kate gives her a handkerchief and Joan, inebriated on joy and champagne calls loudly, 'Kiss the bride!'

A chorus of whistles and cheers rises into the air as Rebecca's mouth meets Nathan's in a heart-stoppingly tender and prolonged kiss.

'The car is here,' someone close to the window announces.

'We'll all wait outside for you,' Bernard says impishly, his trimmed beard twitching with the ecstasy this day has brought him. 'We have to send you both off properly.'

'God help us,' says Joan glancing at the ceiling in supplication, 'he is still pushing.' She shepherds Bernard out of the door with the rest of the guests.

Left alone together at last Rebecca crouches down in front of her husband's wheelchair. She rests her hands on his knees, kisses his mouth, smiles at him lovingly and kisses him again.

'How do you feel? Are you tired? You mustn't tire yourself.' She kisses his pale, clean hands and looks at him rapturously. 'There are no words to tell you how proud that dedication makes me. I can only say that I'll try to make your life so beautiful that all the pain and tragedy in your past will be as though it never existed.'

'Rebecca, you've already brought me all the beauty a man could ever want.'

'This is just the beginning . . .'

He looks at her, she seemed about to add something more but now her lips are closed and she is smiling at him ambiguously. Not now, she thinks, I shan't tell him now. I'll save it for him, for this evening, when we are together in the same bed for the first time in four months. When we can hold each other and sleep, our limbs and our hearts entwined. Then I'll tell him. Nathan, my wedding gift to you . . . a child . . . our child. Yes, Nathan, I am having your baby.

'Nathan, I love you . . .'

They kiss lingeringly, their hands on each other's faces. Her wine sweet breath warming his cheek. The strength in her loving hands seems capable of lifting him bodily from the wheelchair so that he feels he could walk back into the real world without fear or pain. His heart seems to have become too large, too swollen with love to remain confined in his narrow chest. He takes her hand and kisses the wide, gold band, remembering what it is and who it is that brings him such unbearable joy.

'We're married.' His voice is wondering, his eyes say he still does not believe that such happiness can at last be his. 'Mrs Rebecca Roth.' His fine, curved lips pucker like a school boy's. His face opens in a broad smile of astonishing beauty. He is a different person, all that physical pain and mental anguish had happened to another man in another life, another dimension. It is as if he had truly died and had been reborn through this woman's devotion. He holds her tightly as she rises, kissing his lips. Was the taste of a man ever more sweet on her lips?

'Oh that feels so wonderful,' she says lowering her head to his shoulder as he gently strokes her hair. 'You can't imagine how wonderful it feels to have your arms around me again, comforting me. To kiss you and feel warmth in your lips. To gaze at a man whose eyes are filled not with pain but with love. You were so sick, my darling, but I never gave up hope. I knew that one day we would walk out of here together, arm in arm, strong in the love that we share.'

The sound of the car horn wakes them from their trance. With Dr Jackson alongside her Rebecca pushes the wheelchair to the entrance of the building, outside which the guests and the car are waiting.

'Just a second . . . ' Nathan tells Dr Jackson as he is about to open the doors. He places the palms of his hands on the armrests of the mobile chair and with a tremendous effort of will and faith he levers himself up and forward so that his unsteady feet can locate the floor beyond the footrest.

'No . . . Nathan . . . ' Rebecca cries, taking a step toward him and stopped by Dr Jackson.

'Let him.' The doctor stares at her. 'You gave him the strength, now give him the chance to use it.'

The poet rises slowly, painstakingly, his lips tight shut, beads of perspiration breaking out on his pale forehead, but he is more determined to do this thing, to stand, to walk out of here with Rebecca beside him, than he has ever been to do anything in his life. Finally, standing, swaying slightly, using the chair for support he looks at Kate who has his walking stick. She holds it out to him with a smile of encouragement. He manages a soft thank you. Jackson moves the wheelchair out of his path.

'How do I look?' Nathan asks Rebecca.

'Beautiful,' she says tearfully, smoothing the side of his hair. Her hands are trembling, her knees quite suddenly weak. 'Nathan, could I hold your arm . . . ?'

'Lean on me,' he tells her, offering his arm. He glances at Jackson. 'I'm ready, Doctor.'

The doors are opened. Slowly, painfully, Nathan Roth walks into the unexpectedly bright sunshine of this early January day. He smiles slightly, nervously, before his expression becomes sombre with the gravity of this moment. His first steps in a new life. The guests are assembled at the bottom of the steps. Patrick's children run forward eagerly, lift their small fists and a shower of confetti flutters down over Nathan's shoulders, and into Rebecca's hair. Bernard steps forward, his voice quavering with emotion as he says fervently, 'Welcome back to the world, Nathan Roth.'

The poet's shoulders convulse as tears come into his eyes. He lifts his face to the sun, embraced by the woman who made this day, this moment, possible.

'The pain and suffering are over, Nathan, my darling,' she says, her voice becoming elevated. 'You can rejoice in being alive. Alive!'

Postscript

.. suicide is, after all, the opposite of the poem.'

Anne Sexton, 1928–1974.

Contemporary Romances

Once a Lover £1.95   **Diana Anthony**
Set in New York and San Francisco, *Once a Lover* is the moving love story of Lainie Brown, a young artist, and Jean-Paul Vallier, a blinded sports superstar. Then he regains his sight and Lainie fears she will lose his love. But she learns painfully and joyously why she is so worthy of Jean-Paul's enduring devotion.

Celebration £1.50   **Rosie Thomas**
Bel Farrer, a wine columnist, was a high-flying career girl. But beneath her glittering professional appearance was a vulnerable heart. Both the titled aristocrat bound by an ancient code of honour, and the reckless, carefree playboy claimed her heart and she had to make a choice.

Perfect Dreams £1.75   **Carolyn Fireside**
The world of high fashion, Hollywood and the jet set is the backdrop for this rich love story. Gabrielle Blake, a photographer's model, is independent, intelligent and lovable. Among the rich and famous men who fall in and out of Gaby's life is Terry Baron, a young journalist who finally rescues her when her career collapses. But is it too late for them to rescue their love for each other?

Perhaps I'll Dream of Darkness £1.35   **Mary Sheldon**
In this compelling and beautifully written story of love and obsession the lives of a teenage girl and a burned-out rock star entwine fleetingly — with disastrous results. Probing deeply into her characters' lives, Mary Sheldon creates a portrait of frustrated passion that leads to tragedy, and captures both the grace and terror of obsessive, idealistic love.

FONTANA PAPERBACKS

Belva Plain

– the best-loved bestseller –

Evergreen £2.50

A rich and tempestuous story of Anna Friedman, the beautiful, penniless Jewish girl who arrives in New York from Poland at the turn of the century and survives to become matriarch of a powerful dynasty.

Random Winds £2.50

The absorbing and poignant story of a family of doctors – Dr Farrell, the old-fashioned country doctor who dies penniless and exhausted, his son Martin who becomes a brilliant and famous brain surgeon, but is haunted by his forbidden love for a woman, and Martin's daughter Claire, headstrong, modern and idealistic, whose troubled romance with the unknown Englishman provides a bitter-sweet ending.

Eden Burning £2.50

A romantic saga set against the backdrop of New York, Paris and the Caribbean. The island of St Felice holds many secrets, one of which is the secret of the passionate moment of abandon that threatened to destroy the life of the beautiful fifteen-year-old Teresa Francis. A story of violence, political upheaval and clandestine love.

FONTANA PAPERBACKS

Fontana Paperbacks: Fiction

Fontana is a leading paperback publisher of both non-fiction, popular and academic, and fiction. Below are some recent fiction titles.

- ☐ SEEDS OF YESTERDAY Virginia Andrews £1.95
- ☐ CAVALCADE Gwendoline Butler £1.95
- ☐ RETURN TO RHANNA Christine Marion Fraser £1.95
- ☐ JEDDER'S LAND Maureen O'Donoghue £1.95
- ☐ THE FINAL RUN Tommy Steele £1.50
- ☐ FOR LOVE OF A STRANGER Lily Devoe £1.75
- ☐ THE WARLORD Malcolm Bosse £2.95
- ☐ TREASON'S HARBOUR Patrick O'Brian £1.95
- ☐ FUTURES Freda Bright £1.95
- ☐ THE DEMON LOVER Victoria Holt £1.95
- ☐ THE UNRIPE GOLD Geoffrey Jenkins £1.75
- ☐ A CASE FOR CHARLEY John Spencer £1.50
- ☐ DEATH AND THE DANCING FOOTMAN Ngaio Marsh £1.75
- ☐ THE 'CAINE' MUTINY Herman Wouk £2.50
- ☐ THE TRANSFER Thomas Palmer £1.95
- ☐ LIVERPOOL DAISY Helen Forrester £1.75
- ☐ OUT OF A DREAM Diana Anthony £1.75
- ☐ SHARPE'S SWORD Bernard Cornwell £1.75

You can buy Fontana paperbacks at your local bookshop or newsagent. Or you can order them from Fontana Paperbacks, Cash Sales Department, Box 29, Douglas, Isle of Man. Please send a cheque, postal or money order (not currency) worth the purchase price plus 15p per book for postage (maximum postage required is £3).

NAME (Block letters) _____

ADDRESS _____

_____

_____

While every effort is made to keep prices low, it is sometimes necessary to increase them at short notice. Fontana Paperbacks reserve the right to show new retail prices on covers which may differ from those previously advertised in the text or elsewhere.